TEAROOM
mysteries

Dear Reader,

I had a lot of fun writing *Tea and Touchdowns*, but to be honest, I wasn't always an enthusiastic football fan. Growing up, it was always the main event on Sunday afternoons: football and pretzel rods and maybe, if we were lucky, something homemade from my mother's kitchen, such as molasses cookies (look for the recipe in this book).

But between the Chicago Bears winning the Super Bowl when I was in eighth grade, and then cheering for my high-school team for the next few years, my interest was piqued. This book was special for me to write, because I got to work on it during my son, Paxton's, first season playing tackle football. So fun! The timing was perfect, as I was personally invested in the sport, and my heart was on the field.

I hope you enjoy the heart in this book and the thrill of the game. I also hope you can feel the crispness of autumn and the dry hay beneath you on a hayride through the Richardsons' dairy farm and laugh at some of the pranks that are key to the story. Jan and Elaine are busy women, as usual, and they were fun to capture once more in a couple of weeks of their lives.

Enjoy the season. And don't forget to pause in the busyness of life to enjoy some tea and pastries!

Erin Keeley Marshall

Tearoom Mysteries

TEAROOM
mysteries

Tea and Touchdowns

ERIN KEELEY MARSHALL

Guideposts
New York

Published by Guideposts Books & Inspirational Media
110 William Street
New York, New York 10038
Guideposts.org

Acknowledgments

Every attempt has been made to credit the sources of copyrighted material used
in this book. If any such acknowledgment has been inadvertently omitted or
miscredited, receipt of such information would be appreciated.

Scripture quotations are taken from *The Holy Bible, New International Version*.
Copyright © 1973, 1978, 1984, 2011 by Biblica, Inc. Used by permission of
Zondervan. All rights reserved worldwide. www.zondervan.com

Cover and interior design by Müllerhaus
Cover illustration by Ross Jones, represented by Deborah Wolfe, Ltd.
Typeset by Aptara, Inc.

Printed and bound in the United States of America
10 9 8 7 6 5 4 3 2 1

Tea and Touchdowns

CHAPTER ONE

Jan Blake gripped the reins and nudged her horse forward with her boot as she'd been instructed.

The air was cool, even for an October Sunday afternoon, and she was glad for her gray flannel shirt and red vest. A breeze boding of coming rain draped the pasture and nearby woods in a cozy sort of gloom. Since the sun was hanging out behind thick clouds, Jan prayed the storm would hold off on this opening day of Lancaster's Fall Fest. Dry skies would also be better for sales at the merchant booths in town and at picturesque spots along the riding route.

Although Jan wasn't an experienced horsewoman, she was enjoying her mount, a gentle-natured buckskin named Triscuit. Leaves crunched beneath the hooves of a dozen horses and their riders, who were a mix of locals and tourists in town for the fall colors and the much-anticipated homecoming football game between the Forrest High Pirates and the Claremore Raiders. As alums of Forrest High, Jan and Elaine loved living back in Lancaster for this time of year.

Jan patted Triscuit's tan neck and smoothed her black mane. She was slowly feeling more comfortable in the saddle. It was good to try something new when life took a turn. She wondered what Bob was doing right then in Baltimore and smiled to herself. He'd been gone only a few weeks—he'd moved there for a job, an opportunity of a lifetime—and she knew he was adjusting to the distance as much as she was. But she was happy today, despite the deep sense of loss she'd felt since he left, and she clung to that happiness. Elaine Cook had offered to man their Tea for Two booth on her own so Jan could take part in the first trail ride of the week. It was a generous gesture, one of many Elaine had been offering lately, Jan thought with gratitude. Elaine seemed to be very concerned for Jan's emotional state since Bob's move.

But pockets of joy were coming more and more frequently now for Jan, faster than she'd expected, and the fog she'd felt when Bob first left had begun to lift. Ultimately, she was happy for him. And she was the one who had chosen to let him go without her, after all.

She pulled gently on the rein with her right hand, and Triscuit responded by moving to the center of the trail. She looked around, glad she was still in Lancaster and not in Baltimore, glad she still owned Tea for Two with her cousin Elaine. She took a deep breath of the crisp air. Yes, she'd made the right choice.

The trail meandered through trampled meadow grasses crisping in the autumn air and into forested areas shaded by tall oaks, maples, and evergreens. The whole area included acres of three adjoining properties on the outskirts of town:

the Richardson dairy farm, Dr. Tyson and Claudia McInnis's Orchard Hill, and the Donahue Stables.

An hour ago she'd driven up the winding drive of the Donahue property and seen the sprawling white house that presided over two paddocks and two large white outbuildings she learned were a barn and indoor arena. After some shuffling of horses and cinching of saddle straps, and taking instruction from the stable hands, she and the other riders were ready to go.

Jan felt as if she'd put in a full day already. First thing that morning, she and Elaine had made the easy drive in Jan's old Camry from downtown Lancaster to their booth site. They'd chosen a spot near a number of other booths in a clearing where the three properties met, accessible by a tire-worn path a hundred yards from the main road. The owners of the three properties had worked with the town's selectmen to arrange a community gathering area there for festival events.

A circular seating area had been set up with log stumps and hay bales for chairs around a large fire pit in the center. A couple of white, open-air tents had been erected nearby, with space for additional temporary seating that hadn't been delivered yet. It would be the site for the community bonfire. It would also draw people to the dairy farm's corn maze, the orchard's apple trees, the stables' trail rides, and the sales booths. Elaine was back at the booth now.

When they'd arrived there in the morning chill, Annie Richardson of Richardson's Dairy Farm was eyeballing the placement of their tables for her husband, Gavin, and his dad, Ethan, while their three kids unloaded coolers of milk and cheeses and other products they planned to sell. The What-Not and Oldies But Goodies and A Little Something stores were setting up too, and some members of the Lancaster Community Church were assembling a backdrop for puppet shows they'd put on for kids. Jan had waved to her friend and the town librarian, Priscilla Gates, who had been nestled among boxes of used books she was selling. Jan was also glad to see that Dr. Tyson and Claudia, who owned the orchard, brought along two of their employees to help set up their bulky booth, from which they'd sell all kinds of apple goods like homemade applesauce and cider. All in all, the fair had an unfussy but organized and charming feel.

She looked around again at her riding companions, most of who were visiting with each other. Most were locals she knew, as well as a family of three—two parents and a middle school–aged daughter visiting the area. And she was delighted to share the ride with three students from Forrest High in Penzance, the school that Lancaster's teens attended.

She'd fallen behind most of the group and was now riding close to Dori Richardson, a senior at Forrest High, and another student, sandy-haired Chris Cosgrove. Chris worked at the library and had helped Elaine and her cousin retrieve some security camera footage last year when they were investigating a crossword puzzle mystery. He was a 4.0 student and was Forrest High's quarterback as a junior last year. Until an hour ago at the stables, Jan hadn't seen him for months.

She caught their eyes and smiled at their banter about the game the next weekend. "The whole town has football fever, don't they?"

Dori grinned back from her perch on an older paint horse, and a smirk spread across Chris's freckles. His lanky frame sat atop an Appaloosa. Both looked comfortable in sweatshirts, jeans, and hiking boots.

"Definitely," Dori answered. "Do you like football, Mrs. Blake?"

"I do. I've sat in the Pirates' bleachers more times than I can count. You can't beat football season around here."

They agreed, and Dori looked mischievously at Chris. "Too bad you turned traitor on us."

He made a face. "Hey now, that was my parents' fault. I got dragged into it."

Dori's ponytail bounced playfully, a little lighter brown than Jan's short cut. "I'm only teasing. Everyone misses you."

Chris must have noticed Jan's quizzical expression. "We moved to Claremore over the summer." He looked a little regretful but shrugged.

"He's the QB for the Raiders now, too bad for us," Dori quipped.

"Ah." Jan made sure she looked impressed as she pushed up her glasses. "Congratulations. But I'm guessing that feels a little complicated."

"No kidding." Chris shook his head.

Jan thought it must not be easy transferring right before the last year of high school, especially to a rival like Claremore. The two schools had battled fiercely for decades, even long before she and Elaine were students at Forrest High.

"Trace and Derek are like lost puppies without you," Dori teased again, but not without a hint of support in her tone.

"Well, yeah," he chortled. "Maybe that'll make it easier to beat 'em Friday night."

Jan knew the big game was strategically scheduled to cap off the festival. Both teams were strong this year, with sights on the state tournament and more than one player from each side hopeful of college scholarships. "With your GPA, you could probably get academic *and* athletic scholarships," she suggested to Chris, hoping to cheer him.

He shrugged again. "Maybe. There are a few of us trying to get the scouts' attention." He nodded toward the third teen, who was riding a football field's length ahead of them. "Trace, for one."

Jan followed his gaze toward Trace Donahue, Forrest High's star player, the quarterback who'd replaced Chris. Trace was leading the group with his mother, Bridget. Trace's family owned the stables and horses. And Jan had taken instruction from Derek Jameson, the other friend Dori mentioned. He was yet another Pirates senior player and an extra hand at the stables during the busy festival week. He'd stayed back to get things ready for the next trail ride that evening. They all seemed like nice kids.

The rest of the group had rounded a bend that cut through the woods and were out of eyesight, so Jan urged her horse a little faster, and the teens kept up with her.

Suddenly Triscuit's ears pricked up. Half a breath later a horse's whinny from ahead pierced the air, followed by a scream. A flurry of birds shot out of the trees and scattered into the sky, staccato *thwaps* of their wings echoing through the air.

CHAPTER TWO

With a glance at each other, Jan, Chris, and Dori pushed their mounts to a fast trot. Dori and Chris took the lead. Jan brought up the rear, holding tightly to Triscuit and hoping she wasn't stretching her riding skills too much. The blaze of leaves that still clung to tree limbs whizzed by in a smear of fall colors.

Above a few snorts from the horses and her pounding heart, Jan thought she heard another sound like laughter from the trees off to the left, but all she saw were tree trunks, branches, and fluttering leaves. Then a second wail, a woman's, rang out louder.

What was happening?

Dori and Chris disappeared around the bend. Seconds later Jan caught up and managed to slow Triscuit a few feet from the other riders, who had already dismounted and were circled around a form on the ground. Here and there horses stamped and snorted or tossed their heads in agitation. Jan saw Trace Donahue try to calm a couple of them while also

7

paying attention to whoever was on the ground. Jan scanned the scene to determine which woman wasn't standing.

"My leg! My leg! It's broken!"

Jan's heart beat faster and she moved closer.

"It's Mrs. Donahue!" Dori said urgently. Her brow wrinkled in concern.

It was true. Bridget Donahue was lying on her back, rocking side to side and reaching for her right leg while she howled in pain.

"Mom, can you hear me? It's Trace. We're going to get you help!" Trace handed two sets of reins to Chris and squatted by his mother. He and Bridget shared the same blond, toned looks. "Can you tell us what happened?"

Most of the riders were just standing still, stunned into silence.

"Did anyone call for help?" asked the burly man from the out-of-town trio.

Orin Bond, the town postman, spoke up. "Everything was fine, and then her horse got fidgety and began to buck."

Overwrought, Bridget shook her head fiercely and gave another yell. Tears flowed down her face and smudged mascara around her eyes. "Something scared Leopold! He never does that!" she cried as she cradled her leg. "Who did this? *Who did this?*"

Trace tried again to get her to explain what might have scared the horse, but she said between sobs that she didn't know. "But someone did this to me," she cried. "I know it!"

An enormous black horse stamped and snorted behind her. His reins were one of the sets Trace had handed to Chris. The animal's sleek ebony coat shimmered over his muscled frame. Jan assumed he must be Leopold. He was beautiful. He stamped again and nodded deeply toward his owner, then gave a shake of his mane.

Orin and Russell Edmonds started to help Bridget sit up, but she swatted their hands. "Don't touch me! The pain!" She kept on about Leopold. "He would never hurt me! Someone did this!"

Trace looked regretfully at the men and shook his head. They backed off, and everyone seemed too befuddled to know.

Everyone reacted differently to pain, Jan reasoned, and then she remembered something. "Dr. Tyson!" She nearly had to shout over the cries, but she got most of their attention. "He was back at the Orchard Hill booth earlier. One of us needs to get him…a better rider than I am."

"I'll go," Russell offered as Jan placed a call to Dr. Tyson. Russell was on the trail ride with his schoolteacher wife, Kit, and their spunky seven-year-old, Marcella, who looked shaken. He squeezed the girl's shoulder, then seconds later he was back on his horse and off at a gallop.

Trace sat down next to his mother and got her to lean against him. He just kept nodding and patting her arm. The rest of the group inched away, giving them space.

Jan felt in the way too. Even though she felt terribly for Bridget, she couldn't do anything to help her at the moment.

She decided to see if she could find anything that might have scared the horse.

She looked around but couldn't see anything on the path that seemed likely to have spooked Leopold. Just some leaves and twigs and pinecones on the trail and the trees on either side. Maybe something in the woods...

She dismounted and held out her reins to Kit. "Would you mind holding these for me, just for a couple of minutes?" she asked in a low voice. "I want to take a look in the trees."

Kit took the reins and Jan moved to the tree line.

She pushed back a couple of low-hanging branches. The bark felt cool and rough to her fingers. A few feet off the path, the temperature dropped some more, and she could smell the pungent soil and decaying greenery that cushioned the ground. Being in the woods felt sheltering and a little spooky at the same time, especially in autumn.

She shook off that last thought; she needed to keep a grip on logic and not get carried away by the drama, or her imagination. She took a deep breath and gave herself a pep talk. If there was anything unusual to find...well, in the mysteries she and Elaine had investigated over the past year and a half, Elaine was always saying that Jan was good at picking up on the little details.

She thought about what she did know so far. Although she didn't know Bridget well, she figured the woman had to be experienced on horses to make them her life's work. And although Jan didn't know what Leopold's temperament was, whether he was typically high strung, his owner obviously had an expressive personality, Jan thought, and then chided herself. The woman was hurt. Some people were just louder than others when they were in pain.

So much for what she did know, she thought. She felt very out of her element—from taking up horseback riding that day to realizing she didn't know how to find her way through the woods. It was sort of funny, really.

She picked her footing carefully and decided not to go too far. Her boots crunched the undergrowth for several winding yards. It was darker in the woods, where meager sun rays were hard pressed to make it through all the clouds and foliage down to her level. She checked the ground as she scooted along, then looked up into the trees for an animal that might have startled Leopold. The atmosphere in the forest was still, muffled from the loudest voices on the trail.

Jan thought again about Bridget's claim that something— or someone—purposely caused her fall. Had Jan really heard laughter in the distance? Was it related? She couldn't have imagined that...or had she? Admittedly, there had been a lot going on, so it was possible the sound came from the chaos of the group. But it really seemed like it had come from the woods. If she had heard correctly, then Bridget may have been right that someone provoked Leopold to buck—and stuck around long enough to laugh about it. It didn't make sense. Who would do such a thing? And why?

Jan looked back toward the trail and saw several riders turn, apparently at something approaching. Seconds later she heard the faint thump of hoofbeats and the rumble of an engine, and then Russell slowed his horse and Dr. Tyson pulled up in a golf cart. Jan headed out of the woods toward them.

But as she took her next step, she glanced down and gasped at the sight at her feet. Instinctively, she lurched backward. She stumbled and almost fell before she braced herself on a large maple trunk and her other hand flew to her mouth as she scrambled to catch another look at a bolt of color she'd spotted in the undergrowth.

There it was again. Four feet from her boots a snake with red, yellow, and black rings coiled and raised its head. Its forked tongue flicked in and out beneath glowing eyes that were staring right at her.

CHAPTER THREE

Jan told herself to be calm. She'd be fine. Wow, if she thought she was out of her comfort zone before!

She'd come so close to stepping on the creature. She'd never been overly afraid of snakes, but she wasn't a fan of them either. And this one had startled her. It looked so unusual, not the average brown, black, or green she'd expect to find in a central Maine forest. It looked like pictures of venomous coral snakes from her kids' science books back in their homeschool days. Those were very dangerous, but she didn't think they were found in Maine.

She studied it. It didn't move except for that flicking tongue. Shimmering and bright, the reptile really was beautiful, but yikes. *Just don't move,* she silently willed it.

Then it occurred to her: Could this snake have been closer to the trail a few minutes ago and spooked Leopold? If it had been, then a bucking horse and a tumbling, hollering rider could have sent it slithering back to the safety of the woods. Only a few yards separated it from the trail.

But how did this snake get here? If it really wasn't native, it wouldn't just be randomly slithering around. Had it been intentionally placed? She shouldn't jump to conclusions. She didn't want to create more upheaval around Bridget by announcing its presence, but neither did she want to dismiss this creature that seemed so out of place. She thought quickly.

Jack. Jack Weston was a game warden who worked for the Maine Department of Inland Fisheries and Wildlife. The headquarters were in Augusta, but Jack worked in the Lancaster area, and had incidentally also taken interest in her daughter, Tara. Jan had definitely seen more than a few sparks fly between them, but right now, she was more interested in what he thought of this snake than her daughter. She had a feeling he'd want to get a look at it.

Stealthily, still watching the snake, she moved back and took a photo of it with her phone. She found Jack's contact information, sent the photo, and had him on the line in no time. She quickly explained the situation. "I don't want to create another scene after Bridget's accident, but if this snake had something to do with it...well, it also just doesn't look like it belongs here. If it's someone's lost pet, I figured you might know how to get it back to its owner."

"Sure, Jan. Tell me where you are on the trail."

She described her location as best she could until he seemed to understand.

"I think I can be there in ten minutes."

She thanked him, disconnected, and didn't dare move another muscle or make another sound.

Thhp...thhp. The tiny, glistening fork-tongue flicked in and out, almost too fast to see.

Jan was thankful for her sturdy boots that protected her feet and legs. She glanced at the group on the trail. They were partly blocked by branches, but Bridget looked like she was sitting more quietly now. Jan knew Dr. Tyson could help calm her, if anyone could.

Antsy for Jack to get there and anxious not to lose sight of the snake, Jan started to feel impatient. *Come on, Jack.* She knew from Tara that he'd renovated an unused bay of his garage for his office, which was outside of the main part of town, away from busyness but still fairly local. She tried to guess where he was by now on the drive out to the woods. Jan couldn't see Kit at all but knew that if everyone dispersed before Jack arrived, Kit wouldn't know what to do with Triscuit. She didn't want to keep the woman waiting, especially since Kit had a young daughter to get back to the stables, and Marcella had looked upset about the accident.

Minutes passed while Jan waited. She watched several riders help Bridget into the golf cart. It soon drove off. Jan knew the rest of the group would be looking for her because Trace wouldn't want to leave anyone behind, but she really didn't want people tramping into the woods and sending this snake slithering off into oblivion.

Then she remembered she had Kit's number and jabbed a quick text to her.

Checking out snake. Jack Weston coming. Don't want to call attention back here. Ask Trace to wait 5 mins pls?

As she was about to hit Send, she heard the trees rustle between her and the trail, and Jack appeared between the leaves. She must have been distracted because she hadn't heard his truck pull up. It was good to see him.

A broad grin broke across the thirtysomething's friendly face. "Hey, Jan. How're you doing? I got here fast as I could." He was wearing an official game warden jacket and carried a long grabbing stick and a clear rectangular container with a lid. He checked the ground without moving closer. "Where…?"

Her pointing finger answered him.

His eyes searched the ground, and after several seconds he nodded once. He quietly set the container on the ground and removed its lid, setting that next to the box.

He trained his focus on the animal and moved closer within the stick's reach of it. "If this thing moves before I can grab it, you get yourself out of the way, okay?"

"Got it. No desire to be snake bait." She swallowed. "Do you think it's venomous?"

"I don't. We don't have venomous snakes around here, and the state has lots of rules about not keeping them as pets. The big question is, where did this guy come from and how did it end up here? Heh, that's two questions. Let's hope I can catch a snake better than I can count." He shot a smirk toward her before his brow wrinkled and he angled for a different position over the snake.

"Like you," he went on, "my first thought was this is a coral snake. My new guess is it's a milk snake. There's a variety of those that look a lot like the coral snake. They aren't venomous."

"That's a relief."

"Yes, but that type isn't indigenous to Maine either. So we still don't know why it's here today. Now please step back, Jan."

She obeyed, and his arm shot downward and the leafy ground erupted with writhing. A second later he held up the pole with the striped snake wriggling furiously from the end of it.

Jack moved back a step, holding the pole away from himself and Jan. He deposited the snake in the container and secured the lid.

The snake curled into a corner. They both watched it for a minute. Its scales were brilliantly colored and shiny. Jan felt like its slitted eyes were glaring at her, then Jack straightened and looked at her. "I'm not positive what type it is, but I can find out when I get back to my office. This was a good find on your part. Lucky you didn't get closer to it. Any snake can bite if it feels threatened."

She nodded. "So you don't think it's indigenous?"

"No. Which means that…"

"Someone put it here?"

"Or around here, yes." He tipped his head and pursed his mouth, as if trying to come up with a likely scenario. "Or I suppose it could be a pet that got loose. There aren't so many state regulations against keeping nonvenomous snakes as pets."

"And it ended up right here at the very moment our trail ride came through?"

She could tell he shared her doubts. She couldn't do anything more now, though, and she was anxious to fill Elaine in on what a ride it had turned out to be. So much for trying something new! "I better not keep my group waiting any longer."

WHEN JAN GOT back to the booth at last, she was glad to see business hopping, even though she wanted a few minutes of Elaine's time to share all that had happened and to voice a few more questions that had been forming in her mind. She also intended to follow up with Jack to find out his plans to try to locate the snake's owner, and a confirmation on what type of snake it was. But that would have to wait too.

"Have fun?" Elaine greeted her warmly when Jan slipped behind the booth.

"Mm-hmm," she responded simply while reaching in a bin under the table for two more bags of treats to replace the ones Elaine was ringing up for an elderly tourist couple. She and Jan had decided to sell a new pastry during the festival, a twist on Jan's beloved maple croissants: maple Cronuts, which was a mix of a croissant and a donut. She placed the bags next to several others on the table and shuffled everything distractedly while she waited for the couple to move on.

Elaine shot her a quizzical look but kept telling the couple about what the week offered. When the man and woman left, Elaine took a sip from her stainless tea mug before speaking. "It's been really busy here. These Cronuts are selling like the wind. Did you have a good time?"

"I'm so glad! And yes?" Jan shook her head, accenting the question mark. "I'll tell you about it later. It was a little more than I bargained for."

Elaine looked curious, but a pair of women in fall jackets, bulky neck scarves, and ankle boots approached the booth. Jan said hello to them before moving aside so Elaine could help them. She knew she'd do better behind the scenes for the short time they had left before closing up for the day.

As Jan went through the motions of keeping the table filled with bags of Cronuts and filling tea samples while Elaine ran the register, she reviewed the questions she'd already thought of: Where did the snake come from? Who did it belong to since it wasn't naturally found in those woods? And did it escape and end up there accidentally, or was it placed there on purpose? If on purpose, who put it there and why?

But there were also several new questions forming, questions that mattered if someone had purposely left the snake on the path. If so, then why was Bridget the target? Or was she? It was also possible someone wanted to spook any of their horses and Bridget happened to be the unfortunate victim.

She reviewed the trail riders: The three Edmondses, Dori Richardson and Chris Cosgrove, Trace and Bridget Donahue, the visiting family of three she'd met that morning who were in town to see a niece cheer for Forrest High, Orin Bond, and herself. She had no clue why any of them would be the object of a trick like that. Someone could have gotten seriously hurt. As bad as it was that Bridget probably had a broken leg, it could have been much worse.

She handed a bag of Cronuts to Macy Atherton, who'd just walked up. Jan smiled. Macy could be picky, but her crusty front hid a kind heart, Jan knew. "Thanks for stopping by,

Macy," she said cheerfully. "I hope your guests enjoy those Cronuts. They're a special twist on my maple croissants."

Macy harrumphed. "I hope they're not dry." Macy's short gray hair fluttered on another breeze that smelled of rain.

"Try to get home before the storm hits," Jan said, and Macy looked skyward, where the clouds continued to darken.

Elaine checked her watch. "It's almost five o'clock, so let's pack up and head home."

CHAPTER FOUR

Elaine couldn't get Jan's story out of her mind the next morning while she showered and then dressed in tan slacks and a melon-colored merino turtleneck. She ran her short brown hair through the barrel of a curling iron several times while she mulled over the events as Jan had described them and wondered what they all meant. Jan had seemed more and more certain that she'd heard laughter from the woods about the time the accident happened. Why would someone plant a snake and try to scare a horse on a simple trail ride? Elaine couldn't deny the quickening of her pulse at the chance of a new intrigue to unravel.

Sunshine was streaming through the windows of the parlors as she reached the bottom of the stairs, ready for the day. Elaine smiled to see their employee sorting silverware in a drawer across the hall in the east parlor. "Morning, Archie!" she cheerfully greeted him. "Nice to have you back. How was your trip?"

It was his first day back at work after returning from a New York City vacation with his wife, Gloria. Elaine was curious to hear how his meeting had gone with an art authenticator. They hoped she would verify whether the painting the cousins had found at Mainely Bargains was an original by Archie's father, whom they'd all been surprised to learn had been a talented and renowned painter before Archie was born.

"It is a nice morning," he answered in his refined English accent. "And we enjoyed our trip immensely, thank you, although it is good to be home."

"I want to hear all about it."

"Perhaps if we finish our morning preparations," he said, "we can sit a spell and I can fill you in before we open. Although there isn't a great deal to tell yet."

"Did the authenticator—I can't remember her name—did she give an idea when she might have information for you?"

"Beatrice Miller-Pyle. And she hopes to give me a call in a couple of weeks."

That didn't sound too bad, Elaine thought. The painting had taken decades to come into Archie's life, and he must be chomping at the bit to hear the truth about it; she figured she could wait a couple weeks for her own questions to be satisfied.

He turned toward the window then and changed the subject. "The storm seems to have passed overnight. Your maple tree fared better than some."

Elaine went to a corner window framed in polished wood trim. Minus many of its fiery leaves that were scattered over the lawn, the tree in their front yard looked fine. But along Main Street, branches lay in the road from nearby properties. Workers were clearing the larger ones and tossing them onto truck beds. One worker was hauling a limb from Sylvia's doorstep next door. Sylvia was outside shaking her head and picking up a few leafy twigs. Though her property looked a mess at the moment, she was dressed smartly, her dark hair pulled back in a sleek ponytail.

"She's lucky that didn't hit her house," she told Archie. "I must've slept hard. I didn't hear any of it."

Elaine moved into the west parlor to make sure everything looked in order for the day. Tables and chairs were in place, and Archie had already placed silverware rolled in napkins at each place. On her way back toward the kitchen, her eye caught sight of the empty place on the parlor's far wall. The painting had hung there before they'd packaged it up for the trip with Archie to New York.

Before they'd learned the painting was so valuable, she and Jan had wanted to display it where everyone who came through the parlor could see it. The painting had been of special interest to Archie since the moment he saw it when they brought it home. He had been shocked to see a symbol in the scene that he recognized as his father's. The symbol combined three initials, HAB, layered over each other.

Archie hadn't known his father to be a painter—as far as Archie knew, he had been an official for the British government. But recently, Archie had confirmed that his father, whose name was Henry Arthur Bentham, was not only a painter, but a world-famous one, who'd gone by the pseudonym Harley Archibald Benningham. And yet it still surprised and delighted him to see such a lovely painting done by his father's hand.

It was a tranquil image. Archie's father had painted the length of a room, with a good-size window at one end. Vintage kitchen appliances, a café table with newspaper and tea, and a small vase of flowers, were the setting for the painting's main focus: a beautiful, brunette woman dressed casually in morning clothes. She was seated at the table with her legs crossed, sipping tea. The tea was one of the things that had drawn Elaine and Jan to the painting originally. In the painting, the woman was gazing out the window, her face in profile. She was looking outside at a lovely park.

The painting had a melancholy yet peaceful quality about it that drew Elaine in whenever she looked at it. It occurred to her that she'd like to have a print made so they could continue studying it while it was in New York. She had a snapshot of it on her phone and jogged her brain to think of a place where she could have a print made.

There was a one-hour photo store near Nathan's home in Waterville. It only took a minute to find the store's Web site on her phone, and with a few clicks she placed an order for an eleven-by-fourteen print. After sending a quick text to Nathan asking if he wouldn't mind picking it up for her before his next trip to Lancaster, she felt content knowing that she, Jan, and Archie could refer to the picture anytime they wanted to until the painting was safely back at Tea for Two. Her gaze rested once again on the image on her phone screen.

"It is a mystery, isn't it?"

Surprised, Elaine turned and patted the Englishman's arm. "Quite." Her answer sounded British to her own ears. Archie's influence, she supposed. She recalled not being sure they were making the right decision to hire such an overqualified man as their second employee, but she had grown to appreciate and enjoy Archie's heart and good work, not to mention his vast knowledge of the world of tea and so many other things. His résumé was like none other she'd seen. He'd been everywhere and done so many things, and that was saying something coming from her, a woman who'd lived all over the world as a military wife.

"I'm befuddled about where to look next to learn more about my father—I mean, besides the Googling we've done, which revealed almost nothing." They'd searched for information on Henry under his pseudonym, only to find that he had remained almost entirely out of the media's gaze, which wasn't as difficult back then, but still impressive.

"I know, I'm wondering the same thing. Jan and I were talking last night and we think it would be helpful to hear more about your memories of this apartment, as well as your father and his military history. And there's still so much to learn about the style of his paintings."

"Those are good ideas. As for the apartment, I was so young when we lived there, I don't remember a great deal. But I do know it was near the Soho area, which attracted artists."

They'd learned from Heather Wells, the antiques restorer in Waterville, that the stretcher bar across the back of the painting's canvas came from an art supply store in Soho.

Archie continued. "And I certainly would like to know more about his military days, if we can find out anything. The war was not a subject he welcomed talking about."

"That's understandable." Archie's father wouldn't be the first soldier who lived with difficult memories. In all her years being married to Ben, a lieutenant-colonel in the army, Elaine had heard her fair share of PTSD stories and the difficulties of returning to civilian life, where the average person couldn't truly relate to wartime dangers.

They headed back to the kitchen, where Jan and Rose, the first employee they'd hired, were mixing and forming croissants, cookies, and scones for a busy Monday. Rose's thick hair was plaited past her shoulders and looked like a braided loaf of bread.

A purr filtered through the kitchen door that opened to the screened porch.

"Would you check on Earl Grey, Elaine?" Jan's face was flushed from a wave of heat as she leaned toward the open oven to remove a pan of pumpkin bars.

The cat purred again when Elaine opened the door to the porch. "Good morning, mister." She reached down to stroke the cat's silky gray neck. He looped his tail around her wrist and purred luxuriously until she scooped cat food from a lidded container and listened to the kibble pitter-patter into the small bowl they kept for him. She refilled his matching water bowl and returned inside.

From the office off the kitchen, she retrieved her list and went to the granite-topped island, where she could read under the pendant lights. "Rose, you still okay to stay until six today?"

"Yes, and the rest of the week. Brent's got a late class tonight, so it works out well." The two had met in culinary school and had been dating for a while. Brent had a six-year-old, a dark-haired, blue-eyed daughter named Emma. It was good to see Rose so happy. She'd become like part of Jan and Elaine's family.

"I'll just be another few minutes," Jan said, swiping her wrist across her forehead.

"No rush. We're in good time." Elaine checked the oven clock to be sure. "I'll open with Archie and then help you pack the car."

Rose and Archie could handle the tearoom while they were at the fair. But their extra hands would be helpful unloading booth supplies each night. Rose would also have time after the tearoom closed to do some baking for the next day, and Archie would see to the dishes and table linens before the cousins returned.

Elaine opened the front door and swept the porch and sidewalk. Along Main Street, stores were opening, their owners cleaning up storm debris to make the street presentable for the locals and visitors who would populate Lancaster for Fall Fest.

When Elaine returned to the kitchen, Jan's son, Brian, was there eating a leftover blueberry scone.

"Just wanted to be sure you've got a handle on things, Mom. I know these festival weeks stress you out, especially without Bob stopping by to lend a hand."

Jan waved off his concerns. "I'm fine, Bri, but thanks."

"But…"

"Really."

Thirty-three years old with a medium build, brown hair, and eyes like his father's, Brian Blake was protective of his mother. Elaine was secretly pleased to see that he'd wasted no time taking her hint to look out for Jan after Bob had moved away.

But Jan looked a little impatient as usual when anyone mentioned Bob leaving. In fact, whenever anyone showed concern about how she was doing without Bob nearby, Jan downplayed it. It had to be a cover for her true feelings, Elaine figured.

Elaine tried to seem nonchalant as she set bags of maple Cronuts into the bins for the booth. Jan had to be heartbroken, losing her husband more than a decade ago and now for a second love to move far away...

"Of course I miss him. But I'm happy," Jan said pointedly. "I chose to stay, remember." A plastic sleeve bag of sample cups dangled from one hand, and she gripped a stack of napkins in the other. But a second later, the middle of the napkin wad pinched out of her small hand and cascaded on to the kitchen floor.

Jan blew out raspberries, and Rose, Elaine, and Brian stopped to help her gather up the napkins. Jan hooded her eyes at her son in a playful threat as she tossed the whole stack into the garbage. "I'm okay. But I need to get to work and so do you." She steered him out the door and took the napkin from his scone and tossed it into the trash with the others. "Have a good day, Brian. And bring my granddaughters and Paula by this week, will you?"

That was that. Elaine gave a knowing look to Rose when Jan's back was turned. Elaine said nothing more to Jan about Bob on their way out the door, but she'd continue to keep her eye on her cousin.

CHAPTER FIVE

The drive out of town was a colorful sight. Pirates pennants hung from lampposts, and banners were strung high across Main Street, along with posters and more banners to announce the Fall Fest. With the addition of nature's own colors that autumn had unfurled, the street looked ready for a celebration.

"I love this time of year." Elaine drove slowly past painted displays that Forrest High Pep Club students had done on the windows of A Little Something, Oldies But Goodies, the Bookworm, and Gift Me.

"Remember those days?"

"Doesn't seem terribly long ago, does it?" Elaine turned to head out of town and broached the subject that had hung over their heads since last evening. "You feeling okay about being out there today?" She wasn't sure how spooked Jan had been, thinking that a mysterious person had been hiding in the woods near her.

But Jan made little of that concern too. Her expression was clear and seemed full of fresh perspective. "I don't think there was any real danger yesterday. I'm over the creeps, for the most part."

Elaine nodded. "Good. Because I'd love to help figure out where that snake came from, and I've got some ideas."

"Go on."

"Pet stores. We could start narrowing down where it might have come from. I say let's call a few stores in the area to see if they've sold any striped snakes that look like that one." She had a good idea of what it looked like from the pictures Jan had pulled up online to show her last night.

"I'd also like to call Jack later about putting out notices that he found the snake, in case it's someone's pet that really did get out and ended up there by accident."

"Good idea. And I want a look in the woods for myself."

"That would be good—maybe you'll notice something I didn't."

Minutes later they arrived at the clearing. Soon after that, they had the booth set up and were serving a steady stream of customers. The mood was lively, but there was a lot of buzz about Bridget's accident and the snake, news that had spread like wildfire.

What Elaine hadn't anticipated, however, were twitterings about a part of Lancaster's history she hadn't thought about in ages. Jan seemed surprised too. They'd already heard murmurs from a few customers by the time two women in well-cut clothes and manicured nails walked up and admired the treats Jan and Elaine had assembled.

"Landry came home last night gushing that Old Man Warner's back for his gold," the taller highlighted-blonde said in conspiratorial tones to her strawberry-blonde friend.

Even after Elaine handed each woman a Cronut sample, Elaine wasn't sure they knew she and Jan were standing there.

The blonde continued. "It's all over town. This morning, the gal who does my hair…"

"It looks great, by the way."

"Oh, thanks," her friend smoothed her waves. "Anyway, someone from my stylist's bridge club called her last night, saying it was the old guy for sure."

"That's hilarious. I didn't know anyone believed that legend." The redhead handed Elaine two bags of Cronuts with a flash of white teeth. "I'll take these. They're fabulous."

"Landry and his friends are saying Warner left the snake by his grave so no one would go near the gold," the salon-blonde said with a grimace. "How spooky is that?" The women giggled.

Stories about Old Man Warner were coming back to Elaine. He had been a grumpy tycoon who'd struck it rich in the California gold rush in the nineteenth century, then crossed the country to resettle in Maine. He was the original owner of these three properties until he lost them in a gambling bet.

Elaine recalled one Saturday night her junior year when she and a few friends hiked through these same woods and found the old curmudgeon's grave, isolated and lonesome looking, beneath an enormous oak. The rumors circled each October that Warner returned every few years—always random years, but oddly enough always in autumn—for his gold that was said to be buried near his grave.

"And my stylist said to her bridge-club friend that Warner's the one who spooked that horse. It happened near the grave, you know." Both women shook their heads and chuckled as they popped bites of Cronut into their lipsticked mouths.

Like the redhead, Elaine hadn't thought anyone truly believed there was hidden treasure to be found, but it did make for a good legend. And stormy nights like last night only added to the spooky mystique. It was no wonder Old Man Warner had been "resurrected" this year. The women moved on to the dairy booth.

"Ay-yi-yi," Jan laughed quietly.

An hour passed before the pace dwindled enough so they could pause to eat the sack lunches they'd brought. Elaine was anxious to check out the woods by then, so Jan gave her as many quick details as she could remember about where Bridget had fallen.

Phone in hand, Elaine set off on foot for what she fig-ured would be a half-mile trek. She waved over her head at another urging from Jan to be careful and wondered whether it would have been smart to ask Nathan to join her, just in case. But whoever was in the woods yesterday wouldn't have camped out there until now. What would be the point? Feel-ing good enough about her safety and reminding herself that Nathan was busy at his auction house, she kept going, assured that it was best she didn't interrupt him just to help satisfy her curiosity.

Right now, mere curiosity was their main motivation for finding more about what happened yesterday. Neither of them really knew Bridget Donahue, and they certainly had enough to do to stay busy and forget the whole thing. But Elaine loved investigating, and she knew the incident was eating at Jan.

Getting a look at the scene now and calling a few pet stores later on felt proactive.

As the voices from the booths faded behind her, Elaine was glad to get some exercise on such a beautiful day. When she dressed that morning, she'd chosen her old pair of hiking boots that had traveled through a lot of countries when she and Ben had been overseas. No matter how much time passed, thoughts of Ben would always bring a joy deep down, she knew, along with wishes that they'd had more time to enjoy retirement before he passed away.

But she had Nathan now. Her heart swelled. Brilliant, kind Nathan. A new gift from the Lord who was so suited to her, and she to him. Theirs was a relationship built on friendship and long history as well, one that went back decades to a childhood friendship born even before she'd laid eyes on Ben. God was good that way, to give her a sense of coming full circle into this new love with Nathan. He was a good man, and good to her too.

With each step her boots squished rain-soaked layers of leaves that had been crunchy before yesterday's storm. The part of the trail she was on cut through meadow grasses, but she could see trees up ahead. Though the air felt brisk and cleared her lungs, the noon sun was warm on her head, and she was glad for the sunglasses she'd dropped into her tote at home that morning. She was tempted to tie her jacket around her waist but figured the temperature would drop more comfortably in a few minutes beneath the trees.

She reached the wooded section and rounded one bend before she saw a second and knew that must be the one Jan described. A section of the trail looked more disheveled, possibly where Bridget fell. There, hoofprints had plowed deeper into the dirt, the fallen leaves and older debris pushed aside as if something bulky had disturbed them. Turning to her left, she set her jaw and tramped into the woods at that place, sending a couple of birds soaring with perturbed calls.

Although she did want to get a look around the accident site, she had to admit she was curious about the old man's grave. It had been so long since she'd laid eyes on it, and frankly she'd forgotten about it at all until that morning, but the distant recesses of her memory told her its location was not far.

She remembered that she and her friends had found the headstone under a large oak tree. The forest had about forty years of growth since she'd been there as a seventeen-year-old girl, so she kept her eyes peeled for the broadest trunks.

As she pushed back low-hanging growth on some saplings vying for space, she realized she'd been watching her boots with every step. She shook off concerns that another snake would appear and kept going. It was a little unnerving that the only sounds were the ones she was making, but she refused to spook herself wondering if anyone outside those woods could hear her.

About fifty feet from where she'd abandoned the trail, she pushed back another branch to keep it from slapping her face and blinked as something at the end of it brushed her cheek. A swatch of shiny black fabric was stuck to the branch's tip, as if it had been torn from a piece of clothing. Stitches of gold thread were woven through an edge of it.

She stuck the scrap in her jacket pocket and stepped around the branch.

And there it was in front of her. A weathered gray head-stone, darkened by moisture and time, poked up a couple of feet from the earth. Tilted at an angle, with bits of moss growing in the letters etched into the rock, it still stood its ground. Time and the elements had worn away the precision of the numbers and words, much like waves flush away creations on a beach, bit by bit.

Fordham Cyrus Warner, the name read. He had been born on February 2, 1830, and died July 19, 1891. The stone was plain other than those facts. With no other indication that he'd left anyone behind who'd cared about him and no other graves nearby, the life of Fordham Warner seemed lonely and regretful.

Elaine felt drawn to the place, this fading symbol that someone had lived and died here long before her own story had begun. What had his life been like? To have enough zest to risk so much in the gold rush, to gain a fortune courageously, only to lose it because of a mistake that forevermore cemented his identity as the town legend, a grumpy hermit. She'd never heard any stories about him being cruel or bad—just curmudgeonly. But he had been a real man with more to him than the few details that made up his entire identity in the town's collective mind.

Any heart can become hardened by loss if left alone, that much she was sure of. A wave of gratitude filled her as she thought of her friends and family who'd filled up her empty spaces, many times quite assertively, to keep her from losing hope and vitality after she'd lost Ben.

Maybe Warner hadn't had that kind of community. Whatever his history, she hoped someone had cared for him in life. Everyone needed someone to hope the best for them. She couldn't help but feel some compassion for him—no one should be ostracized or made the butt of jokes for their mistakes.

But then again, there *was* a sign that someone had visited. She stepped closer and looked more carefully at the small, tidy pyramid of pinecones a few inches from the base of the headstone. Like a unique bouquet of sorts, they sat atop the ground cover, with no leaves or twigs over them, as if they'd been set there recently.

CHAPTER SIX

"How does it look?" Jan finished hanging a wreath of dried fall florals, faux apple slices, and cinnamon sticks on the front door.

It was seven thirty, and Main Street glowed with streetlamps, reminding Elaine of an evening scene on a postcard. Only a handful of festivalgoers still strolled past the shop windows. It was quiet enough to hear faint strains of music float from the marina and the putter of a boat out for an evening cruise or on its way home for the night. It was the kind of setting she loved to file away in the "cozy at home" nook of her heart. That nook continued to fill with every month that passed at Chickadee Lake.

"I love the golden shade of those mums in it," she answered as she observed the wreath next to Jan. "And I can smell those cinnamon sticks." Their fall décor was turning out beautifully on the front porch, she didn't mind telling herself. In addition to Jan's wreath, Elaine had brought home several pumpkins, the traditional orange and a couple of white ones, which they'd arranged on either side of the steps up to the door. "The wreath looks great."

"Claudia McInnis made them to sell at their booth. It was either this or a pinecone-and-pheasant-feather swag at A Little Something's booth. I liked that one too, but I think apples and cinnamon fit our tearoom better." Jan tipped the wreath a smidgen to the left and stepped back. "There."

"Speaking of pinecones," Elaine ventured as they chose porch rockers to relax in for a while, "I don't think we can assume the stack of them on the grave had anything to do with the accident or the snake." During supper she had shared with Jan the thoughts that had crossed her mind about Old Man Warner. Compassionate Jan had understood. "But if you did hear someone laughing in the woods, Jan, that person could have been the one who left them. Whoever it was took care putting them there."

Jan crossed her ankles. "Agreed. I'd never given the 'real person' part of his story much thought before now, I'm sad to admit, but I feel glad that someone seemed to break from the tradition of poking fun at him, whoever it was. Now, about those pet store calls." Jan had begged off supper cleanup to call stores before they closed.

"Shoot."

"For starters, I called Jack first to find out more about the snake. He'd already checked into it and said it's a Pueblan milk snake."

"And he's still sure it isn't native here?"

"They're native to Mexico."

"Maine's a long way to slither."

Jan smiled. "I also asked about his plans to locate its owner. He already talked to *The Penzance Courier* about a missing-snake ad in their pets section starting Wednesday morning. So in the meantime I offered to put a stack of missing-pet flyers at our booth and here too. He liked that idea and is having some printed to drop off tomorrow."

"And how about the pet stores?"

"I called a few. Two chain stores in Waterville and Augusta haven't ever carried Pueblan milk snakes. Two small pet stores in Augusta and Penzance don't sell snakes, period. But I did find two stores in Portland and Bangor that sold that type in the past."

"You covered some ground."

"I wouldn't have checked that far away, except the Penzance store manager knew someone who knew someone else who lived in Bangor years ago and owned milk snakes." Jan rolled her hand through the air. "The manager couldn't remember if any were Pueblans, though, and admitted it was a long shot. But it prompted me to look for stores in Bangor. After calling two stores there, it seemed worth checking in Portland, since it's a bigger city too."

Elaine hugged her sweater around herself. "Did anything turn up?"

"Nope. Not a single one has carried that type. They're usually special-order animals."

"So that seems like a dead lead."

Jan nodded and both women fell silent as they looked over the town.

The soft hum of another boat carried from the lake behind the house. The sound was broken suddenly by the thud of footsteps clumping up the wooden steps and along the side porch. A teenage boy in athletic wear came around the corner. Elaine hadn't seen him before but was surprised when Jan grinned and stood up.

"Derek, right?" Jan gave him a friendly smile and held out her hand, which he shook.

He was average height and strong looking with brown hair peeking from beneath a ball cap, and he seemed at first impression to be fairly serious. He removed his cap and nodded to Jan, then acknowledged Elaine with a soft "ma'am."

"Pull up a chair, Derek," Elaine offered. "What brings you to our tearoom this evening?"

He seemed nervous for some reason as he sat down and cleared his throat. "Well, I came because I heard you've solved some mysteries." He looked hesitantly from Elaine to Jan.

Jan's eyes widened and seconds passed in silence before she offered encouragingly to Elaine, "Derek works at Donahue Stables. I met him yesterday when he saddled my horse."

"Ah. It's good to meet you, Derek." Elaine grinned and held out her right hand to shake his. His handshake was firm despite his unsure manner. "And yes, we do love a good challenge to sort out." She loved being able to say they'd had some success at it.

He adjusted his position in the chair, rotated his ball cap several times in his hands, and seemed to search for his next words.

"Your friends on the ride were telling me that you play football for the Pirates," Jan continued with a glance to Elaine, obviously picking up on the tension.

Jan's efforts to draw him out worked. A sparkle lit Derek's eyes. "Yeah. I mean, yes, I do play football. Number 44."

"What position do you play?" Elaine asked, following Jan's cue to help the young man feel comfortable so they could find out what brought him to Tea for Two.

"Wide receiver. I just came from practice."

"We'll have to look for you in the game this weekend."

His polite responses held notes of pride, and he seemed to relax talking about something he obviously enjoyed. He cleared his throat again.

Elaine spoke gently. "You seem like a man with something on his mind, Derek. Why don't you tell us how we can help?"

The teen shrugged and began. "Well, I...I'm not sure. It's about the accident. Mrs. Donahue's."

Elaine sat up straighter. "What do you mean? And have you heard how she's doing?"

"Yeah. I mean yes. Trace said at school that her leg's broken and she's got him running all over the house for her..." He looked startled by his own words. "I guess I shouldn't have said that part."

But the cousins smiled, and soon a lopsided grin crossed his face too. "I didn't mean to say anything bad about her."

"No harm done. But what was it about the accident that you wanted our help with?" Jan pressed gently.

"Well, it's our team. There's a lot of pressure on us to win Friday's game against Claremore. And sometimes the teams like to prank each other. Dumb stuff like filling our cars with popcorn." He laughed, and his words started to flow then. "And one time we swapped their jerseys with junior high jerseys before they played Augusta. That was unfortunate for them." A grin peeked through before his seriousness was back. "But this game. It's big, you know? And a few years ago Claremore got a reputation for playing dirty when a couple of their players egged our locker room and spray-painted our shower walls. Destructive stuff."

Elaine thought she knew where he was headed. "You think they're back to their old ways?"

"I do."

"And you think yesterday's accident wasn't really an accident," Jan concluded.

"It seems fishy to me. I know Mrs. Donahue thinks someone did it to her. Trace says she's still upset about that."

"But why? Who does she think would do something like that?" Jan added.

He nodded to Elaine. "I'm not exactly sure. But Trace says she's convinced that her horse wouldn't have bucked for any old reason. To be honest, he and I both would agree with that. Leopold's the best." He looked at Jan. "As for who Mrs. Donahue might suspect, she really doesn't know."

Leopold. The name sounded regal for a horse, Elaine thought, although she had never seen the animal.

Jan sat forward. "I've heard she's a big advocate for Forrest High. She was in the tearoom for a meeting of the Boosters Club last month. If she is such an advocate for the school, is it likely that someone would have something against her?"

"See, that's the part I can't figure out," Derek answered. "She does a lot for Forrest High, and she never misses a game. Plus, why would someone want to mess with the mother of one of our players? It's true she can get pretty loud with her cheering, which I guess can bug some people. But I'm not sure anyone was trying to prank Mrs. Donahue."

Elaine and Jan waited.

"I think it was meant for Trace."

Elaine blinked. She was not expecting that comment.

Derek leaned forward. "Trace is our quarterback. He's key to our chances of winning Friday, and our opposition knows it." Derek's tone sounded firmer, more urgent and deliberate. "I think someone at Claremore was trying to keep Trace from playing this weekend."

CHAPTER SEVEN

Derek's statement hung in the air. He'd voiced something Jan had already considered—that Bridget just got in the way—but Derek had further narrowed it down to Trace. And a Claremore suspect. It was an unexpected theory.

Jan spoke first. "Do you suspect anyone in particular from that school?"

He shook his head. "No. I just think they're the ones with motivation. And Trace was helping lead that ride, which is typical. I asked him if he was up front near his mom, and he said he was. It would have been very easy to catch Mrs. Donahue off guard instead of Trace."

Jan was tracking with his logic but needed more to go on. "Let's think this through. Bridget Donahue was sure someone planned that accident—she was convinced Leopold wouldn't buck without a very good reason. What about Trace's horse? Would someone have expected it to spook more easily?"

Derek's mouth narrowed. "Trace's is a good horse too. I've spent a lot of time at the stables, working and hanging out with Trace. I know the horses nearly as well as he does, enough to know that any horse can get spooked if the conditions are there."

"Like encountering a striped snake?"

"Yeah, like a snake."

"Bridget has heard about it by now?" Elaine wondered out loud.

"She has," Derek said. "But she doesn't think even that could've made Leopold buck. I don't know though."

Jan thought for a second. "Do you happen to know anyone who owns a snake with black, red, and yellow stripes?"

He slowly shook his head as he appeared to give it some thought. "I don't know if any of the Claremore players own snakes."

"How about anyone from Forrest?" Jan thought the question had to be considered.

"No."

"Well, we don't know if the snake had anything to do with Mrs. Donahue's accident, but we also can't rule it out. Its presence near the trail was odd. Hopefully its owner will see Jack's ads and flyers," Jan said, then had a further thought. "If someone comes forward to claim it and has a good reason for how it got in the woods, that might mean either the accident was just coincidence or something else entirely."

Elaine was nodding. "But if someone planted the snake to try to scare any of the horses, they might be reluctant to come forward and admit guilt."

Derek looked concerned. "Especially since Mrs. Donahue got hurt." Then he held out his hands, the ball cap swinging from one. "See? It would really help if you could find out if Claremore is behind this whole thing."

"I see," Elaine said. "Let's assume for the moment that someone did intentionally scare one of the horses. How would that person have been able to pick out one specifically from the dozen on the trail ride? It's tough to know if anyone was a target when they were all clustered together."

He nodded. "I've thought about that too. I guess since I've been on lots of trail rides with both Mrs. Donahue and Trace, I've seen that their normal way of leading a group is for him to stay in the lead most of the time. She tends to hang back and talk with the first guest riders."

"I was behind the group when the accident happened, so I didn't see if she or Trace was first in line," Jan said.

"Trace confirmed it was Mrs. Donahue that time," Derek answered.

"But someone who'd been on a trail ride with them in the past might have remembered that he's usually in the lead and could have taken a reasonable risk that Trace's horse would have been first in the order again on Sunday," Jan said thoughtfully.

"But it seems pretty risky to try and target one particular horse, with a snake or some other method. And where was that person? In the woods? Could he or she have been spotted?"

All great questions from Elaine, but ones none of them had an answer for yet.

"How well do you know the Donahues?" Jan asked Derek next.

"Like I said, Trace is one of my best friends. Has been for as long as I can remember. Their house is like a second home to me. My folks both work a lot, so I've helped at the stables since Trace and I were young. Kind of a trade back then—my extra help for them keeping an eye on me until my mom got home from work. Now they pay me."

"Do you live near them?" Elaine wanted to know.

"Nah, I live closer to the high school. Nothing fancy like theirs."

"Do you know anyone with something against any of the Donahues?" Nothing had been mentioned about Trace's dad. Clive was his name, Jan recalled.

"Not really. Mr. Donahue is pretty quiet and travels for his work. He does some kind of investment training. I don't understand it. Mrs. Donahue can be a prankster herself," he admitted. "She used to play jokes on Trace and me. She'd sneak up and surprise us a lot or put green food coloring in our macaroni and cheese. Once she put sealed pouches of that kids' play slime inside our barn boots, which felt really weird to step into. And I've lost count of the times Trace and I would want to crash in front of the TV after working hard in the barn, only to have whoopee cushions sound off under our sofa cushions when we sat down."

Elaine laughed out loud, and Jan smiled at the image. Bridget Donahue sounded like a fun mom. And it sounded sweet to Jan that Bridget made efforts to connect with the boys on their level. She obviously knew what kids would get a kick out of.

"She hasn't done any of that for a while though," Derek said. "She's really busy with Boosters and PTA and running the stables. Hers is a name you hear a lot at school events. The Donahues carry some weight in the district. And now with

Trace being number one for college scouts to watch…" His sentence dropped off.

"If Mrs. Donahue likes pranks herself, maybe a friend of hers went too far getting her back," Jan suggested, playing devil's advocate to Derek's theory that Trace was targeted.

"Yeah, I thought of that." But Derek still looked doubtful. "It just seems more like a high school thing to mess with a snake like that. And the timing with the homecoming game seems like more than a coincidence."

Derek suddenly stood up and said he needed to get home. Putting his cap back on his head, he added, "If you could do anything to find out if Claremore's trying to get Trace benched, I'd appreciate it."

Jan and Elaine looked at each other. They had already started looking into it of course, little did Derek know. Their curiosity had been piqued, and with Derek's clear concern, it gave them all the more reason to investigate.

"Of course we'll help, Derek." Jan raised her finger. "Oh, and one more thing. Have you told Trace about your theory?"

"Yeah. He wasn't all that concerned. He figured I might be right, because he doesn't know who would do that to his mom. Actually, he hopes someone had it in for him instead of her. But he didn't notice anything odd on the trail, and he isn't thinking much of it. That's his way. He's a lot more chill than his mom, who can be pretty focused when she wants to get things done."

Derek looked frustrated. "But Trace doesn't have as much riding on this game as some of us do. He doesn't need scholarship money to go to college. He wants to win the game, sure. But just for the win, not necessarily for his future. Some of us need the best chance we can get to go to college, which means we need him healthy to play this weekend."

Elaine sent a meaningful glance Jan's way before responding. "We totally understand. We'll do whatever we can to help."

CHAPTER EIGHT

T uesday morning ushered in a bright fall day at the booth, with a few clouds scattered across the sky and the sun warming the cool air.

"I think a visit to Claremore's head football coach would be good," Jan told Elaine. "They'll probably be practicing after school all week."

Elaine was pouring two samples of orange cardamom tea for their customers, and then sipped some herself as the couple walked away. "This is one of my favorites," she said to Jan.

"When you're not sneaking espresso?" Jan was fully aware of Elaine's "secret" habit.

Elaine looked at her mock-defensively, then conceded with a smile and a guilty shrug.

The morning zoomed along, but they made sure to take turns covering their booth to give each of them time to walk around among the shoppers and view the offerings at the other booths. Not only were the other booths run by fellow business-people, but Jan and Elaine considered those people friends.

When it was Elaine's turn, she decided to stop first at the church's booth because she could see them beginning a puppet show for toddlers and preschoolers who weren't in school all day. Elaine waved to the mothers she recognized and several people behind the scenes that she knew from church, including Pastor Mike.

Michael Ryder was narrating the story of Jonah and the great fish and putting lots of dramatic inflections into his voice. He caught Elaine's eye, and she gave him a silent applause. He grinned back but didn't miss a beat describing Jonah's decision to run away and his days in the fish's belly. The handful of children enjoying the special weekday event were active participants, scooting to stand near the puppets and jumping around with delight. A few of the mothers even had a chance to peek at the nearest booths and still keep an eye on their kids.

She moved on to visit with Annie Richardson. Annie saw her while she was putting a couple of cheese wedges into a paper bag and ringing up the purchases for the older man standing there. Elaine picked out a bottle of chocolate milk while she waited for him to finish and walk away.

"Taking a well-earned break, Elaine?"

Elaine liked Annie. "Jan's got things under control. She enjoyed talking with Dori on the trail ride Sunday."

"From what Dori told me, it sounds like that was some ride. Poor Bridget." Annie undid the clip that held back her auburn hair, then finger-combed it back into submission and refastened the clip.

"Do you know her very well?"

Annie said she did. "We're both in the PTA, so our paths cross quite a bit. She's something, that's for sure." It wasn't said insultingly, but with something along the lines of affectionate exasperation. "And Dori knows Trace and has spent time at the stables with some of the other high school kids."

"Yes, Jan and I talked with Derek recently." Elaine thought she might be risking coming across as nosey, but Annie didn't seem to mind.

"Yep. Derek has probably spent more time over there than any of the kids. Truth be told, I think he's one of the reasons my daughter likes working there. As a mom, I really can't complain about Dori's friends. I like all of them." Annie's smile was warm. "And even if Bridget has gotten pushier at times than some people would prefer, everyone knows her heart is in the right place and she's working hard for our kids."

There it was again, a suggestion that Bridget could ruffle feathers. "What's behind Bridget's reputation?"

"You mean what has she done to earn it?"

Elaine nodded.

Annie hesitated, and Elaine was glad she didn't seem to relish in gossip, which wasn't Elaine's thing either.

"Bridget's a friend. And she's a great mom, don't get me wrong." Annie spoke for Elaine's ears only as shoppers mingled a few feet away. "She'd do anything for Trace, like we'd all sacrifice for our kids. But sometimes I think her drivenness might get excessive where he's concerned. She pressed for more Boosters funds to be allotted for new football equipment, when lesser amounts went to girls' tennis and boys' soccer for their new uniforms."

Elaine could understand why that wouldn't sit well with the teams that might have felt cheated. But still, she didn't know the details of how it happened or why and couldn't judge based on the little information Annie shared.

Annie greeted a customer who paused to look over the merchandise. When the woman moved on, Annie opened up some more to Elaine. "As a mom, Bridget tends to be more protective than lenient, which personally I think can be great in the right balance. She likes to have the kids at her house, possibly to keep her son close. Again, not a bad thing. She certainly has a home to handle large numbers. Dori seems to like Trace's new girlfriend, Keri. For what it's worth, I think hanging out with Keri brings some levity Trace needs right now with football pressures on his shoulders. But now I'm just chattering on. Bridget's a good person. Her injury really was unfortunate, and I hope she recovers quickly."

Elaine tracked with most of Annie's jumping conversation but wasn't sure whether any of it had any bearing on the accident. New customers had come up to the booth, so Elaine knew it was time to move on anyway. She paid for the chocolate milk, wished Annie a good day, and went to see the McInnises.

Dr. Tyson and Claudia were an elderly African American couple who'd run Orchard Hill since the days when Dr. Tyson was the doctor at the Lakeview Clinic, which their son and daughter-in-law now ran. Since they'd gotten older, they relied more and more on good staff to do the manual labor at the orchard. They were a wonderful couple Elaine and Jan both enjoyed seeing often in the tearoom. And they'd even learned a while back that Claudia used to babysit Rose long ago.

Their booth was decked out in all things apple-related to celebrate one of autumn's best fruits.

"Hello there, Elaine Cook!" Claudia was easy to pick out of a crowd because her cap of pearly-white hair was eye catching. Also because graciousness flowed so easily out of her. She was sitting in a chair surrounded by customers while her workers hefted apple baskets onto wagons to make it easy for customers to transport to their cars.

Jars of apple butter, apple pie spice, cider gallons, and applesauce lined makeshift shelving behind the tables. Baskets of fresh apples in several varieties filled a wide area around the booth.

Elaine took Claudia's outstretched hand and felt the soft richness of Claudia's aged skin. She complimented her on how inviting the booth was and told her she wanted to make a few purchases after they visited a while. At Claudia's invitation, she took a seat in the empty chair next to her.

"Jan told me Dr. Tyson was such a help on Sunday."

"He was glad to be able to take care of Bridget. He'd be here now, but he took the cart home to do a few things. He should be back soon and will want to say hello to you."

"Jan didn't say whether he went with Bridget to the hospital."

"He did go. Her son needed to finish the trail ride and make sure there were no more troubles. So Tyson drove her to the hospital."

Elaine confided to Claudia that she and Jan were looking into what had caused the accident, and she thought it was worth asking Dr. Tyson if he'd noticed anything out of the ordinary.

At first Claudia said no, but she was glad they were trying to find out what had happened if there seemed to be doubts whether it had been a true *accident*.

Elaine was about to speak again but stopped when Claudia looked like she was thinking over something.

"Come to think of it, he did find something. I had forgotten this, but I suppose it may be important. When he came back from the hospital, he handed me a key he found when he was helping Bridget on the trail."

"A key?"

"Yes, a regular old key. It was on the ground near where she fell, and he picked it up, meaning to ask if someone had dropped it. But Bridget kept him so occupied that he realized he hadn't told any of the other riders about it. It's back at our house. We think it must belong to one of the high school students who went on the ride."

"Why is that?"

"Because it was on a key ring with one of the high school logos on it. Claremore."

Elaine remembered Jan telling her that Chris was on the trail ride and he had recently transferred to that school. Like Jan, Elaine hadn't talked with Chris Cosgrove in a long time, but she did remember who he was. Dori and Trace, the only other high school students on the trail ride, all went to Forrest High. She told Claudia she would ask Chris if the key was his, and Claudia was happy to text her husband to bring it back to the booth when he returned.

Back at Tea for Two's booth, the line was dozens of people deep, and Elaine jumped in right away. She and Jan needed to work together instead of taking shifts for a while until the rush died down. Soon, Dr. McInnis showed up in a golf cart and handed the key to Elaine. It was a plain silver key on a ring with a Raiders mascot on it.

"Thank you, Dr. Tyson," Elaine told him with a friendly pat on his arm. He nodded to both cousins and left, and Elaine tucked the key into her jacket pocket to look at if the crowd left her with a slower moment.

It could mean something or nothing, Elaine decided. The key could be Chris's, or someone else's from Claremore. To be honest, Elaine hadn't known initially what to think of Derek's idea that someone from Claremore might have been behind the accident. But that key could change her mind.

CHAPTER NINE

The afternoon was a blur of selling Cronuts and tea. Jan loved seeing familiar faces and thought the festival was turning into an all-out reunion as people flocked to town not only for Fall Fest but for homecoming week. She and Elaine caught up with many former schoolmates, some they hadn't seen since high school, now dispersed all over the world.

"As much as people change, they all stay somewhat the same, don't they?" Elaine commented.

It was true. While everyone they caught up with had certainly matured over the years, personalities were still familiar—the class jokester still cracked funnies at the booth, the girl once voted Friendliest still grinned beautifully when she complimented their Cronuts, and the ones Jan remembered being down to earth in high school seemed to have lived their lives well. The academic ones still liked to talk information, the athletes sports, the band members music. She couldn't help wishing Bob was still in town for this. Many of these people would have remembered him from Forrest High too.

It was late afternoon and the crowd had thinned some when Jan recognized a woman coming toward the booth. She'd seen the petite blonde only once since high school, back on one of the cousins' initial return visits to Lancaster when they were considering making an offer on their house. In spite of all the visiting and recalling of names Jan had done today, she panicked a little when the woman's name didn't immediately come to mind. Jan tried to place her by high school club and snapped her fingers when it hit her: journalism club. She scrambled for a name as the woman drew near.

"Jan and Elaine, how are you?" she asked a moment later from the other side of the table.

The swing of her bob did it. "Lucy Rodgers, it's been a while!" Jan straightened, relieved her memory had recovered just in time.

"I got the afternoon off unexpectedly, and now I get to catch up with both of you. It's my lucky day." Lucy was pretty with a natural style and simple makeup.

They chatted while Lucy paid for a bag of Cronuts and told them about her job as an administrative assistant for a construction firm in Augusta.

"Did you hear about the accident a couple of days ago?" She didn't give them much chance to answer. "I'm friends with Bridget, you know. Ever since college. Poor thing, I'm so glad she wasn't hurt worse, just her leg, but I couldn't help thinking it's lucky it was her leg and not her vocal chords. Oops, I shouldn't have said that." She covered her mouth in playful remorse. "I'm one to talk."

Between Derek saying that Bridget was capable of ruffling feathers in her school positions and that she was keeping Trace hopping since her accident, and Lucy basically saying Bridget talked a lot, Jan wasn't sure what to think of Bridget Donahue.

"Have you seen her since she got hurt?" Elaine spoke up.

"No, actually not for a while, but you know what a small world Lancaster can be. News travels fast. And now all the buzz about the old legend."

"We've heard that too. Silly, don't you think?" Jan asked.

"Oh, for sure, but it's fun to play up the old stories this time of year," Lucy replied, then winced a second later. "And I heard about the snake. *Ew.* Makes me shiver. I do hope Bridget is up and running quick. You know…well, maybe you didn't know, but I dated her husband, Clive, in college before they ever met."

"Really?" Elaine handed her another Cronut, which Lucy took without pausing.

"It's water under the bridge now. She got the good life, and I got the divorce. But no worries, I'm doing fine now."

That seemed like an odd statement, Jan thought. Sort of cynical, but then again, it sounded like Lucy was coming out of a tough season, which could wear on anyone's spirit.

"I'm sorry to hear you and your husband split up, Lucy," Elaine said.

"Thanks. But I really am doing fine."

Contrary to Lucy's claim, Jan sensed the breakup wasn't completely water under the bridge. She wanted to show Lucy kindness, and she couldn't help sensing a passive-aggressive frustration in Lucy toward Bridget. Lucy did come across as simple and quiet next to Bridget's more flamboyant style and personality. Bridget's life could seem enviable to someone who might have felt outdone by her over the years.

Jan remembered what she and Elaine had talked about with Derek—the possibility that Bridget's own peer might have played a prank on her. Did Lucy fit that description? Possibly. The smaller crowd allowed for more chitchatting time, which was good in a way because Jan wanted to know more. But she didn't feel comfortable prying into Lucy's divorce, no doubt a sensitive topic for Lucy, who really was quite sweet.

Elaine interrupted Jan's thoughts. "We heard Bridget can be a jokester."

Lucy's hair brushed her chin. "Yes, she can be. Bridget used to play jokes all the time in our sorority house. She got me once by rigging my room phone so when it rang and I picked up, it wouldn't stop ringing. It was one of those older styles, you remember. Talk about annoying! I had to listen to that thing for twenty minutes before I found someone who knew how to fix it."

"Annoying sounds right," Jan said, amused. "But you have to admit it's pretty funny too."

"I guess," Lucy managed around a bite of Cronut. "Funny looking back, but not so much at the time."

There it was again. A hint of genuine exasperation in Lucy toward Bridget. But it disappeared once more, and Lucy perked up.

"Have you ever pranked her back?" Elaine couched her frankness in a friendly tone.

"Sure. What goes around comes around, right?" A mischievous expression took over Lucy's features.

"Do tell," Jan said enticingly, very curious indeed about Lucy's feelings toward Bridget.

"Nah, just silly stuff," she said with a smirk. "It'd bore you, and it's been a while. I think I got her for her birthday a while back." Then she seemed to hurry to rationalize whatever it was she'd done. "In a sweet way, nothing nasty."

Jan wasn't sure why Lucy would think they'd assume she'd acted meanly, much less need to assure them she hadn't. But, Jan second-guessed herself, maybe she was trying to read too much between the lines and trying to find anyone with a motive. Maybe Lucy wasn't really sending mixed messages after all.

"I've never been much of a prankster myself," Elaine offered, "so I'm curious how people come up with their ideas. Do you ever hear of that stuff between her and other friends of hers?"

Lucy looked like she was losing interest, or maybe growing weary of discussing Bridget. Despite second-guessing her intuition mere seconds ago, Jan felt her confidence return. She *was* getting the impression that Bridget had a history of stealing the show from Lucy, at least from Lucy's perspective.

Lucy swallowed and answered Elaine. "Sometimes I'll hear bits and pieces at church, but nothing that I remember specifically. I will say one thing for Bridget Donahue, she'd do anything for her son."

"And he took good care of her after she fell Sunday," Jan offered.

"They're a good family. I think she goes overboard for him at times. That's got to wear thin on a seventeen-year-old kid."

"What do you mean?" Elaine wasn't shy about asking.

"Last year she was his biggest fan to the point of sending prayer requests through our church prayer chain for the good Lord to shine His favor over Trace's games."

Well, yes, probably excessive, Jan agreed without comment. But there could have been background circumstances, personal details, that Bridget didn't share that were complicating things for Trace at the time. She had to give Bridget the benefit of the doubt. There were times when mama bears needed to guard their cubs, each in her own way.

"Lucy, it's been nice to see you," Jan said, before adding one more question for her old friend. "Did you make it out to the festival on Sunday?"

Lucy tucked a blonde curl behind her ear. "No, not Sunday. After church I went to my sister's house for the afternoon."

Soon Lucy moved on to the Richardsons' booth, but something about the woman kept Jan watching as Lucy visited with Annie. The two women were laughing at something between them that Jan couldn't hear.

Jan didn't think she was off base sensing there was more to Lucy's friendship with Bridget than laughter and jokes. Could Lucy have returned a prank on Bridget on the trail? Maybe it was time to pay a visit to Bridget.

CHAPTER TEN

H ello there." Nathan was wearing jeans and a casual, cran-
berry-colored sweater.

Elaine's heart skipped a beat as she held the door open for
him. "Hi yourself. I'm almost ready." She was looking forward
to supper with him tonight. It had been a few days since they'd
spent any quality time together, so it would be extra good to
see him. But she was also itching to run the details of this latest
mystery by him. He often had helpful input and looked at situ-
ations from a different viewpoint than hers, which she valued
more and more all the time.

She pulled on a favorite cardigan and began to button it
and cringed at the realization that it was hard to make the
buttons meet across her middle—surely attributed to all those
Cronuts she'd sneaked. She'd have to take it down a notch,
literally, with all the snacking. She slipped her handbag over
her arm before taking his.

Jan was coming down the stairs as they were heading out
the door. Already in her robe and slippers, she looked ready to
settle in for the evening. Elaine cringed a little inside, hoping

her date with Nathan wasn't tugging at her cousin's wounded heart too much.

But Jan smiled brightly. "Have a nice time, you two."

"You're all set for a comfy night in," Nathan replied.

"I am. It might be my only quiet one this week, and I plan to milk it for all it's worth. Hot tea, maybe a good book or a puzzle magazine. Can't wait."

Elaine gave her cousin a sympathetic smile and was surprised to see Jan's expression flicker.

"I'll be fine, Elaine. Don't you worry. I might even paint my nails, woo-hoo." She chuckled, reminding Elaine of the time she'd pulled out all her nail polishes and helped Jan with a manicure before a date with Bob. Jan hadn't been used to that kind of primping, but they'd had fun. "Have a good supper," Jan said firmly.

Elaine didn't want to keep Nathan waiting, so she allowed herself to be led out the door, with a prayer on her lips that her cousin wouldn't get too lonesome. Just to be sure, she'd text Brian on the way to the restaurant so he could check in with his mother. That's what sons—and cousins—were for at times like these.

"Do you want to know what I think?" Nathan's blue eyes shone in the candlelight at the table for two. Seated at a restaurant he'd been wanting to try, about thirty minutes south of Lancaster, they were halfway through lobster tails and had updated each other on work and their kids. Elaine had just shared with him again her ongoing feeling that Jan wasn't being honest with herself about her grief over Bob leaving.

She smiled warmly. "One of the reasons I love spending time with you is because you help me see things from a different perspective. So I'm all ears."

He regarded her affectionately. "I think all Jan needs is your normal daily routine and friendship."

Nathan's answer was kind, as Elaine expected. But then again, he wasn't around Jan as much as she was, which could make it hard for him to see what Elaine did: Elaine knew that Jan was hurting. Elaine was of course there for Jan, but she suspected that Jan needed extra support, which Elaine was also making sure to offer her cousin. Elaine said as much to Nathan, who just smirked around his bite of asparagus.

He pointed his steak knife at the half-eaten loaded sweet potato on her plate. "Good, huh?"

Absentmindedly, Elaine looked at the food she hadn't finished. It had been a huge meal. "All of it was delicious," she said. And it had been. The lobster with butter sauce was the best she'd had in years, and that thought was followed by a mental note to wake up early to work it off with a walk the next morning.

She gave Nathan her best direct look and waited to catch his eye. Did he really not see her responsibility to look after her cousin? She'd been so thankful for a couple of close friends who'd seen her through the tough first weeks after Ben's death. Sure, Bob was still alive and well. But so far away from Jan...

Nathan smiled at her, and she could see in the next moment that he did understand her. "All I'm saying is maybe you're projecting on to her how you think you'd feel."

She felt his eyes search her heart.

"I'm not going anywhere. You know that, right?"

His gentle words moved her. "I know." She smiled tenderly. He seemed to believe she was projecting a fear of losing him on to Jan. She didn't think she was, but she deeply appreciated his reassurance regardless.

Now he looked relieved. "Good. I'm perfectly content with my auction house in Waterville, and I have no plans to change that on you. In fact, since we've been together, I've felt more settled than ever."

She knew that's how he felt, but it was always good to hear. He'd shared long ago with her how his first marriage had fizzled because he and his wife had grown apart. Talking with him now made her wonder if her own loss of a spouse was making her extra sensitive toward her cousin's situation. Of course it was. How could it not? But that wasn't a bad thing. It helped her relate to Jan. Still, she'd keep Nathan's comments in the back of her mind.

He also assured her that his bill of health had been squeaky clean at his recent doctor's visit. "I'm here," he repeated.

Elaine squeezed his hand. She hadn't meant her concerns for Jan to worry Nathan, and she admitted that to him. She did still think she was doing exactly what he was suggesting for Jan. She was being as supportive as she knew how, taking every opportunity to make Jan feel surrounded by love. Between

Brian and herself, they'd make Jan feel supported every day. Her resolve only strengthened.

UPSTAIRS AT THE tearoom, Jan was curled up on her sitting room couch in her robe and fuzzy socks. She'd finished most of her chamomile tea and slices of apple from the Orchard Hill booth and was letting her thoughts wander through the details of their mystery.

It had occurred to her that Jack Weston might have some additional insights about a possible connection between the snake and the accident. There'd been too much going on right after the accident, and she hadn't thought to ask when she'd called him to confirm that the snake was a Pueblan milk snake and to find out about his plans to locate an owner. So she sent a text to him to see if he thought the sight of a snake would make a well-trained horse buck.

But instead of the ping of a return text, her phone chimed with a FaceTime call. Bob. Her heart lifted.

His first words were "You look relaxed."

"I am," she said luxuriously. "We've been really busy with the festival, and it's been a lot of fun. But it's good to veg for a while and talk to you."

Jan filled him in on the mysterious happenings she and Elaine were looking into. He encouraged her that they would figure it out. "Now those Pirates just need to beat the Raiders on Friday, and the week will be golden."

She laughed. They talked for a while and promised to be in touch again in a day or two.

As soon as she disconnected, her phone chimed with a second FaceTime call.

Brian. She clicked Accept.

"Mom, how was your day?"

"Hi, Grandma!" both of her preteen granddaughters piped up. Brian, Avery, and Kelly smiled back from the screen. Avery was blonde like her mother, and Kelly had Brian's dark hair.

"Hi, Brian. Girls, how are you? I'm so glad to see you."

"We just wanted to say hi," Brian explained, and the girls asked her if they'd see her that week.

"You're coming out here one night, right?" Jan thought Brian had mentioned that when he stopped by the other morning. "There's the bonfire tomorrow night and the corn maze Thursday. Then Friday's the parade and game."

"I want to come for all of it, Grandma," Kelly piped up, but Brian quickly moderated her comment.

"We'll see. We need to check with your mom first." Then he explained to Jan, "We've been really busy. I'm not sure what Paula has in mind, or what else we have going on, but we'll be there at least one night for sure."

The girls updated Jan on their activities and schoolwork. Paula was grocery shopping, so Brian was holding down the fort. He said he'd be toast if he left the supper dishes for her to clean up when she returned with a dozen grocery bags she'd need counter space for. They talked a few minutes, Jan assured Brian she was enjoying her evening, and they disconnected.

Jan laid her phone next to her on the sofa and sipped her lukewarm tea. She'd been doing quite a bit of reassuring Brian lately. As he'd been trying hard to reassure her, Jan reminded herself. He and Paula ran a busy household, and she'd look forward to spending time with them soon, even though she had seen Brian more often than usual recently.

This swapping of parent-child roles was something to get used to. She'd always been the one looking out for her kids, but now she felt her son taking an almost parental concern toward her.

Families were there to help each other, she figured, and thought of Bridget Donahue. She hadn't remembered much about Bridget when she'd visited the tearoom, but her memory had been jogged talking with Brian and the girls. She recalled hearing Bridget talk about her son when she was at Tea for Two with the other Boosters. As the memory grew clearer, Jan remembered that Trace seemed to monopolize her conversations.

If Derek's theory was true, and someone wished to play a prank on Trace, or to make his horse buck so he'd get hurt and couldn't play on Friday night, wasn't it a long shot that Trace's horse would be the one and only horse to react to a snake? Why hadn't any of the other horses bucked?

There were a dozen horses and riders on the trail that day, and Trace and Bridget couldn't have been that far away from each other or the other mounts, even with one of them usually taking the lead. But none of the others had acted nervous, much less begun to buck. What made the difference for Leopold?

Jan racked her brain to recall as many details of the ride as she could. Bridget had done more of the talking, sometimes lingering back a bit with the other riders, while Trace had often been slightly ahead of his mom, in the true lead position as Derek said they typically were on trail rides. Those roles fit with the images Jan was developing of the mother's and son's different personalities—outgoing Mom, and quieter, more "chill" son, as Derek had pegged him. If someone had known they'd take those positions, that meant they'd probably somehow participated in a trail ride before. Plus, it would seem more difficult to pick out Bridget's horse than Trace's since she was among the other riders instead of right up front. If someone had suspected Trace would be in the lead, then Derek's idea that Trace's horse was the one who was supposed to have spooked made sense.

She wanted to get some clarity. She'd go see Bridget in the morning. She wasn't sure how that would help, but somehow she needed to get a sense of the woman for herself.

Jan looked at her phone, wishing to hear back from Jack. She wanted his take on the snake angle.

One thing was sure, whatever the motivation and whoever was the intended target, the stunt had been foolish. That is, she reminded herself again, *if* it was a stunt and not just an accident.

There were still the flyers and newspaper ad coming out in the morning. If the snake's owner came to claim it and had a reasonable and innocent explanation for how it ended up on the path, Jan wasn't sure how much she and Elaine could help Derek. Still, that'd be the best news.

But what about the laughter? Jan kept coming back to that. If someone was laughing over Bridget's accident, Jan was inclined to agree with Derek's concern that someone intended to cause the accident.

But it helped Jan decide that she'd go see Bridget in the morning and the Claremore coach after school. She thought Elaine would want to go with her on that trip. She Googled the Claremore High School Web site and found the head coach's name easily enough. Coach Lawrence McTeague had been employed by the school for five years. He ought to know his players pretty well, Jan hoped.

Her phone pinged.

A horse could buck if it sees a snake. Anything's possible. Although I'd guess a well-trained horse would more likely refuse to move or would step backward instead of bucking. Sorry not much help.

Jan would find out tomorrow if Bridget agreed with Jack.

She could ask Dori Richardson and Chris Cosgrove whether they heard someone laughing. She added keeping an eye out for them at the bonfire tomorrow night to her mental to-do list.

Of course, if word got out that someone was hiding in the woods, laughing near the gravesite... Jan could already hear the rumors flying that Old Man Warner was laughing at someone's failed attempt to get near his gold.

This was shaping up to be some Fall Fest week indeed.

CHAPTER ELEVEN

When Jan had first seen Bridget Donahue at the stables on Sunday, they hadn't had time, with everything going on, for more than a customary hello to each other. Guests were arriving and taking direction while saddle straps got cinched and riders were matched with horses according to size and temperament.

Trace and Derek had seen to all of it and kept the mostly novice riders organized until everyone was ready to go. Then Bridget entered the barn and introduced herself to the group and did a quick spot check to make sure the boys had done their job sufficiently.

Before Sunday, they'd met only briefly at Tea for Two, so when Jan called Bridget Wednesday morning to see if she could stop by the stables to talk, Bridget sounded guarded. Jan told herself the horsewoman's reaction was understandable, considering Bridget could still have fears that someone wanted to harm her.

"It isn't very easy for me to get around these days, Jan."

"I don't want to inconvenience you, Bridget. I'll be happy to drive out there, and I'll bring the tea and treats. You relax. I won't stay long."

Jan was glad Bridget didn't press her over the phone about the reason for visiting. Jan preferred to talk face to face.

Sitting in the Donahues' sprawling white kitchen now, she sensed that Bridget was more at ease. The plate of tearoom pastries sat on the quartz counter between them next to a tin of plum oolong tea from an online club Elaine had discovered. The women made small talk while the tea steeped.

Bridget was an attractive woman in her midforties, with medium-length dark-blonde hair, which she'd arranged in a partial up-do that softened her strong jawline. Thick gold hoop earrings brought out her hair's highlights, and her drapey ivory sweater looked comfortable over coordinating lounge pants. A bulky cast covered her right leg from mauve-painted toenails up past her knee.

Even seated on a kitchen stool or pushing herself on a wheeled cart with her good leg, Bridget had a commanding presence. Jan's ongoing impression was that Bridget had more than her share of business savvy. But as she talked with her, Jan saw touches of humor and even vulnerability through Bridget's polish.

Jan learned the family had owned the horse property for the past six years after moving east from their previous farm in Ohio to be closer to Trace's grandparents. Jan didn't catch which side of the family. The management of the property fell to Bridget, while her husband, Clive, traveled frequently overseas on business. Trace was their only child, born three years after they'd lost a stillborn baby girl. So as picture-perfect as Bridget's life might have seemed to someone like Lucy, Bridget hadn't been immune to her own struggles.

"How long will you have to wear the cast?"

"The doctor says a couple of months. It's broken in two places, one spot more seriously than the other."

"I'm sorry."

She sighed. "I suppose there's never a good time to break a leg, but right in the middle of Trace's season is probably the worst." She shook her head. "Not sure how I'll manage the bleachers on Friday night. And trail rides are out for me for a while too, of course."

When Jan asked if she had enough help at the stables, Bridget said she'd hired high school students for busy seasons in the past, so she had several people she could call who might like to earn extra money for Christmas shopping.

"Speaking of your staff, I met Derek Jameson on the ride. What a sweet kid."

"We love Derek. He works for me quite a bit." Bridget added that he knew his way around the property almost as well as Trace. "He's like another family member."

"That's what it sounded like." This was the opening Jan had prayed for. "Actually, Derek is why I wanted to stop by." She explained his visit to the tearoom and his suspicion that someone had meant the accident for Trace, mentioning the snake, the laughter in the woods, and her confusion over what it all might mean.

A muscle twitched in Bridget's jaw. "I hadn't considered that Trace might've been in danger. I was sure it was meant for me."

"Are you still convinced it was purposeful, Bridget? And, I hate to ask this, but do you know anyone who might've done it? Or why?"

"That accident was no accident, Jan. Now hearing that someone was laughing in the woods makes me even surer of it. Leopold would *not* have bucked like he did over a snake. Something else made him do it. Someone had to have been in those woods. But I can't think of who."

"Do you think it was just a prank that got out of hand?"

"I am known for playing jokes," she admitted. She smiled. "I got Annie Richardson last month, and I'm expecting her to retaliate. But she wouldn't have done *that*. But yes, I suppose someone might have been getting me back... But to not come clean after I broke my leg... really? That's a step too far."

Even though Jan couldn't see Annie playing a potentially dangerous joke, she would have had to consider her a suspect if it weren't for that fact that Annie had been helping man the Richardsons' booth that afternoon. She would remember to ask Elaine if Annie was at her booth *all* afternoon Sunday. "Can you think of anyone besides Annie?"

Bridget looked at the ceiling. "Let's see... well, my husband for one. But he's out of town. And anyway, if he were behind it, he definitely would've owned up to it. A couple of people from church have recently gotten me back for things, so I'm the one who owes them now, I suppose. And I haven't played any pranks on my Booster Club or PTA friends for a while.

We're all so busy in the first months of school. We don't usually mess with that kind of thing this time of year."

She looked at Jan. "That's part of what's got me thrown by this accident. I haven't pranked anyone in a while, and nothing very significant. I don't understand the timing or the unknowns about what happened on Sunday...And now to think it might have been meant for Trace? I'll have to talk with Derek about it, Trace too. I wish Derek had come to me first."

"He probably didn't want to worry you."

She nodded. "Trace never mentioned Derek's concern to me either. But I suppose he also knew I'd worry about him. And those two can be pretty tight-lipped. I'm the talker of the bunch." Her expression said, *Take it or leave it.*

Jan tried a different tack. Sounding casual, she told Bridget she'd seen her old friend Lucy Rodgers.

"I haven't seen Lucy in a while. She's one who'd probably want to return an old joke." But the next instant, Bridget again looked dubious and shook her head. "But I'm sure she already played the last one on me, which was a long time ago. So she wouldn't have thought she owed me one."

Jan waited for Bridget to explain.

"It's been a couple of years. We haven't been in touch lately. I feel bad that I didn't call her when I heard about her divorce. I should have." Bridget's regret for her old college friend appeared to be real. "Last time I saw her was on my birthday two years ago. For days before that I'd been getting anonymous gifts of specialty coffees in the mail. Everyone who knows me knows I detest coffee. Then on my birthday, Lucy showed up at my door with a basket of gourmet teas, which I love. She admitted to sending the coffee, and she took me out to lunch and gave me a card. It was really sweet. We had a nice time catching up." Bridget held out her hands. "Plus, now that I think about it, Lucy's never been an animal person. I know she'd never mess with a snake. There's no way she'd bother with that kind of prank. The motivation isn't there, and it just isn't her."

Then Bridget turned the conversation back to her horse. "Did you know Leopold was trained as a circus horse?"

"I hadn't heard that, but how interesting." Jan really was fascinated by Leopold's unique history.

"He's so used to seeing other animals around, and dealing with chaos. He's far too well trained to buck like that over a snake."

Bridget had said the same thing right after her fall. Obviously, she hadn't wavered in her belief that the snake wasn't the cause of her accident, and Jan had to believe Bridget's knowledge of him counted for something. Between Bridget, who clearly knew her horse, and Jack's opinion that a snake might only make a horse halt or back up, maybe a snake *didn't* cause the accident. "Do you know of *anything* that would've made Leopold buck like he did?"

"Actually, yes," Bridget said. "I meant to explain this earlier. During his days in the circus, Leopold was trained with hand signals, one of which told him to buck as part of the show. Not in fear or aggressiveness. Just as a trick."

She demonstrated the signal by holding out her hand at her waist, keeping her arm straightened and her palm up, and then swiftly raising her hand to make a fist. She kept it like that in the air for several seconds. "That's it. He would've bucked just like he did. Unfortunately I wasn't ready for it." Her mood grew quiet. "That's the only thing I can think of that rationally would have made him buck. Of course, there could have been independent factors, but again, Leopold is very well trained. Animals can be unpredictable, sure, but I didn't see anything that would have frightened him to such a degree that he would have bucked."

"Agreed," Jan said. "About those hand signals. For that to happen, someone had to have been nearby, which we're already considering because of the laughter I'm quite sure I heard." Jan thought for a moment. "Also, some of the other riders said Leopold got agitated right before he bucked."

"He did," Bridget said in her frank way. "But that much could have been from the snake, I suppose. Or, if he heard someone laugh in the woods like you did, he might've been on alert."

Her host's tea was nearly gone, so Jan quickly got up to refill their cups to keep Bridget talking. "Who besides you knows that signal?"

"Trace and Derek, of course. And Chris Cosgrove and Dori Richardson too, simply through all the time they've spent here. All of them are Trace's friends who've worked, or at least have ridden, here. Chris and Dori not as often as Derek. But Derek was at the stables, and Chris and Dori were riding with us."

Jan was quiet, thinking.

Bridget seemed to study her reaction before she added, "I've never seen any of our employees try the signals on Leopold on their own, without Trace or me around. But it is fun to watch him perform, and they seem to enjoy it too, which I haven't minded at all. The signals are just the type of unique info that comes up now and then when we're working with the horses. I trust all of them to respect the boundaries of their jobs."

"Sure," Jan replied. "Maybe someone else learned the signal. Could Trace have taught anyone else?" There was no telling how far that bit of info had spread in Trace's circle.

"I mean, people could have picked up on them during demonstrations. Owning a circus horse is a conversation starter with our guests who visit for classes and trail rides. Our family are the only ones who ever ride Leopold, but there's no telling how many people know that the signals exist and have seen us perform them with Leopold."

Jan thought about that. "So one of the riders could have picked up the signal during a demonstration at some point, then made the signal without anyone noticing. I was too far back to see everyone around the bend, but I think it's possible."

Bridget pulled out the tea ball from her cup and placed it on a nearby saucer. "Yes, I suppose it's possible."

Together they listed the people on the ride. They figured for now the out-of-town family could be crossed off the list because it was a long shot that they knew of the signal, and Bridget hadn't even met them before Sunday. It was Orin Bond's first trail ride, and she didn't know him well either, so what reason would he have had for trying to make a horse buck? Chris and Dori were back with Jan. Besides Trace and Bridget, that left only Russell, Kit, and Marcella Edmonds.

Jan would give Kit a call, but she knew in her heart their family had not caused the accident, unless little Marcella had somehow heard at school how to make the fun circus horse buck and wanted to try it for herself. Jan would have to phrase her questions tactfully to Kit and pose it as if she was simply wondering whether Kit had noticed anything unusual—and to see if Marcella was feeling better about witnessing the whole thing. Jan hoped so. She was a sweet little girl who obviously had been rattled by the eventful ride. The more Jan thought about it, the more she knew it was worth contacting as many as she could from the ride to see if they'd remembered anything more out of the ordinary that they hadn't bothered to mention yet.

To Jan's thinking, the news about Leopold's history opened the door wide to the number of people who might've been in the woods on Sunday. Even Claremore players, as Derek suggested. If someone was playing a joke that went badly, if that person had a lot to lose by coming forward, or feared Bridget would file charges... That could have been motivation to keep quiet. A Claremore player could lose a lot, including his place on the team, scholarship chances, reputation. She shared those thoughts with Bridget.

"I can be outspoken at times, I know. I'm not shy about getting things done for my son's school. But I'd hope no one from Claremore would want to hurt me. This whole thing shook me up, it's true. But I've got great neighbors and friends, even in Claremore. Plenty of people from there come out to the stables all year long. We might disagree at times, but I don't feel in danger."

"That's good to hear."

Then Bridget looked stern. "But back to my son. If Derek is on to something, and that Claremore team is up to no good where Trace is concerned, I've got to get that coach on the phone. Trace has earned the right to play this weekend, and I'm not going to let anyone stop him. Our team is counting on him to win."

CHAPTER TWELVE

Coach McTeague was a burly man who would look as comfortable on a military base as on the Claremore Raiders' field, Elaine thought. The cousins arrived at Claremore High School a few minutes after five o'clock. Several sports teams were still practicing, along with the marching band and flag squad. Jan hadn't mentioned to Bridget that she and Elaine were going to visit the coach that afternoon. It wouldn't have dissuaded Bridget from making her own call, she knew, and Jan wasn't going to get in the way of a mama bear.

When Jan filled Elaine in on the visit with Bridget, Elaine shared her surprise that several of Trace's friends knew about the circus hand signal. Derek, Chris, and Dori were only a few of possibly dozens of high school kids, and there could be just as many adults. At the moment, Chris was the only one of the three who would have any motivation for playing a prank on Trace—his new identity as a Raider. But just because he moved to the opposing team's town didn't mean he would put aside friendship and history as former teammates to take a cheap shot to win a game. And to top it off, he was on the trail ride, not in the woods. Dori too. And Derek and Trace were like family, and Derek was back at the stables when the accident happened.

They had to consider that other students had learned the signals. Bridget had acknowledged that as a possibility. They wanted to talk with Trace themselves but had decided to look for him at the bonfire later that night, to respect his mother's right to talk with him first.

Elaine took in the typical after-school scene behind the high school. The football team was dressed in pads out on the field, cross-country runners were scattered, either stretching or jogging on the track, and soccer players were scrimmaging on another field nearby. Along the bleachers at the edge of the track, cheerleaders were practicing as well, and the band and color guard were moving through their formations to the school song in an adjoining parking lot. Maroon and gray colors from all around them heralded that this was Raiders' turf.

Elaine and Jan waited for a cluster of runners to pass before they crossed the track on to the area of the field where a couple of large water jugs held down benches that were littered with water bottles, helmets, gloves, and stray football equipment. Two players in pads, mesh practice jerseys, and pants were getting their wrists taped by official-looking students Elaine guessed worked in the school's training room. Without his helmet on, one of the players looked familiar to her.

"Hi, Chris," Jan called out to him.

That was why the teen looked familiar. Elaine remembered Chris Cosgrove.

"Hey, Mrs. Blake, Mrs. Cook," Chris called back. He looked surprised to see them.

"I hope you didn't hurt your wrist, Chris," Jan said as she drew near.

"Nah, it's just sore. I'll be fine for Friday." He didn't look in pain and acted as if a sore wrist was par for the course, which it no doubt was in football.

Elaine's son, Jared, hadn't played the sport, and the mom in her had been relieved back then.

Chris was looking at them curiously.

"We were hoping to talk with your coach when he's done here," Elaine explained.

"Um, okay. Practice usually ends at five thirty, so he should be free soon. I'm about to go back out there. Can I give him a message for you?"

He was searching their faces, obviously trying to figure out why in the world they'd have business with Coach McTeague. Two middle-aged tearoom owners who didn't even live in Claremore or have high school–age children. It must've been clear as mud to him, Elaine thought, amused. But she answered cheerfully, "Thanks a bunch. Just let him know we'd like to talk with him."

That seemed to confuse him more than ever.

Jan changed the subject. "Actually, I wanted to ask you a question too, Chris."

He raised his eyebrows. "Sure, Mrs. Blake. What is it?"

"You, Dori, and I were following behind the other riders when the accident happened on Sunday."

"I remember. Dori was teasing me about moving." He didn't look upset.

"That's right," Jan noted. "When we hurried to catch up after knowing something went wrong up ahead, I thought I heard laughter."

"Really?" Chris shook his head, looking at the ground as if trying to see the events in his memory. "I guess I was too focused on finding out what had happened up around the bend. I didn't hear anything except Mrs. Donahue's screams and the horses' hooves."

"You're sure?"

"Yes, I'm positive. But I'll keep thinking on it and let you know if something else comes to mind."

"Thanks, Chris. I guess you probably need to finish practice now, huh?"

"I do, yeah. But it was nice talking with you." With a nod, Chris snugged his helmet back on and jogged out to rejoin his team.

"I hope things are going well for Chris here," Jan said to Elaine. "It's his senior year, and he was a star at Forrest. As much as I'd like to see the Pirates beat the Raiders, I wonder how it'll be for him on the line against his old team. I feel sort of bad for him."

"He'll be fine. It's one year, then he'll be off to college somewhere."

Jan frowned. "Hopefully he'll be able to go. With his grades and football skills, he ought to have a chance. But not all of them will be so lucky."

Together they observed Chris and the other players. As quarterback, he connected pass after pass with the receivers, and no one fumbled anything. Their defense looked just as strong. They were a well-oiled machine. And they were fast. The Pirates had their work cut out for them for sure.

"I'm thinking it's too bad for the Pirates more than for Chris," Elaine countered. "Maybe his family's move was the best thing for his future. He's really good. And here he doesn't have Trace Donahue to compete with for attention."

Chris did seem to have settled into a comfortable camaraderie with his Raiders team. And Coach McTeague, although he appeared gruff and imposing, seemed fair and encouraging at the same time. The other coaches led impressively too.

At five thirty-five, the team was excused and trooped off to the locker room to change and go home. Chris hung back with his coach and approached the cousins with him. "Like I said, Coach, I know Mrs. Blake and Mrs. Cook from Lancaster. They wanted to talk with you."

The women shook the coach's hand, and Elaine explained to him why she and Jan were there.

Although she was tactful and didn't lay blame without any concrete reason, the coach looked taken back at the idea that his players might have considered harming an opposing player.

"My men would be off the team immediately. They know it. Competition's one thing, but I've made clear that I won't tolerate dirty play. They play with integrity or they don't play."

The man was to the point, that was for sure. Elaine liked him immediately. She looked at Jan, who clearly liked him just as much.

Coach McTeague turned to Chris. "Son, you know anything about this?"

Chris's eyes grew wide and he shook his head vehemently. "Nothing, Coach. We want to win the right way too, sir. If I'd heard anything, believe me, I'd have stopped it. And not just me, but most of the team."

The coach nodded. "I know of Trace Donahue. The whole family. He's a good kid. Good player. Mom can be a little nutty. She already called me about this today. Look, I've got nothing against them. I'm sorry to hear she's hurt, and I speak for my team when I wish them well. We're gonna have a good, honest game Friday, and that's all I've got to say. Ladies." He tipped his baseball hat and walked away. Chris started to follow him.

"Chris, sorry, just one more minute." Elaine pulled the key from her purse and held it out to him. He instantly reached for it.

"My key! Where'd you find it?"

"Have you been missing it a while?" Jan asked.

"Not too long. Maybe a couple of days?"

"Dr. Tyson found it on the ground when he was helping Trace's mom on Sunday," she said.

"I must have dropped it then. Thanks so much."

He turned and jogged away.

"I think that might have been the fastest clue we've ever tracked down," Jan said as they went back to the parking lot. "If the key didn't turn out to be his, I was thinking there might be something to Derek's theory about someone from Claremore causing trouble on the trail that day. But he had a perfectly good explanation for why it was there."

Elaine was grinning as she started the Malibu.

Jan looked sideways at her. "What are you smiling about?"

"Your reaction to Coach McTeague. Your eyes were huge."

"I was wondering if he was expecting a salute or a 'yes sir' from us. I think if you put him and Bridget Donahue in a ring together, it'd be a toss-up who'd win."

Elaine laughed outright, figuring her cousin probably had that nailed.

ON THE WAY back to the tearoom, Jan and Elaine made a side trip to Forrest High. Its field, where the game would be played on Friday, proclaimed proudly in black and gold that this was the land of the Pirates.

In a grassy area outside the fieldhouse, groups of students were working on their class homecoming floats. They had two more days to finish transforming chicken wire, Styrofoam forms, tissue paper, and portable motors into moving, active masterpieces of engineering and art, complete with Pirates mascots throwing footballs to jersey-clad players on makeshift fields with goalposts and scoreboards—showing a shutout score in the Pirates' favor, of course. Jan and Elaine stopped to compliment the teens' handiwork. Those floats would be the highlights of the homecoming parade after school on Friday.

They learned from some students who were leaving that the head football coach, Rob Delaney, had an office in the fieldhouse that was accessible by its own exterior door. They found it propped open a few inches and knocked when they heard voices inside.

"Come on in!" Coach Delaney was as collegiate looking as Coach McTeague was soldier-like. Shorter with a slighter but chiseled build and fair hair, he greeted the women with friendly authority and got their names before introducing himself and his defense coach, who was also in the room. "What can I do for you?"

They explained their reason for stopping by, that they were looking into Bridget Donahue's accident and were following up on a lead about the two teams pranking each other. With her Boosters Club and PTA involvement and Trace's role on the team, the family could have been easy prey for pranksters. Jan purposely didn't mention Derek's visit to them or his concern that Trace was a target because she didn't know if he'd shared that with his coach, and they didn't want to raise issues for him with his team.

"Bridget herself admitted she can make waves to get done what she wants to for the school. We're just wondering if you've noticed any intense competition ramping up with your players, or if you've heard of any stunts on your team by Claremore. Possibly to rattle your players this week."

Neither coach had heard of anything, but they promised to keep their eyes peeled and didn't welcome any activity by either team that would get in the way of a fair game. They thanked Jan and Elaine after a few minutes, and the cousins left.

On the way back to the car, someone called out their names. Turning, Jan saw Dori Richardson run to catch up to them, her book bag strap slung across her chest. The bag looked full, and Dori seemed to be struggling with the zipper.

"Hi, Dori!" Jan welcomed her with a shoulder hug. "Lots of homework?"

Dori looked confused by the question until Elaine pointed to the heavy-looking bag, whose contents were threatening to spill out. "Oh no, this isn't all homework." Wisps of brown hair played around her face as she gave an exasperated sigh and a roll of her eyes. She abandoned her troubles by letting the bag hang open. "This silly zipper broke today of all days, when I have so much to carry. I'm taking some things for the float to work on at home. And I have a couple of books to read up on for my job in the trainer's room." She smiled at them through her frustration.

"So that's how you're friends with Trace, Derek, and Chris," Elaine stated.

"And the rest of the team. Actually, I help all the teams in the trainer's room, not just football. I heard you were talking with Coach Delaney just now."

"News travels fast," Jan kidded and led the way to the parking lot.

Walking in step with the cousins, Dori spoke dramatically. "Tell me about it. It's hard to keep anything under wraps around here."

The women smiled at her, then Elaine got serious. "Dori, you must see a lot and hear a lot of talk in the training room."

"Yeah, I guess so."

"Probably more than what some of the players would say when their coaches are around," Jan added, thinking she knew where Elaine's comment was leading.

Dori's smile wavered, a sign that she did indeed hear quite a bit.

"How are the players handling the pressure?" Elaine asked next.

"I think they're doing okay. Is there some reason you're asking?"

"We're just trying to find out if there's been any talk about pranks between the teams," Jan said.

"Oh, that stuff. The guys make tough comments all the time about taking them down, destroying them. Macho stuff. But that's all meant for the field. None of them would really do anything to risk this team."

"Do you know much about the Raiders players, whether they'd cause trouble for this team?" Elaine asked next.

"I know some of them a little. I've heard more about them from Chris since he's gotten to know them better. There are a lot of friends between the schools, including on the football teams."

"That's good to hear. How's Chris doing at Claremore overall?" By now they'd reached Elaine's car and stopped to finish their conversation.

"He's getting used to it. He already knew some of the football players from all the years they've played against each other. Our guys miss him a lot though. The beginning of the season was rough for us with Chris gone and some positions shuffling. That took some time to adjust to. But it seems okay now." Dori said Chris was still around a lot on the weekends to hang out with his Forrest High friends.

"By the way, when we were on the trail ride, did you hear anything that sounded like someone laughing in the woods around the time Bridget fell?"

Dori considered this but said no, she hadn't heard anything like that. Then she said she had to get going. "My parents won't let me go to the bonfire until my homework is done."

They agreed she couldn't miss that and hoped they'd see her there. With a big smile and a swing of her ponytail, Dori shifted her bag, dislodging some papers that fell to the asphalt. Jan bent to pick them up to help the overloaded girl and realized they were actually a thin, folded newspaper.

Dori didn't reach for it but asked, "What would happen though if Chris's new teammates wanted to be sure he'd play his best for them?"

"Like a test of his loyalty?" Elaine responded.

She shrugged. "Not really that. I know Chris wouldn't do anything to our team, even if he was put up to it. But Derek told me he talked with you. That's been on my mind. I know Chris made a few mistakes with the Raiders players at the beginning of the season by talking too much about his years here. He told me that much. Who knows…he could've made some of the Claremore players mad, or at least worried that he wouldn't bring his best to their team. Maybe that would have made them try something." Then she looked more confident. "But if he knew they did anything on that trail ride, there's no way he'd let them get away with it. I guess I'm mentioning it because if Claremore was behind that accident I wouldn't want it to come back on Chris, like the fall guy, you know?"

That was interesting logic, Jan thought.

"Do you mistrust any of them in particular?" Elaine asked her.

"No, I don't. I mean, some players are better guys than others, on both teams. Just because their coach warned them not to do anything to the Pirates doesn't mean some won't want to try, especially if the new guy would make a good scapegoat. I don't know," she said again. "It's just a thought."

Jan considered this. Regardless of what Coach McTeague claimed, would any of Chris's new teammates he hadn't developed friendships with yet have dared to play a foolish stunt on Forrest High's star player? If more than one person was involved, it could explain how Chris could be on the trail ride while someone he was working with was in the woods. Despite Dori's assurance about him, was it still possible that Chris had been motivated to prove his loyalty to his Raiders teammates by turning against one of his old ones?

They said good-bye, and Dori got into her small car a couple of spaces down and drove off while Jan was buckling her seat belt in Elaine's passenger seat. Elaine was commenting on the evening coming up when Jan realized she was still holding the newspaper she'd retrieved for Dori. She unfolded it to see a *Penzance Perspectives* masthead.

"How long has it been since you've read our old school newspaper?" She apologized for interrupting Elaine but held it up for her to see.

"Oh, wow, a long time. That ought to be fun to look at sometime."

Jan would ask Dori if she wanted it back, but in the meantime she looked forward to getting up to date on the current events in the halls of her alma mater.

CHAPTER THIRTEEN

Elaine and Jan discussed the possibilities on the way home. By the time Elaine pulled into the Tea for Two driveway, she had fewer than thirty minutes to get ready for the bonfire before Nathan came to pick her up.

Jan's daughter Amy's van was already parked there.

"Brace yourself, the twins are here," Jan said from the passenger seat. Elaine knew she welcomed the playful attack. Max and Riley were Jan's youngest grandkids and her only grandsons. At six years old, they were bundles of cuteness who kept everyone hopping.

Speaking of grandchildren, Elaine hoped to fit in a FaceTime visit with Lucy and Micah, her grandkids in Ohio.

"Grandma, we're going to fire you!" Max shouted from the door to the garage.

His matching brown-haired brother smacked him on the arm. "No, Max, we're *going to the fire* with her!"

The boys kept shout-talking as Jan and Elaine entered the kitchen. Amy shushed them while she and her husband, Van, finished takeout sandwiches at the table. Their boys' plates were still littered with broken chips and sandwich remnants.

Van pointed to two paper bags on the island. "Help yourselves. We brought extra."

Elaine thanked them, then excused herself to go change upstairs. Archie was swiping a cloth across an east parlor table and looked up when Elaine's footsteps echoed softly on the wood floor.

"How'd it go today, Archie?"

He stood and placed the rag on a nearby cart. His brow furrowed, making Elaine hope that nothing had gone wrong at the tearoom.

"Was business good?" she asked.

"Yes, yes, of course. I'm finishing up in this room and then I can stay a while longer if you need anything else."

"I think we have a handle on it. Thank you, though. But are you sure everything is fine? You look troubled."

His mouth twitched. "I received a call from Beatrice Miller-Pyle this afternoon. It was somewhat disappointing."

The authenticator in New York City. Elaine caught herself before asking if anything had happened to the painting and asked instead if he'd heard something unfortunate related to his father.

"No, no. But that's part of my dismay. Ms. Miller-Pyle informed me they received a large project from the Met and will have to push back the work on your painting for several weeks, perhaps months."

Elaine's hands dropped to her sides. "You're right, that isn't good news."

He shook his head and looked ready to return the cart to the kitchen.

"That's all she said—weeks or months? That leaves us hanging indefinitely."

"Yes, it does," he agreed. "I told her as much, and she did apologize and say she would return to your painting as soon as she could. But she asked that we understand the situation she is in and the size of the job from the museum."

"I suppose so. But I think we ought to consider whether it's worth looking into a different authenticator."

He nodded.

"If Heather Mills, or Ms. Miller-Pyle, can recommend someone else who's reputable, we may be better off." Elaine checked the time on her phone. She might still be able to catch Heather at her shop. "Let me see what she says."

Archie disappeared around the corner while Elaine's phone call connected with Heather's restoration business in Waterville. She explained the delay and waited while Heather retrieved her file on the painting.

"I'm sorry you've hit a snag," Heather commented coming back on the line. "I do have one name to give you, but he is located in Phoenix, Arizona, so not close at all. He is supposed to be very good, and well versed on your painting's era. Back when I originally searched names for you I checked for experts during the years we believe the painting was created as well as any with special knowledge of Harley Archibald Benningham. This man's name came up, which is why I kept him on file. I'm sending you his contact information now."

A moment later Elaine's phone pinged, showing she'd received something from Heather.

"Phoenix is a couple of hours behind us, so you may still reach him today if you hurry," Heather said and wished her luck.

Elaine thanked Heather and placed the call to Arizona.

After three rings, Dr. William Vanderpool answered his own phone with a pleasant but gravelly voice that gave away his advanced age. "Yes, Mrs. Cook, Harley Benningham was a very talented painter. And like Benningham, I too am a veteran of World War II. I was old enough only at the very end of it, but I did serve a few months. After the war, I lived in London—different sections—during the years that he did, during reconstruction."

Quick math told Elaine that Dr. Vanderpool was likely around ninety years old. "Did you ever meet him?" She could only hope for such luck.

"No, our paths never crossed. But it was while I lived overseas that I first saw his work. And then when I studied art in college, I learned more about his technique and have actually come to own one of his originals, which is quite rare these days."

Elaine was elated at this good turn. Maybe it was a godsend that the New York authenticator got backed up. "I'm glad I was able to get a hold of you, Dr. Vanderpool. You see, we are in a tight spot knowing whether to have the painting sent to a different expert who may be able to look at it much sooner for us. As of now, we have no idea how long we might have to wait."

Dr. Vanderpool was very accommodating and said it would be of personal interest to him to shift some things in his own schedule, if they could have the painting shipped to him. "I don't travel like I used to, and I have had to cut back my hours, but this I will make time for."

Before ending the call, Elaine was able to confirm that Dr. Vanderpool's own Benningham original was not the same as hers, but he remembered the scene on hers. She promised to call him back in a day or two, after she'd made her decision.

She had her next step in place, which was to ask Archie to speak with Beatrice Miller-Pyle again and have the painting shipped to Arizona. She didn't want to give the full green light on these new plans without Jan's and Archie's input, since they'd invested time and interest too, even though she owned the art.

Archie came back into view and told her he'd just spoken with Beatrice Miller-Pyle and gotten the name of another authenticator, a colleague of hers with a separate business, also in New York City. "She assured me she still wanted to work on the painting, so I told her I'd call back soon once we've made our decision."

Of course, Elaine never for a second considered this *her* decision, but she was always grateful for how thoughtful Archie was. "Archie, you know this is *your* decision."

He smiled. "I know. Thank you."

She updated him on her talk with Dr. Vanderpool, and he said he saw the value in having the older man look at it. They decided to shelve the subject for the evening, since Elaine needed to be ready for Nathan to pick her up very soon. And she still wanted to let Jan in on their options for the painting and to ensure Archie was making the best decision.

Upstairs she changed into jeans and a colorful cable-knit sweater, brushed her hair, then sat on her bed and was soon connected on FaceTime with her daughter, Sasha.

"Hey, Mom. You look nice. Are you seeing Nathan tonight?"

"I am. We're going to the bonfire soon, but I had to catch up with you. It's Fall Fest week."

"How fun. So the homecoming game's Friday. And I assume there's a dance…Saturday maybe?" Sasha earned a living as a fitness trainer and was also a biathlete who kept in top condition skiing and running. "Who are the Pirates playing?"

Elaine visited with her daughter and then called her son, Jared. It did her heart good to see her family's faces and hear about Lucy's and Micah's elementary school activities. It was a short call, but she even got a chance to say hello to her daughter-in-law, Corrie.

After catching up with her family, she returned downstairs for her jacket in the office and had enough time to eat her sandwich and visit with Van and Amy.

Jan pointed to the counter, where the day's newspaper was opened to the classifieds. The ad about the snake had been circled in red ink.

"Let's hope it draws the right attention so we'll find out who the owner is," Elaine said. Their stack of flyers at the booth had only raised the volume of the snake-talk. No one had come forward to claim it yet, and Elaine wasn't sure the ad would help, but she knew Jack had to try.

She told Jan she had another idea about the painting, which she'd explain when they both got home later that night. The doorbell rang as she finished her sandwich, and she hopped up to answer it.

Instead of a hug right away, Nathan said hello and held out a large envelope that Elaine recognized from a photography store.

"The painting print! Thank you for picking it up for me."

"No trouble at all."

She returned his hug then and went to put the envelope on her desk before leaving with him. Jan's family wasn't ready to leave the tearoom yet, so Elaine was able to enjoy some time alone with Nathan. The evening air and Nathan helped slow her heartbeat from its fast pace. She settled into his car and was glad to be with him. "You look handsome in that black turtleneck. It brings out your eyes."

"Thank you." His expression warmed her.

They talked work on the way down Main Street, and then Elaine was itching to get his opinion on her latest idea to send the painting to Arizona. "It's an extra cost, but something tells me to go ahead and do it. Not just because I'm impatient to learn for certain whether it's an original by Archie's father— which, I admit, I am—but also because Dr. Vanderpool seems to have such an interest in Harley Benningham's work."

Nathan thought it might be a worthwhile risk. There was always the possibility that the painting could be damaged in shipping, although he assured her that was unlikely considering the professional reputation of both authenticators, who had to be accustomed to packaging high-priced works of art. "I hope you're on to something and won't have to wait months for answers. Archie too." He winked at her. "You're a genius."

They parked a good distance from the bonfire and joined other people on the trek from the line of parked vehicles to the gathering area and tents. She and Nathan visited with a number of her neighbors, and as they reached the huge blaze, they soon were swallowed up into the larger crowd warming themselves around the fire.

Among the familiar faces, one stood out to Elaine. "I think that's Orin Bond over by the food tents." She tried to be as unobtrusive as possible pointing him out to Nathan. "He was on the trail ride with Jan." Already she was heading toward him, with Nathan following close behind. If she could bend his ear for a minute, she could save Jan tracking down one of the trail riders. Every little bit helped.

She called out to him and he turned, smiling when he saw her. "Elaine Cook, nice to see you."

Elaine introduced Nathan and Orin and chatted about this and that, and then suggested they get something to drink. It looked somewhat easier to talk under the shelter and lights of the tents. She steered them to a table with drinks and handed Orin a full cup. "Cider?"

When he took it appreciatively, she dove in. "Jan tells me you were on that crazy trail ride last weekend."

He winced over the first hot sip. "I was indeed, my first time out to the stables when I wasn't delivering mail. I'm not much of a horse fan. But I'm out there so much for my job, and it's a beautiful property. I wanted to see more of it beyond the mailbox."

"Jan says it's gorgeous. I haven't ridden there yet myself."

He took another tentative sip. Elaine picked up a cup for Nathan and another for herself. "Jan said Bridget's accident threw everyone for a loop because no one saw what happened."

"It did. I felt so bad for her."

"Jan did too. She keeps replaying it in her mind and little details are coming back to her. Has that happened with you?"

He looked disinterested. "I haven't thought much of it, to be honest. It was unfortunate, but I don't think anyone meant to hurt Mrs. Donahue, despite her protests. That snake? Someone's joke, maybe? Did you know that old gravesite was nearby?" He gulped some cider and winced again. "Maybe that was the big joke, putting a snake near the grave to spook all of us. Although it could have also just been a fluke." He shrugged. "This cider is so delicious."

She took a sip. "Yes, it really is." Clearly Orin wanted to move on.

CHAPTER FOURTEEN

The bonfire was blazing by the time Jan and her family found parking spaces a quarter-mile from the clearing and walked the rest of the way past a long row of vehicles. Jan thought there must be two hundred people gathered. She knew Elaine and Nathan were already here somewhere, but she couldn't pick them out in the crowd yet. The flames licked at the chilly air and wafted pungent wood smoke and the scent of dried logs everywhere.

Instinctively, she reached for a grandson's hand and noticed that Amy and Van had already locked hands on their young sons, who'd easily dart off and get lost in the dark if their parents weren't vigilant with them. Brian had joined them too, along with Avery and Kelly. When Jan asked him about Paula, he surprised her by grimacing.

"She decided to paint our bathroom this week and wanted to stay back to work on it."

"She wanted Dad's help but he brought us here instead," Kelly stated practically, to her dad's chagrin.

"She said she'd be fine," he explained, but Jan thought she detected guilt in his tone. "I'd have stayed to help, but the girls wanted to be here." He gave his younger daughter a playful look of reprimand. "No tattling on me."

It was too bad Paula was tied up at home while her family got to enjoy the evening. Paula had been out grocery shopping the night Brian and the girls had FaceTimed her. Jan had felt bad that Paula wasn't able to relax at home with her family, and she hoped the couple were able to stay connected even though Brian had been spending extra time looking after Jan lately. Unnecessarily, she pointed out to herself. She'd have to do what she could to support them. It was no good causing discord between her son and his wife.

She saw friends and neighbors seated under the tents and thought it was a nice touch to see the town's selectmen serving behind tables laden with hot cider, cocoa, and ingredients for s'mores. Jan waved to Eldon Carter, their chairman, whose steady nature made him good at his role. In his midforties with light-brown hair and green eyes, he worked as a locksmith.

Jan took the Styrofoam cup of cider he held out for her and helped Amy, Van, and Brian check the heat on cocoa cups for their children. "Is Misty here?" she asked Eldon. His wife taught English at Forrest High.

"I think she went to look for more plastic spoons."

When Amy's family ran into friends and Brian's daughters pulled him closer to the fire, Jan stood off to the side and took in the scene. Across the tent, Elaine and Nathan were at the crowded s'mores table talking with Julie and Chuck Yeaton, who were managing the bounty there.

The decorating committee had outdone themselves. Hay bales and smiling scarecrows had been propped up on the out-skirts of the food tents, and strings of white and orange twinkle lights spanned the insides of the canopies. Aromas of dried leaves, evergreens, wood smoke, and marshmallows mingled with the conversations around her.

The musky spice of the cider warmed her inside while she people-watched. Kids ran back and forth between the fire and the tent to refill on s'mores. High schoolers in Pirates black and gold clustered in groups, side by side with a number of Claremore students in maroon and gray. In the shadows just outside the fire circle, Trace Donahue, Derek Jameson, Chris Cosgrove, and three girls, two of them in Claremore sweatshirts, were laughing. A handful of other teens from both high schools joined them with shoulder punches and pats on the back.

Jan pulled back to a corner of the tent where she wouldn't be noticed. From all appearances, their banter was good-natured and all of them were smiling. Even more interesting, it seemed like Trace was there with a girl in a Claremore sweatshirt, a pretty redhead with long, loopy curls and a smattering of freckles across her nose. More attentive to each other than anyone else, they were standing close and holding hands. Annie Richardson had told Elaine that Dori liked Trace's new girlfriend, but Jan didn't know the girl was from Claremore and not Forrest High.

She felt someone approach and turned to see Bridget Donahue push herself forward in her wheeled chair.

"How are you, Bridget?"

"I'm managing, thank you. The committee did a good job tonight, don't you think?"

"It's all top-notch. The decorations, the food. It's just right and nothing is overdone. And everyone seems to be having such a good time. Did you have a part in all this?"

"As far as helping boost attendance, yes. This is like our community pep rally. Each year the Boosters encourage our students to make a strong appearance at the bonfire. When they do, we end up with more fans at the homecoming game."

"It seems to have worked. I've seen a bunch of Pirates. And Claremore students too actually. And Trace and his girlfriend seem to be having fun," she added as an afterthought.

But Bridget didn't look pleased. "Keri is a Raiders cheerleader. Can you believe it? As if Trace doesn't have enough on his mind without the distraction."

Jan kept silent.

"Oh, by the way, I asked Trace if he knew anyone who might know about the hand signal. I stopped him after he named ten or twelve friends. But like me, he has been consistent about telling people that the signals are only for us to use professionally with Leopold."

Well, that was good to know. Jan looked around and realized she was surrounded by people who potentially knew about the signal: school friends of Trace's, community friends who rode the stable horses and sent their children for lessons. They needed something to help narrow down the suspect pool, but where that would come from she had no idea. She said a quick prayer that God would point the way.

With smiles, she and Bridget watched the students having fun around the bonfire, and then Bridget excused herself, and Jan decided to go meet the teens for herself. When she walked up, Derek said hello and introduced her to the others. She looked knowingly from black-and-gold to maroon-and-gray. "Honestly, this is good to see."

They laughed.

"We're getting along now, but all that ends Friday on the field," Chris joked, making several of the others laugh more, and Jan couldn't help wonder again whether Chris was confused about where his loyalty lay. She also wondered what Derek thought of Chris's humor. He hadn't laughed at Chris's joke.

Jan turned to Trace and Keri. "Looks like you've got quite a role too," she said to the girl. "Cheering for the team who's bent on defeating your boyfriend's?"

Keri leaned in conspiratorially. In a voice loud enough for the others to hear, she teased, "I'm secretly cheering for Trace the whole time." Her friends erupted in whoops or calls of *traitor*, depending on sides, while Trace stood there grinning.

She left the teens and moved closer to the fire, where Misty Carter, Elaine, and Nathan were visiting. Firelight shone on their faces. Tall and willowy like a long-distance runner, Misty flipped her long sheath of ash-blonde hair behind her shoulder and scooted to make room for Jan on her hay bale. Jan caught enough of the conversation to hear Misty talking about what a busy week it was for high school teachers like herself. Apparently keeping their students focused on schoolwork was a greater challenge than normal with so much extracurricular fun going on. "But I understand. It's all part of being young and school spirit and all that."

They grinned along with her and agreed.

"I told Misty about our mystery, Jan," Elaine commented next. "I thought she might have some insights since she's at the high school every day."

Jan asked her if she'd heard any talk about Bridget's accident or school pranks.

"I did hear there's been some forking of yards and TPing. That stuff happens, no matter what sport, and it's pretty innocent. I haven't heard anything more. I've got several football players in my English classes, and it's been pretty typical talk from them."

"I just met Keri. Bridget doesn't seem too happy about her."

"Now, that I did hear from Trace's own mouth. She hasn't been too keen on the time he's been spending flirting. Bridget has big goals for her son in football."

Elaine rolled a piece of hay between her fingers. "When Nathan and I got here tonight, we introduced ourselves to all of them and wished them luck Friday. While we were talking, Bridget came up and pulled Trace aside for a minute, away from Keri. I didn't understand the look he and Keri gave each other, but now it makes sense. I'd say they're both well aware Bridget isn't Keri's biggest cheerleader."

"Pun intended?" Nathan nudged her playfully, and they all laughed. "If that's the case, Trace could be feeling pressure about more than just winning this football game," Nathan offered.

"Maybe so," Misty said. "It seems like he and Bridget have a good relationship overall, so it could be a little stressful not to have her support when it comes to his girlfriend. But maybe I'm assuming too much. I only know what I see and hear at school. Whatever the case, they're all good kids."

They asked her what she knew about Chris Cosgrove, and Misty said that he, too, was a pleasant kid, great student and football player. She couldn't see him giving in to pressure to prove his loyalty to his new team. "They all seem to be friends off the field. Any of them would get into a lot of trouble by creating problems for the other team."

Elaine asked her how well she knew Bridget.

Misty hesitated. "I consider Bridget a friend, even if she does have her idiosyncrasies. I don't know anyone who has a deep-seated issue with her. It's more a case of people rolling their eyes and groaning at times when they hear about the next mountain she aims to move. At the same time, most of us feel grateful toward her for all she does for the school. She has a good heart, and she works hard.

"Many of us wouldn't be willing to put ourselves in a position of criticism as she has done. With her leadership, the PTA has gotten us new math textbooks and funded special field trips, even weekend-long ones, for real-life experiences for the students. And the Boosters, which she heads up too, pay for the majority of the athletic and band uniforms, and even the scoreboard on the field." She paused and rubbed her lips together like she was searching for tact. "It's just that in the process, she doesn't seem to mind stepping on toes if others want to do something else with the funds. Or, really, if anyone wants much of anything different than she does."

Jan wasn't surprised to hear Misty reiterate things Elaine had reported hearing from Annie Richardson about Bridget. But the most surprising information Jan heard all evening came from a late arrival. The bonfire had been left to dwindle, and Jan's kids had already left with their sleepy children, when she spotted Jack Weston coming toward the tents where she, Elaine, and Nathan were helping pack up food and drinks and take down tables.

She started to tell him she'd seen the newspaper ad but stopped at his look of frustration.

"I'm afraid the flyers and ad—all the publicity—backfired, Jan." Jack tugged a hand down his face. "The snake is gone. Someone took it from my office today."

CHAPTER FIFTEEN

Instead of going to bed when they got home, Elaine and Jan took comfy quilts and mugs of tea out to the screened porch and stayed up talking into the wee hours. Earl Grey must have heard the door open and close because in no time he purred his way on to the porch and Elaine's lap, where he lay curled up enjoying a nap while Elaine stroked his back.

With the night air chilly on Elaine's face—one of the few body parts she hadn't bundled beneath layers—she and Jan reviewed the perplexing events and every motivation anyone might have for the accident and the snake, which was now a missing snake. They were no closer to locating its owner, realizing that oddly enough its owner might know exactly where it was.

Jack had told them he'd spoken with Arnie Sheffield, the sheriff's deputy, but didn't have much in the way of clues. He hadn't found fingerprints. And Jack had left the office unlocked while he drove to town in the afternoon to grab something for a late lunch. When he came back, the glass tank was empty.

"I think it's still worth our while to talk with Arnie ourselves," Elaine told Jan. "You never know when a seemingly insignificant detail could end up making a difference. I'll see if I can persuade him to drop by here before we go to the booth tomorrow. I'll offer him some maple Cronuts to sweeten the deal."

They listened to the night sounds and then Jan reached for both their tea mugs and went to the kitchen to rewarm them. When she returned to the porch, she handed Elaine a steaming mug and Dori's school newspaper.

"I forgot about this."

"Me too, but it was still on the counter where I left it."

"There's one other thing," Elaine said.

Jan sat back down and adjusted the blanket around her.

"You remember the swatch of fabric I pulled from the twig by Old Man Warner's grave the day after Bridget's accident?"

Jan did.

"The team jerseys and sweatshirts tonight reminded me of it. Jan, it could be jersey fabric."

"It's black, right?"

"Yes, with gold thread."

"Like from a Pirates jersey."

They reviewed what else they knew. There was the snake and the hand signals any number of people knew about. The snake might not have caused Leopold to buck, but its sudden and purposeful disappearance from Jack's office made it even more likely to be connected with the accident. It certainly added to the mystery of it all.

Trace or Bridget could have been a target. Opposing players might have wanted Trace out of the game. Although Dori and Misty didn't seem to think so, Chris could have been put up to the prank by the Claremore team. "The key turned out to be his, which rules out that some other Claremore player dropped it," Elaine said. "But instinct tells me Chris wasn't involved."

"I agree, although it still is possible that a different Claremore player was hiding in the woods."

Elaine knew Jan was right. And now there was Keri, with possibly two motivations—to play a joke on her boyfriend's mother out of hurt for Bridget's disapproval, or because Keri, despite what she claimed, could be more loyal to her own school than to Trace. And then there was still the lingering possibility that Bridget's own peers might have been getting her back for a prank. Lucy Rodgers came to mind, as unlikely as that really sounded. They crossed Annie off the list because Elaine confirmed to Jan that Annie was at her booth the entire afternoon on Sunday.

Jan told Elaine of her plans to talk with the other riders one more time, particularly Kit Edmonds. Kit taught at the elementary school, so Jan would have to see if she could meet up with her late one afternoon.

They knew there could be more people with motivations, and they felt more troubled than ever by the stolen snake. Whoever did that tied him- or herself to Sunday's accident.

They'd considered lots of possibilities but answers still evaded them. No one they'd spoken with knew anyone who owned snakes, much less a rare Pueblan milk snake. With the game less than two days away, it was like fourth and ten at the fifty yard line, and time kept ticking down on the clock. They prayed right there and trusted that God would reveal the path and help them leave no vital stone unturned. And they prayed for the safety of all the players on both teams, and for Bridget Donahue as well.

"I'm getting sleepy now, but I'd like to take a peek at this before bed." Elaine changed course and unfolded the school newspaper in her lap to reveal the full front page. "Oh, look, Jan, did you notice this story? It's about Trace and Derek."

She held out the paper for Jan to see in the dim light that glowed through the kitchen window behind them. The headline read "New and Old: Donahue and Jameson Team Up for Friday's Win." Both in Forrest High black jerseys and shoulder pads, Trace and Derek smiled out from their football headshots placed side by side on the lower half of the page. The top half showed an action shot of a Pirates player throwing a pass, with uniformed players surrounding him during a game.

Jan switched on the lamp on the table between their chairs, and the words instantly became readable.

Cradling the mug in her hands, Jan listened from her blanket cocoon while Elaine read out loud. "In Friday's homecoming game against longtime rival Claremore, the Pirates will entrust their best chances of a win to their senior captains, current quarterback Trace Donahue and former backup quarterback Derek Jameson. Donahue has proven his mettle time and again since taking over the position at the start of this season two months ago. Since the position switch, Jameson also has shown versatility on the field in his new position as wide receiver."

The story focused on some highlights from both of their high school football careers at Forrest High and also mentioned former Pirates player Chris Cosgrove, who was expected to be a tough competitor as the Raiders' new first-string quarterback.

"I'd say those are glowing comments about all three of them," Jan said.

"Definitely. It sounds like both teams had some big changes this year, which I think makes it even more impressive that they both have such winning records."

"True. Both had changes to their quarterback positions, and Derek apparently picked up a new position as receiver." Jan pointed out that the article didn't say what position Trace played before taking over the QB role, but that wasn't something that seemed to matter to the team for this season.

"Well, it ought to be a great game," Elaine said, stifling a yawn. "I'm looking forward to it, but right now I'm looking forward more to getting to bed."

They said good night to Earl Grey, who reluctantly slunk off Elaine's lap and settled onto a cushion on the porch floor, and then locked the door to the kitchen before shutting off the lights at the back of the house and heading upstairs. On the way, Elaine updated Jan about the possibility of having the painting shipped to Arizona in hopes of getting it looked at sooner. Jan agreed that Dr. Vanderpool might be able to offer some additional information with his background knowledge of Harley Benningham's work. Elaine would set it in motion the next day.

She handed the Forrest High newspaper to Jan at the top of the stairs. "Why don't you keep this? Maybe one of your grandkids would like to look through it."

Soon after that, Elaine turned her bedroom light off and welcomed sleep.

CHAPTER SIXTEEN

I think these might be even better than your maple croissants, Jan," Arnie Sheffield said around a mouthful of maple
Cronut. He had arrived at the tearoom in full uniform when
the morning sunrise was fading to pinkish orange over the
east end of the lake.

"Thank you, Arnie. We thought a twist on the croissant
would be the perfect signature treat for our festival booth."

He picked another one from the plate on the kitchen
table, where they were seated. "I didn't take time for breakfast, so thanks. Now, what would you like to know about what I
found—or didn't find—at Jack's office?"

Elaine leaned back in her chair. "Here's what we know: Jack
left his office unlocked when he went out for lunch, which was
later than usual."

Arnie was nodding, not yet free to talk around his bite of
half a Cronut. "'Bout three o'clock, he said."

"And Jack said the snake was in the glass tank when he
left it. The tank he brought to the woods to pick it up looked

plastic," Jan filled them in. "So he must have put it in the more permanent glass one."

Arnie wiped his mouth with a napkin and took the glass of milk Jan offered him. "I asked him if anything was stolen, but nothing else looked touched. Even that portable container Jan's talking about was still there."

"Which means that whoever took the snake came prepared with something to take it away in and wasn't interested in anything else." They knew Jack's office was in a renovated section of his garage at his house, a typical setup for local game wardens in Maine.

Jan was glad for this conversation with Arnie, even if it seemed like there wasn't much to learn. At least it was helping her begin to form some generalizations about the guilty person—maybe not who he was, but something about who he was not.

So although the snake-snatcher was on Jack's property, he wasn't motivated by stealing and had made the effort to plan how to get the animal out of the building without having to take something that didn't belong to him.

"When Jack got back from getting food, did he go outside to see if his neighbors saw anything unusual?"

"He knocked on a couple of doors nearby. No one was home at one house, and the woman at the other one thought she might've heard a vehicle pass on the street, but she was busy caring for her toddler, not looking out her windows."

Arnie was eying the Cronuts, and Jan moved quickly to place another one on his plate. He didn't pause but dove in for another bite. She had some muffins in the oven that she'd offer to him in case he downed the other three Cronuts on the plate. If food was fuel for his memory, then she would help him to all he wanted.

"Arnie," Elaine began, "does it say anything to you that whoever did it wasn't just walking into some random commercial building? Even though the snake was in Jack's office, it was on Jack's personal property. If it were me, I think I'd feel more intimidated, or guilty maybe, for being on someone's property than I would walking into a public place."

"I think I see what you mean," Jan responded. "To me it seems like it would either take more guts or some familiarity with Jack."

Jack was an authority figure in town, but a personable one, and a favorite among the younger ages because of his friendliness to them while he monitored summer lake activities.

Jan could see Elaine processing something else. "What is it?"

Instead of answering, Elaine changed the subject and asked Arnie if three o'clock was the time Jack left for lunch or got back.

As he reached for a fourth Cronut, he pulled a small spiral notebook from his chest pocket with his other hand and flipped through it. "Jack left around three, maybe a few minutes after."

"How long was he gone from the office?"

"About thirty or forty minutes."

"So he would have been back around three forty-five at the latest."

"He said he returned at three forty."

"What are you thinking?" Jan asked her.

"Oh, I'm just curious."

Jan knew better. Elaine would fill her in once Arnie left. Arnie wasn't a fan of them investigating on their own, but he'd shown them respect when they'd figured things out in the past. For some reason Elaine didn't want to clue Arnie in to whatever track she was on.

The oven timer rang, and Jan fetched a to-go box and put the last two Cronuts from the plate into it, then added two cinnamon raisin muffins, still piping hot. "Arnie, you've helped us get a better picture of what happened. You've been very generous to come out here so early. Thank you."

The deputy didn't stand right away. He put his crumpled napkin on the table and leaned back in his chair with a searching look toward the women. "I haven't asked you why you wanted to know about it."

"We're just—"

"Curious?" He was grinning reluctantly when he interrupted Jan. "I thought as much. If your curiosity turns up anything, I trust you two will let me in on it. And also that you'll ask ahead of time if you need my help."

"Sure we would." Elaine returned his smile and left it at that.

Once Arnie was on his way, Jan turned to Elaine. She thought she'd guessed why Elaine had asked about the time.

"From three to three forty," she said. "Were you thinking that allowed for school to get out, then a drive from Forrest

High or even Claremore to get to Jack's, take the snake, and leave before he got back?"

Elaine said yes.

It certainly didn't rule out any number of adults either, but the timing of school letting out so closely upon the heels of the snake going missing could be a lead.

CHAPTER SEVENTEEN

Jan pulled a frozen enchilada casserole from the freezer
that she planned to take to Paula, then sat down to finish her sandwich. Between bites she pulled up Kit Edmonds's
number on her phone and texted her to ask if she could drop
by their home after work, apologizing for the short notice and
assuring her she wouldn't stay long.

"We sold out of blueberry crumb muffins by ten thirty,"
Rose was saying as she whisked dry ingredients in a bowl, "so
I've already made two more batches of them on top of the mini-
muffins. You've got to love what festival weeks do for business."

"Worth all the hours, even if we do need a week's
rest afterward."

An earlier conversation that morning had revolved
around how much work the festival required, fun as it was.
Running two separate sales sites made it challenging to get
the behind-the-scenes work done or anything else personal
that needed doing.

So they'd decided to tag-team the booth that day and give
each other a break. Jan would take some time in the morning

to drive to Augusta and then hoped to make it over to the Edmonds' home after school so she could talk with Kit. In between those errands, Jan would relieve Elaine at lunchtime so Elaine could slip away for a couple of afternoon hours to catch up on office work and some other things.

"I'm heading out now to drop off this casserole at Brian and Paula's. Paula is painting, and apparently missing Brian's help, so it sounds like they could use some supper tonight." She wanted to see how her daughter-in-law was really doing and hoped her maternal instincts were misled this time and the couple was as happy as ever. Brian needed to stop worrying about his mother if it meant creating issues with his wife.

Traffic was light on the roads, and the radio kept her occupied and made the drive seem short. During the drive Kit's text came through saying she'd love to see Jan after work and to stop in when she could.

Jan had texted Paula before leaving her garage and received a cheerful invitation to come on by as well. Paula was smiling when she opened the door, and she looked chipper, girlish even, with a streak of light-blue paint on her chin and wearing a denim shirt and baggy jeans rolled to her ankles.

"Come see my bathroom." She pulled Jan inside and thanked her for the meal. After putting the casserole in the refrigerator, she led Jan down the hall to show her work, which was neatly done. She only lacked finishing behind the toilet and around the mirror over the sink.

"I love the color."

"Thanks. I found it on an HGTV blog. I wanted to be sure to get it right. You know how different it can look on real walls versus a little paint chip."

"It's a lot brighter in here," Jan said. "You've got a knack for making a home, Paula." It was true. Paula was gradually redoing each room of the two-story New Englander-style home that had needed a lot of updating when they bought it for a song a few years back. It was not large, but Paula's touches were truly turning it into a beautiful place.

Then Jan cautiously asked Paula if everything was going well.

"Well, it's always a challenge to keep up with work, school, homework, and activities. But we're fine. The girls had fun last night"—she chuckled—"although they were almost late for school this morning because they were so tired."

Jan said she'd miss them at the corn maze in that case, but she understood the girls needed their rest.

"Oh, Brian wants us to take them," Paula replied.

She realized Paula might be concerned about her and chose her words carefully. "Tara's planning to meet me at the maze tonight. She let me know this morning."

Paula brightened. "That's great. Brian will be glad to hear it. And we'd love to see her too. We'll just have to gauge how tired our girls are after school."

Jan complimented Paula's project one more time, then gave her a hug and said good-bye.

Before she made her next stop, she sat in her Camry and called her friend Priscilla at the Lancaster library. After Jan explained what she was looking for, Priscilla checked the database and said her library didn't have any books or other information on Harley Archibald Benningham. "Only a mention in one article shows up, but I don't think you'll find it very helpful. You're right, Jan, the university library would be a better place to check. I can find out what they have through our library link system, but I've got someone at the desk waiting on me right now, so I'd have to call you back."

Jan assured her she was a short drive from the University of Maine's campus in Augusta and would stop by and check for herself. Along the way, she admired the sun rays dappling the Kennebec River and caught a glimpse of Old Fort Western along the water. She loved seeing it and was fascinated by its history as the country's oldest surviving wooden fort, dating back two hundred and fifty years.

But she didn't have time to linger. She drove down colorful tree-lined streets and campus buildings until she came to the Bennett D. Katz Library on Jewett Drive. After speaking with the librarian there, she found a couple of resources that commented on Benningham's work, as well as his life, and one even mentioned his military days. She ran across several photographs, which she copied. In no time she had gathered what she thought would make for a pleasant surprise for Archie and Elaine and was back on the road.

With a little time to spare, Jan decided to swing by the auto-parts store Brian managed to say hello to her son. Once more she guided the Camry through the streets of Augusta. Maybe showing up in person so he could see that she was okay would help him feel free to stay home that evening, if that's what his family needed.

The store smelled of tires and tools when she entered. An employee in a store-logo shirt pointed her to the office at the back of the store, where she found Brian doing computer work at his desk.

He looked up at her knock. "Mom!" He bolted up and came around the desk, placed his hands on her elbows and searched her face. "Are you okay?"

Jan laughed and stepped back. "Can't a mother visit her son at work?" She looked around and saw a few photos of his family and a drawing of a lake scene with Kelly's name on it stuck to a filing cabinet. Then she told him about her trip to the university and his home.

She rose on her toes to kiss his cheek. "I should have brought you a snack, but you'll have to wait until supper at your house. Enchilada casserole tonight, on me."

He gave her a hug. "Thanks for coming, Mom. Great to see you. So you saw Paula? How's she doing?"

"Busy at work on the bathroom. She's doing a beautiful job."

"Yeah, she is. She seems to be having fun with it too, so I've been keeping my distance." He gestured to a free chair. "Please sit."

"Oh no, no. I don't want to hold you up. But I did want to let you know you don't need to come out to Lancaster again tonight on my account." She held out a hand when he started to protest. "I know the girls might want to come, but go ahead and take the night off together. I'll have Tara with me, and your family needs some downtime, I think." It was her turn to search his face. "Everything okay there?"

He looked surprised at the question. "Sure. Yeah, of course."

She let his answer hang on the air for a few moments before moving to leave. "All right. I hope you all enjoy dinner."

They hugged and she headed back to the Camry, praying her son wasn't keeping his distance from his wife *too* much.

"DID YOU FIND what you were looking for?" Elaine asked Jan when she arrived back at the booth to relieve Elaine after lunch.

Jan was sipping what looked like a smoothie she must have picked up at a drive-through on her way back from Augusta. "I think so. I got to see Paula and Brian, and I also have some things to show you and Archie later. Maybe if we have time after work before the corn maze."

"Great. That reminds me: I need to call Dr. Vanderpool to let him know we would like to have the painting shipped to him. Make sure he can put it officially on his schedule before pulling it from the New York authenticator."

Elaine caught Jan up on how much product they had left to sell for the next few hours. "Thanks a bunch. It'll be nice to get current on the office work."

Jan wished her well and turned to help a smiling customer holding two bags of Cronuts.

Two uninterrupted hours at her desk allowed Elaine to get through her inbox. She paid several invoices and placed a few orders for more supplies they'd need to replenish after the festival. Feeling lighter and satisfied with what she'd been able to catch up on, she turned to the next item on her list and found Dr. Vanderpool's number.

But the voice on the line was a woman's, not the gravelly sound of the art expert's. "I'm sorry, Mrs. Cook, but Dr. Vanderpool has had to cancel all of his projects for the next several months. He took a bad fall yesterday and has a long rehabilitation ahead of him."

CHAPTER EIGHTEEN

Jan couldn't believe the sweet-sounding art expert Elaine had spoken to a short time ago had taken such a turn for the worse. Her cousin had returned to the booth cheered over getting her desk cleared off but disappointed to lose what she had been so sure would be a source of wisdom regarding Archie's father's painting.

"On the bright side," Jan told Elaine, "at least you hadn't asked for the painting to be shipped yet. Arizona is out, but all is not lost. There's still the chance Beatrice Miller-Pyle's colleague can fit it in sooner." They decided to ask Archie about it after hours.

The cousins' final swap for the day was for Elaine to man the booth again while Jan made the short drive to the Edmonds home. School was out, and Kit would be home by now.

Russell, Kit, and Marcella lived in a lovely white two-story house with black shutters on one of Lancaster's charming residential streets. Jan pulled into their driveway and admired the stone steps flanked by yellow potted mums up to the front porch. The barn-red door and bay-leaf wreath looked magazine worthy, and the trio of pumpkins on the top step were waiting to be carved soon.

Jan raised her hand to knock and saw the wood blinds separate on the window to her left. Marcella's pert nose and bright eyes peeked out at her. The child looked excited and popped out of view as the slats of the blinds snapped back into place.

A hollered "Mom!" sounded from the depths of the house, and a few moments later Kit opened the door. Marcella was standing next to her, dressed in gray leggings and a red-and-white striped tunic shirt, hair in slightly lopsided pigtails from a busy recess on the playground, Jan guessed.

"Come right in, Jan," Kit said warmly and moved aside to let her enter. "Marcella," she directed her child, "would you please bring Mrs. Blake's drink to the living room? Carefully?"

Obviously proud to be given an important task, and in front of a guest to boot, Marcella walked off responsibly.

"Come on in here." Kit led the way to a sitting room off to the right of the front door. They passed a wide set of carpeted stairs with a dark-stained railing that matched the house's trim work, and Kit motioned toward a sofa in a homey shade of maize next to two coordinating armchairs. The room also had a fireplace and built-in bookshelves. Jan sat on one end of the sofa and Kit the other. Still in her dress pants and blouse from the teaching day, Kit curled her legs up under her and looked relaxed and pleased to take a few minutes to visit.

They were talking about the festival, church happenings, and an update on Kit's parents, Lancaster icons Will and Pearl Trexler, when Marcella reappeared, carefully balancing a tray with not one but two glasses of cider chilling with two ice cubes and a paper restaurant umbrella in each. Her mother helped her set the tray on the coffee table. She shyly accepted Jan's compliment on her service, then ran off to get a glass for herself.

"Is she feeling any better about Sunday's accident?" Jan asked Kit when Marcella was out of sight.

Kit handed a cider glass to Jan. Its tart refreshment made Jan realize she hadn't drunk much all afternoon and was thirstier than she'd realized.

"She's doing fine, even though she still brings it up, usually at bedtime. She'll have to get past some fears of riding a horse again, but I don't think she's scarred for life." Kit's relaxed attitude made Jan think Marcella would recover since she had no anxiety to pick up on from her mother that could feed her own.

"Do you mind my asking what she says when she brings it up?" Jan settled further into the sofa cushions. "I'm asking because Elaine and I are looking into it."

Kit was about to answer when Marcella appeared again with her glass, prepared just like the others. Jan was sure they'd have to change the subject, but Kit held out her arms for Marcella to come near and pulled her daughter to sit close on the sofa.

"Marcella, Mrs. Blake is trying to find out more about what happened when the lady fell off the horse on Sunday."

Marcella twisted to look at her mom.

"Do you think we can help her do that?"

"I guess so." She looked at Jan, ready to help again. She could do more than serve cider. She was, after all, seven years old. "The black horse jumped up and down, and the blonde lady fell. I don't like that horse. It scared me. But we'll get past it, right, Mom?"

Kit nodded against the back of Marcella's head. "Yes we will, sweetheart, and Mrs. Donahue is going to be fine as soon as her leg heals."

Feeling she'd been given permission to find out what the child had seen, Jan forged ahead gently. "Leopold is a strong horse, isn't he? He's actually a nice horse, and he loves Mrs. Donahue, and she loves him. But I'm trying to find out if he accidentally thought someone told him to jump up and down, and that's why he did it. I don't believe he was trying to hurt her."

"Why not?"

"Well, right before he jumped, did you see anyone move their arms funny? Like this?" Jan did the signal for Marcella and Kit as Bridget had demonstrated to her earlier in the week.

The expression on Marcella's face was priceless as she looked at Jan as if Jan had two heads. "Why would anybody do that?"

Jan's smile came easily for the girl. "It is a funny thing to do, isn't it? But it means something to Leopold. See, he used to be in a circus. He performed tricks that he learned, and the way he knew what trick to do was by watching his trainers make hand signals at him, like the one I just showed you." Jan motioned the signal one more time.

Marcella looked a little more willing to accept that reasoning for the silly signal and tried it for herself. It was clear to Jan that Marcella had not known of the signal until now.

"Did you see anyone do that before he jumped, honey?" Kit asked her daughter.

Marcella looked confident. "No. No one did that. You and Daddy and I were behind the others, and I didn't see anyone raise their arms to tell Leopold to jump up."

"They were all holding on to their reins like you were doing?" Jan tried to word her questions as literally as she could so there'd be no misunderstanding.

"Uh-huh." Pigtails flicked her shoulders as Marcella's head moved up and down.

"You're sure?" Kit pressed.

"Yes. There was us. And the lady and the older boy with her. And that other family we didn't know. And the man. They all were riding like they told us at the barn."

"Okay." Jan had managed to follow all that, and somehow she felt she could trust Marcella's sureness. No one on the ride had made the signal—that Marcella had seen anyway.

Marcella's head dipped to the side. "But are you sure that horse is nice?"

"Leopold? Oh yes. In fact, I went to see Mrs. Donahue, and she isn't mad at him at all. He's her favorite of all her horses. And since she knows she can ride him again, then we can feel good about getting back on a horse when we're ready too. What do you think of that?" Jan tried to put fun in her voice.

The corner of Marcella's top lip curved up cutely and her eyebrows lifted, as if to convey she wasn't sold on it quite yet. But behind the doubt, there was also a glimmer of spunky hope.

The child was too cute.

"But if no one on the ride made the signal, then why did he buck?" Marcella asked the question as it was crossing Jan's own mind.

"That is a very good question, Marcella." *Does that mean someone was hiding in the woods? And how do I respond to that without scaring her more?* Jan asked herself.

Kit stepped in. "Mrs. Blake is going to find out. She's very good at figuring out the answers to things like this, so no need to worry."

No need to worry, no need to worry. Jan had to remember that, because even though she and Elaine had gotten pretty good at solving mysteries, they weren't all-knowing. But, she reminded herself, she trusted in the One who was all-knowing. He'd proven time and again to her that He had every answer she needed and knew precisely how to guide Elaine and her to them. They just had to keep taking each next step He put before them.

CHAPTER NINETEEN

After the booth and tearoom were closed for the day, Jan and Elaine took time to sit with Archie in the dining room and update him on their investigations. Chicken and potatoes were baking in the oven. The tearoom was bathed in shadows, the only lights the ones shining in that room and the kitchen. The corn maze would start in a couple of hours, but for now Jan was glad to sit.

"I made that call to the other authenticator in New York today," Archie responded to a question from Elaine. "Unfortunately, he is booked through spring."

Elaine frowned. "That's too bad. I suppose since Dr. Vanderpool in Phoenix can't work on it either, we will have to keep the painting with Ms. Miller-Pyle's company. At least we can assume she'll do a good job, although I was really hoping you'd have more answers about your father without having to wait a long time."

Jan saw her opportunity to lift their spirits. She set the file folder she'd brought with her on the table. One by one she lifted photocopies from it and spread them out. "I thought it might help to have something to study while we wait." She looked pleasantly at Archie. "At least we can feel like we're doing something proactive instead of being at the mercy of a stranger's schedule in New York."

The others' eyes roamed over the photocopied pictures of paintings, and Elaine pointed out characteristics shared with the one she owned.

Jan nodded. "If you take time to read through the text that accompanies them, you'll see critics' comments about Harley Benningham's style. I haven't had time to read carefully myself, but what I have skimmed included quite good comments. It seems the art world was impressed by his talent. It's too bad we don't know yet why he stopped painting."

Archie was looking at two pages at the same time, his gaze lingering over details Jan couldn't see. He had told them he remembered drawing with his father when he was young and recognizing even back then that his father was skilled.

When the doorbell rang, he set down the papers and offered to answer it since most likely it was his wife.

Jan and Elaine had spent a little time with Gloria Bentham and welcomed her with hugs. Gloria looked pretty with her blonde bob curled toward her chin and wearing a wine-colored jacket over her cable-knit sweater and pearl necklace.

"So nice to catch up with you both," she said in an accent that matched her husband's.

"I hope you're all hungry by now, because I think the food is ready." Jan led the way to the kitchen. They all pitched in and the clear end of the table was soon set. Jan's mouthwatering chicken and baked potatoes filled the dining room with a homey aroma while they ate and caught up on everyone's work and the festival.

After clearing supper dishes, they refreshed their glasses and set the teapot to boil and returned to the information Jan had brought home. Taking turns, they read about the different techniques Benningham used to create his signature style, which was a unique take on the realism that was popular during that era.

His art showed detail that made his images appear as if they could move off the canvas, and often had a melancholy tone, much as the painting did that Elaine owned. She went to get the eleven-by-fourteen photo of it, and they each commented on the light used to add dimension and texture and how the artist was able to make the woman's mood so realistic, even though her face was only visible in profile.

"How about this quote?" Elaine held a page up that showed a picture of a residential street scene with a young girl holding a scruffy puppy. "'Benningham's signature strength was in his ability to make each scene, each character, appear as if the viewer could place himself there, to converse with the subjects he painted. One can only marvel at the artist's thoughtfulness in every stroke.'"

"If we only knew why he stopped painting," Gloria murmured.

"I think we'll find out if we keep looking," Jan encouraged.

"It looks like some of his art made it into museums in England, France, and other countries in Europe," Elaine said. "The more I read, the more unbelievable it feels that we came across the painting. I'm starting to think it was a 'God thing.'"

She looked up and wrinkled her nose. "You can probably tell I'm choosing to believe your painting is an original."

"I tend to agree," Archie said. "I'm blown away that I'm learning all this about my father. And whether or not the painting is real, the information I've learned about my father *is*, and that's enough for me. I'll thank God for that regardless of the authenticity of the painting."

Jan agreed wholeheartedly. "Archie, what do you remember about this apartment and the park?"

He inhaled deeply, as if drawing the memories together, and his mouth curved into a small, wistful smile. "Perhaps it is because we've been focusing on my father as a painter, but when I look at the painting now, my first memories are of times we sketched together there. And not only with pencils."

He leaned in and set a finger over the park in the photo version. "For a while I didn't remember anything specific about that park, but in the last day or two I recall times when my father and I took brushes and a bucket of water out to that sidewalk that circles it and painted water pictures on the concrete.

"And I remember my mother there too, but not this woman. I am curious to know who she is, because there is tenderness in how he captured her on the canvas."

Yes, there was, Jan had to admit, raising her curiosity about the relationship between the artist and subject. "Do you mind my asking if your father's marriage to your mother was his first?"

"I never thought otherwise. But I suppose this leads me to wonder."

Quiet descended as they all seemed to digest the possibilities of who the woman in the painting could be. They didn't have answers, but Jan felt in her heart that God would reveal them in His way and time.

CHAPTER TWENTY

Jan stood outside the entrance to the corn maze, which had been lit by rented portable lights. The gathering at the Richardsons' dairy farm seemed smaller than at the bonfire the night before, but even so, the numbers were hardly low. Jan estimated a good hundred or so had come to pay the small fee to go through the maze. All proceeds would go to the PTA, so Annie Richardson, Misty Carter, and Bridget Donahue were tag-teaming the event. They'd rented a cotton candy machine and a DJ, who kept the music flowing. And a tractor lugging a big wagon filled with hay rumbled up and unloaded its riders before loading up again for another trip around the farm beneath the stars.

Together with Tara, Jan was taking tickets after Bridget volunteered them for the job. They were willing recruits and were having fun spending a rare evening with each other.

The cool night and shadows cast by the moon seemed to loosen tongues, surprising Jan with the plethora of tidbits she caught. While she stood there greeting people, she learned of two engagements, a number of Christmas

vacations planned, a couple of family quarrels, an investment that had gone well and an unfortunate one that hadn't,
and four babies expected in the spring. She didn't hear so
much on a daily basis in the tearoom kitchen surrounded by
speechless bags of sugar and flour. No complaints, though.
She wouldn't trade her niche there. But it was nice to socialize, she had to admit, and with her accomplished daughter at
her side. Her heart had swelled with pride to hear from Faith
Lanier that Tara's jewelry was selling out each day at A Little
Something's booth.

Jan had already sold tickets to some of the high school
kids and was feeling happy about the familiarity she was building with them. Elaine was currently navigating the maze with
Nathan and the Yeatons, so when Jack came up to see if Tara
wanted a break to go through the maze with him, Jan found
herself on her own when Derek Jameson and Dori Richardson
walked up.

"Hi, Mrs. Blake." Derek paid for both tickets, making Jan
wonder if it was a date. If so, serious Derek and bubbly Dori
made a cute couple, she thought. Instead of going into the
maze, though, they hung back off to the side while Jan let a
few more people enter. Several minutes later, Trace and Keri
hurried up and the foursome went in together. She was feeling
good about all that until a while later when the four teens came
out from the cornstalks at the same time Bridget and Annie
were standing near Jan collecting the cash earned so far.

The women greeted their own two kids and Derek, and
Annie was cheerful in her hello to Keri. But there was no mis-
taking Keri's discomfort beneath Bridget's aloofness toward

her. What a shame, Jan thought. She wondered whether there was more to that rift than she knew.

The awkwardness spread and the other teens seemed antsy to move on, but Bridget made the first move to head back to the Richardsons' house with the money. After Bridget was out of earshot, Jan overheard Trace whisper an apology to Keri for his mother's behavior. "Sometimes she can be pretty bullheaded."

When Keri frowned and shrugged, Jan caught her eye and offered an encouraging smile, then turned to Trace. "Are you ready for tomorrow night? The whole town's looking forward to cheering on the team."

"I think we're ready as we can be. It should be a good game."

Jan smiled. "Your mom seems to be getting around pretty well."

He motioned a so-so answer with his hand. "She's been trying out the crutches at home. It's hard to keep her down. She said you stopped by. Thanks for doing that."

Jan handed two tickets to an elderly couple and pointed them toward the maze entrance, then looked at Trace again. "She told me about Leopold's hand signals. That's pretty impressive."

"Isn't that amazing?" Keri spoke up. "I've watched Trace work with him on some of those."

"I'd love to watch that myself sometime. I hear a lot of people are aware of them."

"Yeah, a bunch know," Trace said reluctantly. "Derek finally told me he stopped by to see you about it." His expression didn't reveal what he thought of that, but he thanked Jan for doing what she could to help out. "I still think someone was just playing a joke, but I'm glad to have people looking out for her."

"And for you," Jan said, earning a *whatever* shrug from him. "I bet she's glad to have your help."

The tractor was slowing to a stop, so the two excused themselves to go join the next ride.

Annie Richardson was coming up behind her, but before Jan could ask if they were happy with the earnings so far, Chris Cosgrove and two other teen boys wearing Claremore jackets hurried up. They didn't seem to see Jan or Annie there because they were craning their necks to look past the women at the tractor and wagon. Trace and Keri were joined by Derek and Dori, and the four climbed on board as the tractor began to pull away.

One of the other boys pointed and whispered excitedly to Chris. "There's Donahue and Jameson! Let's go!"

They took off in that direction, but instead of running directly toward their friends, they kept to the shadows, weaving around the light put out by the portable lamps. As they disappeared from view, Jan noticed they each had something in their hands.

"What's that about?" Jan asked Annie.

"They're up to something."

"I'm sure you saw Dori get in the wagon."

"She can hold her own, whatever they've got planned." Annie was smiling.

While Jan and Annie took tickets, she couldn't see the tractor or wagon because of the darkness beyond the lighted maze area. But she was keeping her ears peeled and could hear shouts and laughter erupt from somewhere out in the field.

Annie still didn't look concerned and said Dori had told her she knew Chris and the others had been planning something. "So I think they're getting ready to turn the tables right now." Jan thought Annie seemed like the kind of mom who would just go with the flow.

The shouts and laughter continued for a while. Jan was anxious to know what was going on, but Annie kept taking tickets and chatting with everyone who held out money to her. Jan figured she'd better wait to find out naturally instead of crossing the line into meddling.

At last, the rumble of the tractor drew nearer. When it stopped in the same place it had launched, only a couple of young families unloaded from it. Jan didn't see the teenagers for a few more minutes until she heard them coming closer on foot, laughing and teasing each other.

Jan observed them in amazement. When they neared the ticket table where Annie and Jan were looking on, they were such messes that Jan might not have known who they were if she hadn't seen their "before" versions. Hay was all over their hair and clothing, stuck on by what Jan could only guess was shaving cream and…red Jell-O? But they were all cracking jokes and seemed to be having a ball. Keri and Dori were picking straw and goop off each other. With their long hair, they had quite a way to go because it was loaded with gunk.

Jan didn't know exactly how it all went down, but she sensed a story coming that she couldn't wait to hear.

By now, other people had heard the ruckus and come over to the ticket area. One of them was Bridget, who swung on her crutches to stand by Jan and Annie.

Trace saw his mother then and started toward her with his arms open and a huge, goofy grin. "Mom," he crooned, "I love you so much. How about a hug?"

Bridget clearly didn't know whether to reach her arms out or run the other direction, an impossible option in her injured state. She looked horrified but was cracking up laughing too. "Red? Really? Did you have to choose *red* Jell-O?" she managed between laughing gasps for breath and demands for him to stop as she kept wriggling away from his reach.

He grinned roguishly and flicked a pouf of shaving cream off his sleeve on to her hand, clearly enjoying an unscripted moment of fun with her while everyone looked on in awe.

His friends started to cheer him on, and soon others joined in the chant. Bridget looked around wide eyed and panicked, but also soaking up her son's attention.

He reached out as if to pull her into a bear hug while her laughter held her in place as surely as her bad leg did. Just when it looked like her clothes were about to be desecrated, he stopped short... And then he leaned in to kiss her sweetly on the cheek, somehow managing not to get another drop of the mess on her.

The audience let out a collective *aww*, and Bridget searched his face for the cleanest place to kiss him back. "You better get used to doing your own laundry, pal," she told him loudly enough for everyone to hear.

That was easily Jan's favorite moment of the night, and she was pretty sure it was Bridget's as well.

People started to move away, and Annie sent her younger kids, Joe and Ella, to get some old towels to help the teens clean up the worst of it before allowing them into the house to clean up some more.

The five friends and rivals turned and pulled each other into a big, disgusting group hug.

If this was the extent of the pranks between the teams, then Jan figured things were going to be just fine.

Things quieted to a more organized chaos after that. Jack and Tara rejoined her at the ticket table, where she asked Jack about the snake that hadn't turned up yet. He admitted he was frustrated with the whole thing and had even revised the ad in the newspaper with a two-hundred-fifty-dollar reward that Bridget had put up for whoever turned in the creature. It was a good idea. But Jan shared Jack's doubts that a guilty person would ever come forward, even for a reward.

Jan was still mulling over the missing snake as well as Annie's words while she got ready for bed later that night. With her face freshly clean and dressed in her pajamas and robe, she knocked on Elaine's door to see how her cousin's evening went.

They talked about how fun the week had been and who they'd seen at the dairy farm.

"It's a shame that Bridget Donahue is keeping Keri at arm's length when Keri obviously is part of Trace's world." She was caught off guard when Elaine narrowed her mouth as she rubbed lotion into her hands.

"Actually, I'm not so sure about Keri."

Jan hadn't expected a contradiction.

"Nathan and I were near Keri and Trace and Dori and Derek at one point in the maze," Elaine explained. "I didn't hear the context of their conversation, but I distinctly heard them laughing and then he mentioned his mom." Elaine paused, looking at Jan intently.

"And?" Jan asked.

"And then Keri said to Trace, 'I'm sorry about the accident, but I wish it would've taught her a thing or two.'"

CHAPTER TWENTY-ONE

The sky gradually darkened throughout the morning on Friday, the clouds slinking in thickly while Elaine and Jan finished lunch. Since Sunday's storm, they'd had such fortunate weather that week, Elaine thought. Until now.

As the clouds gathered and billowed, she noticed more and more shoppers glance heavenward and start to head for their cars. Now the midafternoon sky was rolling. The cousins and the other booth owners sped up their pace crating product and loading their vehicles before the first drops fell.

Gavin Richardson rumbled up in his farm truck and hopped out to help Annie with their display. On his way past the tearoom booth he stopped to fold up the tearoom's table and easel and carry them to Elaine's Malibu.

"Thanks, Gavin," she called after him as he jogged back to his wife.

"Doesn't look good for the Pirates tonight," he answered.

That was for sure. Today of all days for a rainstorm. From the looks of it, Elaine was pretty sure the parade would be in trouble too.

"The parade's already been canceled," Gavin added, on track with those thoughts. "Better now than midway through it, I suppose. But my daughter will be fit to be tied if all their work on the floats was for nothing. Get home as quick as you can, and you might beat this storm."

They waved more thanks. This weather would crush hearts all over Lancaster, and Claremore as well, for that matter. She had no idea how many people were visiting for the game, but whatever the number, it was large.

"Gavin was right," Jan said on a relieved exhale as she pulled the car door closed. "All the hard work the students put into the floats, only to see them melt into soppy, tissue-paper messes."

Elaine blew raspberries at the whole thing and turned the Malibu toward home. She was pulling into the garage when the sky let loose. A deluge of rain spattered her car before it was fully under cover. Grateful to park inside, she and Jan gathered the remaining bags of Cronuts and hurried into the house to drop their armloads on the kitchen island.

"Welcome back," Rose said, throwing a kitchen towel over her shoulder.

Archie was returning to the kitchen with table linens when he saw the women and offered to get the tea urn from the car. Elaine accepted his help, then hung up her coat and dropped her purse and keys on the office desk, while Jan excused herself to go put her things upstairs.

"Phew! I'm about to declare an official rainy season in Lancaster," Elaine commented when she returned to the kitchen.

"I'm glad you both are home," Rose responded. "That doesn't look good for driving."

Elaine checked a weather app. "There's going to be a lot of disappointed fans tonight."

"And to think how many of them came all the way here just for the game," Archie added, returning to the kitchen to put the urn in the sink.

Elaine had an idea. She peeked out the kitchen door into the east parlor as she considered whether it would work. She preferred to have Jan's thoughts on her budding plan, but she didn't want to disturb her if she was making time for a call to Bob. Jan would be back downstairs soon enough. No, Elaine decided, she'd move forward with her idea and trust that Jan would be all for it.

"Rose, how many cookies would you guess we have in the freezer?" She knew Jan and Rose regularly froze extras for just-in-case times like tonight.

Rose looked up from washing a cookie sheet. "We've still got a few dozen from what we made ahead of time for this week. I can tell you've got something brewing." Rose's eyes sparkled.

"Yes, don't keep us in suspense," Archie said from the sink, where he was maneuvering the spray nozzle to rinse the large urn.

"I'm thinking it's time to add Booster Club pizza party to our list of special events."

Rose's enthusiasm seemed to melt a little. "We'd be ordering pizzas, not making them, right?" She held out a hand. "Don't get me wrong, I'd love to help and I think the whole idea's great, but with time so sh—"

"No, no. I'll see if we could partner with the Boosters and make it an official event. I'm hoping they have some extra funds to pay for the pizzas. Otherwise, it'll be a cookie party," she laughed as she finished.

"Which would be delicious too," Rose said supportively, "but pizzas would draw more of a crowd."

"And keep them here longer, give them something to fill up an evening," Archie said.

"I wonder if there's some kind of entertainment we could add." Rose sat down purposefully at an island stool.

Both employees seemed ready to take on a hosting challenge, which Elaine needed right now. "Did you have anything in mind?"

Rose suggested a slide show set to music, if someone would be willing to throw it together on such short notice. "I'm sure there are slews of football pictures around, with all the parent photographers at the games."

"That's a good idea. It could be tough to pull off in a couple of hours, but we're not aiming for perfection, right? Just low-key fun. It would hinge on finding the right person to do it."

Rose agreed and went to double-check the frozen cookie stash while Elaine excused herself and sat down at her computer in the office. She found a phone number for the stables and soon had Bridget Donahue on the line. She explained that she worked with Jan and hoped Bridget was feeling better every day.

"Thank you, Elaine. What can I do for you?" The woman sounded brusque, so Elaine got to the point quickly as she listened to the rain fall relentlessly outside. "I've been watching the clouds and wondering about the game tonight."

"Ugh. Can you believe this? There was nothing on the radar this morning, and now this. And with the biggest game of Trace's career in a few hours."

Trace and several others. "Exactly. A lot of people were looking forward to this game, but it looks like the weather isn't expected to let up until after midnight, with lightning expected for the next few hours. I called because I'm wondering if there's a Plan B yet. Do you know when a decision will be made whether to cancel it?"

Elaine heard Bridget exhale impatiently. "Not until six o'clock. And then they'd have to decide when to do the makeup. This is awful. The scouts are in town this weekend. I'm sure their schedules are already booked at other schools for the rest of the season. This weekend is our chance."

"Well, I can't fix the rain or make sure the scouts stay in town, but I have an idea to keep spirits up. If you like it I'll need your help." She invited Bridget to contact her network of Booster Club members to put out the word that Tea for Two would host a pizza party that night in the event the game got canceled. "Our parlors could fit the team and their families and the Boosters. We just need to know if the club can foot the bill for the pizzas. We'll provide dessert."

"Well, let's hope worst-case scenario means it's postponed and not canceled, but thank you. This is really kind of you, Elaine." Bridget exhaled again, this time sounding slightly less distressed. "I'll need to check with some of my people, plus the coaching staff. Let me make a couple of calls and get back to you…"

"Bridget," Elaine interrupted before she could hang up, "what would you think about inviting the Claremore team too?"

"Why would we do that?"

At the sharp reply, Elaine held her phone away from her ear, then pulled it back. "It would show sportsmanship, an olive branch of sorts."

"But we never do that kind of thing."

"I understand, but consider how important this game is for both teams. And with the rumors of players pranking each other, and with what happened to you...it might be the best move the Pirates could make. The best one *you* could make. They're still seventeen-year-old kids, after all, who could learn from your gracious example." Elaine hoped she sounded enticing and not guilt-inducing, which wasn't her aim at all. This gesture could help Bridget's reputation and boost the team. Both teams. A win-win.

Bridget seemed somewhat mollified, and she even said she would call someone at the school to handle a slide show. They hung up after agreeing to their next steps. Elaine would move ahead getting the tearoom ready while she waited for Bridget's go-ahead as soon as she heard something conclusive about the game's status.

With Rose's and Archie's commitments to stay until they heard about the game, Elaine felt decently good about this impromptu party. Together they set up a couple of serving tables and raided their stock of paper plates and plastic utensils and cups. And they shifted a few parlor tables to make room for a portable screen, which Elaine made a note to ask Bridget about too.

Around five thirty, Jan came downstairs and stumbled when she came upon the three hard workers who were figuring out where to put the table for the pizza boxes.

"Jan! Welcome to the party." Elaine had changed into casual pants and a black sweater, with simple gold jewelry in honor of Forrest High.

"I was on the phone with Bob. What did I miss?"

"Nothing yet," Rose responded cheerfully. "But we're about to hear that the game is postponed, so we're getting everything ready for a pizza party."

Now Jan drew up her features in bewilderment.

Elaine removed the last bud vase centerpiece from the parlor tables. "I wanted to get your opinion on this but didn't want to disturb you." She brought the vase to a cart with the others. She'd found some gold confetti in their supply of party decorations to sprinkle on the tables instead. "We should be hearing soon from Bridget about whether there's still a game tonight. If not, I offered our place for a pizza party." She explained the details she and Bridget had talked about.

"It's a great plan. I'm just sorry I didn't come down sooner to help."

Jan usually started her day earlier than any of them, so there was no reason for her to feel guilt over enjoying a few extra minutes alone in her room. They all assured her it was fine, and Elaine pulled her aside and added quietly, "Jan, I think this may be a great way to learn more about the relationships between the football teams."

Jan smiled then, looking ready to spy if necessary. "I want to know what Keri really thinks of her boyfriend's mother."

Elaine nodded conspiratorially. She had a good feeling about this night. She hoped it would be a night of discovery about the horse accident. Maybe even the missing snake mystery.

Lightning struck, followed immediately by a roll of thunder that shook the pictures on the walls. The lights flickered, sending shadows shooting across the house, as if God was confirming He heard her thoughts.

CHAPTER TWENTY-TWO

The game was indeed canceled and rescheduled for the following night—much to Bridget's relief, Jan learned from Elaine. While on the phone with Bridget, Elaine mentioned the parade floats and what a shame it would be to lose them, but Bridget told her some students and staff had run outside to cover the floats with tarps before the rains hit, so the parade was a go for three o'clock Saturday afternoon. The homecoming dance, which had been slated for Saturday night, got bumped to Sunday evening.

Although still disappointed to have to wait for the much-anticipated competition, Bridget was in better spirits, Elaine told Jan.

Bridget had found a tech pro among her network that was already moving like a tornado to pull together a slide show honoring the hard-fighting Pirates' football organization, and she even had suggested to him to include a few token slides of the Raiders players too. She'd gotten approval for the pizzas and said they'd be delivered to Tea for Two by seven o'clock, in time for the guests to arrive shortly after that.

With everything set in motion and the tearoom ready for visitors, Rose and Archie said good night and left, and Jan and Elaine threw together some soup and salads for themselves while strategizing who they wanted to talk with at the party. Currently at the top of their list were Keri and Trace. Somehow they needed to play their conversations carefully to find out what Keri meant when she'd told Trace in the corn maze that it was too bad his mother hadn't learned something from the accident. It sounded potentially incriminating but could have been quite innocent.

"You know," Jan began, "this entire week Trace has been near the center of all the possibilities. He's friends with everyone we've found with potential motive. He was with his mother on the trail ride, and the accident could have been meant for him. We've wondered about Chris, who used to play ball with Trace. Keri is his girlfriend. I'd like to hear more of his thoughts about this crazy week."

Elaine agreed that the group of teenagers seemed to have the most likely "suspects," although that term sounded harsh. "Except I don't think we should cross off Lucy Rodgers quite yet."

Jan looked across the table at her. "Lucy? Why not?"

"I've been thinking about our conversation with her the other day. Something wasn't adding up for me, and I just realized what it was. She told us she hadn't seen Bridget in a year."

"Yes."

"And she said Bridget sent prayer requests last year through their church prayer line."

"Yes," Jan repeated.

"So they go to the same church. And Lucy said she went to church before going to her sister's house last Sunday, so wouldn't they have seen each other there a few days ago instead of a whole year?"

Jan considered this. "Maybe one of them switched churches. We can ask Bridget tonight."

"I think it would be good to find out if Lucy had a nice time at her sister's house." Elaine winked. "Assuming she went there."

BRIDGET ARRIVED FIRST with Trace, who helped her get up the front stairs on her crutches while Jan and Elaine ran through the puddles in raincoats and held umbrellas over both of them.

Together they shook off drops on to the extra mats the cousins had set on the front porch and in the entry, then gazed around at the gauzy black fabric draped like a canopy across the ceiling. Strings of golden twinkle lights were tucked inside the folds, giving the effect of starlight. More twinkle lights were strung throughout the parlors. The tables looked festive with their confetti and candy corn centerpieces. They wore broad grins as they took it all in.

"Ladies, you've outdone yourselves," Bridget gushed, surprising Jan with her effusiveness. "And people say *I* get a lot done in short order."

Bridget seemed like she'd been running busily as usual, even with her leg in a cast. But her face glowed with friendliness, and she had a relieved demeanor about her, making Jan glad Elaine had come up with the idea for the party. It was already redeeming a disastrous night for two people.

From a sports duffel Jan only now noticed, Trace pulled out a rubber-banded cylinder and unrolled it enough to show them a Pirates banner. "Mom usually brings this to the games for our sidelines," he said. "We thought you might have a place for it tonight."

It took a few minutes to locate supplies they'd need to hang it on the stair wall so everyone could see it from the east parlor.

"Will Keri be coming later?" Elaine asked while she eyeballed the placement on the wall for Jan and Trace, who held up the banner's ends.

Trace sent a sidelong glance toward his mom, whose lips had suddenly narrowed. "She's coming with a couple of other Claremore cheerleaders," he said tightly. "Thank you for inviting them. A lot of our team members are good friends with their team."

"Elaine gets the credit. It was her idea. We're both just glad it's working out tonight," Jan said warmly, hoping to alleviate the tension apparent between Bridget and Trace over the subject of Keri.

"Bridget," Elaine interjected, "why don't you come with me to plate some more cookies?"

It seemed sort of an odd request for Elaine to involve Bridget, but when Elaine gave a subtle nod on their way to the kitchen, Jan saw the chance to talk with Trace alone.

"Keri seems like a nice girl. I don't know her very well, but you make a cute couple."

"Thanks." Trace grinned. "I like her a lot. She's real sweet and fun."

"And very pretty."

His grin broadened. "That too." Then he frowned. "If I could just get Mom to give her a chance."

Jan wrinkled her nose. "She's not such a fan, huh?"

Trace groaned. "She's obsessed with football. Even more than I am, and I'm the one on the team, not her."

Jan laughed with him. "How does Keri feel about your mom?"

"Mom hasn't exactly been endearing to Keri. Keri's got spunk, so she can handle it, but Mom isn't making it easy. She's so worried about anything distracting me. But I'd be a lot more stressed about football if it wasn't for Keri, you know what I mean?"

Jan thought she did.

"But Mom gets lonely with Dad gone so much. I think that adds to it. At least that's how it seems to me. I'm her main company, aside from kids who come for lessons and trail rides now and then."

And Keri was an intruder on that relationship. That made sense, right or wrong. Jan understood how Bridget might struggle to let go of her control on her son's life, not to mention the comfort of having her kid around. Jan had been through that herself—three times over, and without Peter around at all. It did get lonely. Except now, she smirked inwardly, Brian had returned to hover a lot, to the point that Jan was ready to send him back to his own home. Life flip-flopped in funny ways sometimes.

Jan saw a quiet maturity in Trace. No wonder he was a leader on the team. She guessed it was based on more than just his skills on the field. "Have you been able to talk with your mom about it? Has she gotten to know Keri at all?"

He shook his head and looked a little lost. His end of the banner was up, and as she finished securing her end, Jan wondered if there was anything she could do to help without making the mistake of butting into something that was by no means her business. She gave his arm an aunt-like squeeze and was surprised when he reached over to hug her shoulders.

"Your mom's awfully proud of you, Trace. I can see why."

"Aw, thanks. She's really a good mom."

He turned to go, but Jan wasn't about to miss this chance for one more important question. More people could arrive any minute, so she had to speak quickly. "Trace, as you now know, Derek talked to Elaine and me about the accident."

He turned back with a hesitant look. "I told him I wasn't worried about that."

"No, but he seems concerned for you. And for the game to go well. You've been friends a long time, right?"

"It was tough on him when I got the QB spot after Chris left. But we worked it out."

"I hadn't heard that part. He wanted to be quarterback too?"

"Everyone expected it, including me, since he was second-string QB last year."

So that was the position change Misty had mentioned.

"I know he's bummed about his scholarship chances now, and I totally get that. I feel bad for him." He looked over Jan's shoulder toward the kitchen, probably to make sure his mother wasn't coming back yet. "But I talked with Coach Delaney and asked him to put Derek in at QB for at least a few plays. He deserves a chance, even if we lose the game." He quickly amended that statement. "Not that I think we'll lose if he plays. He's a great quarterback, not to mention he's incredible as wide receiver. Way better than I'd ever be at that position. And he's told me a couple of times lately how happy he is playing that position."

Even if Bridget was a helicopter parent, as some people claimed, she obviously was doing a lot of things right with Trace. And Jan hadn't met Derek's parents, but she knew they were raising a good son too.

Jan had to ask one more question. "Trace, I've got to ask this just because…Elaine overhead Keri say something last night, and we're sure we misunderstood. She mentioned she wished your mom had learned from the accident. Do you think there's any chance Keri might have been involved in a prank on the riding trail on Sunday?"

She cringed a little as he drew back with a touch of defensiveness. "Not to hurt her," she assured him, "but maybe if she's been pranked by your mom?"

He shook his head. "No. She wouldn't have done that." He kept shaking his head. "I mean she *couldn't* have done it. I've wondered myself if anyone at school could have been bent out of shape by Mom's outspokenness. Keri included. But Keri was in Augusta at a cheer clinic that afternoon. And she felt really bad when she heard Mom had fallen. She didn't know anything about it beforehand. Her comment last night was just frustration over not knowing how to win Mom over. I'm sure of it."

CHAPTER TWENTY-THREE

Once guests began arriving, the door didn't stop opening and closing for an hour, while the sky seemed to work hard to overflow Chickadee Lake with its relentless downpour. Elaine stayed busy welcoming guests and keeping the floor as dry as possible.

Several players had been delegated to get the screen to the party and set it up, and a couple of others had volunteered to bring music, which filled the house while pizzas were scarfed down. Coaches crushed box after box and moved them out of the way in the kitchen.

The camaraderie among the Boosters members, coaching staff, players, families, and a handful of friends of both teams made for a lively night. Cheers and laughter flowed as the slides flipped one to the next and players bantered with good-natured jabs across the teams. Chris and his teammates had made sure to bring Raiders foam fingers to pass out as insurance that Claremore was fairly represented.

Elaine made a point to visit with as many people as she could, while also making sure the tables were organized and the trash picked up since there were so many people crowded into the parlors. She was glad to see that the two schools hadn't segregated themselves by parlor, but instead, Forrest High colors blended with Claremore's on both sides of the house. The chairs were filled with people talking and laughing, and everyone seemed to be making the most of a night that could have ended as disappointingly as it began. In fact, the mood seemed high as comments floated around about how the rainstorm was only building the anticipation for tomorrow. And Elaine heard lots of final details discussed about the parade and the floats.

Elaine looked over the partygoers, some familiar students and some new teens, as they rooted for Coach Delaney, who was spinning a cookie on his finger like a basketball. The coach lost control of it but caught it before it hit the ground. With a dramatic flair, he took a big bite, and the group burst out in playful catcalls teasing Coach D to stick to football.

As she was tidying one of the food tables, she heard a few girls whispering behind her. At first she didn't pay it any mind since she was surrounded by multiple conversations, wedged where she was between the chatty girls and a circle of husky football players caught up in their own talk. Elaine poured herself a cup of water and leaned against the table. She wouldn't mind a minute to catch her breath.

"At least that's where he thinks I was on Sunday." Something about the words and the teen girl's secretive tone made Elaine listen closely. She couldn't tell who was speaking, but she tried to remember which girls were in the cluster behind her. She didn't remember all their names, but she knew Keri was one of them. She sipped her water and tried to be as invisible as possible.

"I can't believe he hasn't figured it out yet," the girl practically whispered. "What do you think his mother'll do if she finds out?"

"You mean *when* she finds out," a third girl said with a quiet giggle.

Elaine held her breath, anxious to hear what came next. But when the girls quickly shushed each other, she turned enough to see Trace, Derek, and Chris squeeze through the swarm of Pirates and Raiders sweatshirts and join them, all three grinning broadly as if ready for some old-fashioned flirting.

Elaine managed to count five girls, including Keri and Dori Richardson, as they shelved their private conversation and welcomed the boys over. She tried to place Keri's voice as the one who'd spoken first, the one who wasn't where "he" thought she was on Sunday, the day Bridget fell off the horse. She thought it matched her memory of Keri's pitch. If Elaine was right, who could Keri have been talking about, other than Trace?

A while later, she met Jan coming back from the bathroom at the same time Bridget approached them on her crutches. "I know I said it already, but I wanted to thank you both again. This has been an out-of-the-ordinary but perfect celebration, I admit. I think you've helped save the whole weekend."

They both smiled and said they were happy to have everyone over.

"You did all the work of getting the word out," Elaine told her.

"That was the easy part. One group text to the Boosters, and it was done. Plus the calls to the coaches too."

"And even more good news is that the teams will still get to play this weekend while the scouts are in town," Jan pointed out.

"Isn't that providential?" Bridget looked like a huge weight had been lifted.

"Jan told me about her visit at your home this week," Elaine said.

When Bridget nodded curiously, Jan followed Elaine's lead. "Bridget, you and I talked a little about your friendship with Lucy Rodgers. Do the two of you still go to the same church?"

"Actually, I think Lucy might be visiting other places. At least that's the little I've heard from mutual friends. I think I told you, Jan, I haven't seen her there in a while." Bridget took a sip of her water. "Why do you ask?"

"Just something she said about going to church and visiting her sister last Sunday afternoon." Elaine was thankful Jan sounded nonchalant, not making an obvious link between Lucy and the accident, since Bridget had already told Jan she didn't think Lucy would mess with a horse-riding prank or a snake.

Bridget didn't miss a beat. "Why don't you ask her sister now?"

Elaine and Jan traded bewildered looks.

"How…?" Elaine stammered.

Bridget craned her neck to see over the shoulders of the crowd. "She's one of my best club members. There she is." She waved and called across the room. "Misty!"

The cousins traded another look. Misty?

"You know Misty Carter, right?"

Misty waved back and crossed the room to join them.

"How did we not know you're Lucy Rodgers's sister?" Jan asked her. "They say it's a small world, and it really feels that way. Now that I know, it's crazy I didn't realize it before. You look so much alike."

Misty smirked around a bite of pizza. "We hear that a lot."

"I hope the two of you had a nice visit last Sunday," Elaine said. "It was good to catch up with her at our booth this week, and she mentioned she'd spent the afternoon with you."

Misty dabbed her mouth with a napkin, nodding pleasantly until she swallowed. "We did have a nice time. We went out for lunch and fit in a long walk before it rained. I think we went about five miles, so we got lots of fresh air."

Well, that made it easy. They could officially cross Lucy off the list of possible pranksters. She couldn't have been near the trail ride Sunday afternoon since she was with Misty.

CHAPTER TWENTY-FOUR

W hat are we overlooking?" Jan asked the next morning while making sure the scrambled eggs weren't sticking to the pan. "As much as I want to know what was behind the accident, I really don't want any of those people to be involved. I like all of them. You know, I haven't thought much about the snake lately."

Elaine blew out her cheeks. "No, I guess I haven't either. We've been focusing on the hand signals. What are you thinking?"

"I'm just trying to put myself in the place of whoever left the snake by the trail and then took it from Jack's office, even though I know we can't assume they are one and the same person."

"No. But it's a strong possibility."

"Even though no one has come forward, even after the news-paper ads and flyers and the reward offer, someone around here has to know something about a striped milk snake," Jan insisted. "If that person took the snake back from Jack's office, then it seems he or she cared about whether it got back to its owner—or was the owner himself. Or herself."

"I see. Otherwise, he or she might have just left the snake in the woods instead of risking getting caught in Jack's office."

"Yes."

Elaine put two slices of bread into the toaster and pressed down on the lever. "Wouldn't you think that by now some friend of a friend heard so-and-so talking about his snake during science class or lunch—wouldn't you think someone would have spoken up? These kids seem to know each other pretty well, even across the schools. How could someone in either school hide from *everyone* the fact that they own a rare snake? That would be something a teen would have mentioned to friends, right? At least one friend."

Jan hadn't thought of that, but Elaine made a good point. "If I didn't know better, I'd think a ghost has been playing tricks on us. It's like that snake came out of nowhere and then disappeared. And not just because of the woods and Jack's office. From this whole crazy week."

Elaine pointed a jar of strawberry jam toward Jan. "Someone knows something. That much we do know. I feel like we're close, like we're circling the answers but they're still being sneaky."

"I hope so. Because there's still the chance that someone was merely resurrecting the Old Man Warner legend, someone who knew about the trail ride and decided to leave the snake on the trail near the grave for the riders to see. Just a spooky prank at a spooky time of year in Lancaster's spookiest place."

They stared at each other. But then Elaine reminded Jan that it would have taken a hand signal to make Leopold buck. "And that was certainly done deliberately," she added.

"Unless that person is one of the many who know about it and just added it to the snake prank. This whole thing could have had nothing to do specifically with Bridget or Trace. So who do we know who gets a kick out of the legend, or who loves pranks?"

Together they answered "Bridget," and then laughed.

The truth was, the victim herself was the town's most likely candidate to play a prank.

They talked of other things while they ate breakfast and were cleaning up when Archie and Rose blew into the kitchen together on a gust of air that was downright cold. Jan was glad she'd pulled on a thick, cowl-neck sweater with her jeans. Its golden color would be perfect for the game later, and it'd keep her warm if the wind didn't die down by then. At least they could be thankful the rain had moved on during the night. Outside the kitchen windows, the sun was shining on the waterlogged world.

Archie reported that he'd phoned Beatrice Miller-Pyle in New York City and confirmed that they would wait for her schedule to clear and keep the painting with her for authentication.

"Oh, good," Elaine said to him from the door to the office. "At least that's decided and we know we're on her calendar. Let's pray the Met work moves along quickly."

"My curiosity is growing as to why my father never talked about his military days. I can only assume that his memories of it were difficult enough to want to spare himself, and probably me, from reliving the dangers. So I spent some time last evening looking for anything I could find about when and how he served England."

He had the attention of both cousins and Rose. "Did anything turn up?" Jan asked. They all sat down at the table, and Elaine brought mugs of English breakfast tea.

Archie sipped his before continuing. "Great Britain entered the war on September 3, 1939. I found out from a photograph of him that he joined up right away. I've known that he kept a few photos in a small album that I've stored in my attic. I looked at it more closely last night. I took the pictures off the pages and looked on the backs. Sure enough, one of them had a note in his handwriting. He was in his uniform, which I'd seen once or twice. And he'd written how proud he was to serve king and country. His face was youthful and he was smiling a smile that I don't remember ever seeing so full."

"Did any of the other pictures have writing on the back?" Jan wondered for all of them.

"They all had a date and a few had a short bit about the location of the photograph. One was an image of him and another soldier from the same battalion. Another was of his entire battalion, so it was difficult to make out any faces. There were ten total, and that first one I mentioned was the only one with extensive writing. But I now know his battalion and the name of the other man in the one picture—Bud Connelly."

This was great news. "That might be plenty to go on, Archie," Elaine effused.

"Yes, I was pleased," he said, getting up to bring a brown satchel to the table. He removed a small black leather album and let it fall open. Several square black-and-white photographs were tucked between the pages, but Jan could see they weren't attached. The three women reached for them, looked at the backs, and passed them around.

"Did you check further into the battalion and the other soldier's name?" Rose wanted to know.

"Not yet. It got pretty late, and I wondered if that might be something you would like to help me do."

"Of course," Jan assured him and Elaine went to get her laptop.

While she was up, Archie addressed Rose. "Did you have a nice evening with Brent and Emma?"

The light in her eyes said it all. "We did. We decided to brave the storm and found a place to eat that was pretty empty since not many people were out. Then we took dessert home to eat it with my dad." Her father, Clifton Young, was an orthodontist who lived on Chickadee Lake on the way to Penzance. "How did everything go here?"

"I think everyone had a great time," Elaine answered, back at her chair. "I certainly did."

With the laptop open, Jan, Archie, and Rose made suggestions for what to search. Elaine first searched Henry Bentham and Bud Connelly together. Not much came up except for the infantry battalion they fought in.

"How about searching that next?" Jan suggested.

That search was more helpful and revealed that the battalion fought together for two years until many were captured in battle and sent to a POW camp in June 1941. Several were still missing in action all those years later, which all four agreed would be very difficult on a loved one.

Jan had a thought. "What's the latest date on all the pictures?"

They compared the dates and saw that the most recent picture was dated March 1941. It was a scene of a London neighborhood in shambles.

"He must have seen firsthand much of the destruction to that city," Archie said. "This was taken only two months before his capture."

"And then he didn't add any more photos to the album," Jan pointed out.

"What are you thinking?" Elaine asked.

"Henry Bentham looks happy in these earlier pictures. He still seems to have the energy and zeal for the war effort, as he wrote about on that other photo. But then he was captured, and no more pictures, even though he was eventually released, obviously since Archie was born and raised by him after the war."

They waited for her to continue.

"He didn't include a picture of his military days after his release, as he was leaving the army. To me that suggests his time in the POW camp was the unpleasant turning point that removed any desire to talk about those war years."

Archie had been quiet while Jan talked. "I think Jan is right. My father smiled, but I never saw the openness of his smile like it shows in these pictures."

With a little more digging they learned some more about that particular camp Henry was sent to. From a couple of veterans Web sites that described lack of sufficient food, water, or shelter, plus long days of hard labor under tough captors, they understood more fully that Archie's father had survived very difficult hardships.

Archie seemed downcast at first, which was to be expected after learning what his beloved parent had endured and then kept to himself for so long. But as they talked through the joys Archie had felt growing up as his father's son, he seemed to perk up. His father had loved him very much and had given Archie a good childhood despite the ghosts of the past.

There was still more to learn, but that much seemed enough for one morning.

Archie thanked them graciously for their support and went to put clean tablecloths on the tables and set out the place settings for the first round of customers they expected soon.

CHAPTER TWENTY-FIVE

Jan was putting the lid on a container of cooled raspberry chocolate-chip muffins when her phone rang. Swiping her hands across a kitchen towel, she looked at the screen and tried to guess why Bridget was calling her.

"Jan!" Bridget's voice was urgent. "We need your help. Please say you'll have time to save us!"

When Bridget kept talking, Jan had to interrupt her. "Sorry, Bridget. I didn't catch what the problem is." She hoped it had nothing to do with the woman's broken leg or some other injury.

"I'm sorry." Bridget took a noisy breath and slowed her pace. "It's just that the caterer called me this morning to say that the change of day for the homecoming dance is messing them up. Some of the hors d'oeuvres that they'd made when the dance was set for tonight won't look very good by tomorrow. They aren't sure they can restock all the ingredients and make more of the same food, so I told them I have a great connection with the best baker in the county. I'm hoping I can hire you to whip up a few hundred cookies or mini-muffins or something like that. Some of the caterer's options will still be fine tomorrow, so I'm only trying to fill in some gaps."

This was very short notice, although Jan felt her heart tug to make sure the high school students had a good time, considering the upheavals the weather had caused for their big weekend. She'd find a way.

"How about something a little more elegant?" she asked, committing.

"Jan, you truly are the best!"

With any luck, Jan predicted, she could wrangle Rose into staying up late if need be to get it done. She ran a few options by Bridget, who liked most of them and chose mini cheesecake squares and pecan pie tarts. Jan had most everything on hand for both recipes and would only have to run out to get more cream cheese.

Rose quickly got on board with the changes on the to-do list and set to work on the first triple batch of tarts. "I don't mind coming back tonight after the game too. It could even be fun, an all-nighter to save the dance!" She pumped a fist into the air and gave Jan a cheesy wink, making Jan sure that Rose would be a chipper asset for this mammoth task.

Elaine was up front ringing out customers at the register when Jan told her about the job they'd just been hired for. Elaine was up for the challenge too and told Jan to point her in the right direction in the kitchen, and she'd help get it done. After a speedy trip to the store, Jan set to work on the cheesecake squares. She'd also picked up ingredients for chocolate sauce as a topping. She would have loved to do three toppings for variety, but she figured it was wiser to do one with excellence rather than bite off more than she could chew and risk disaster.

Around lunchtime, she realized she hadn't checked her phone for a while and saw a text from Brian, telling her his family would be joining her for the parade. She sent him back a message letting him know they could watch the parade from Tea for Two's front porch, along with Elaine and Nathan and Rose, Brent, and Emma. Before she could finish chewing her next bite of salad, her phone pinged with a return text from him.

Sorry you'll be alone, Mom.

She wouldn't be alone—she had just listed all the people she'd be with! But she knew she probably needed to talk with Brian soon to find out why he seemed so concerned for her. Maybe an honest chat would clear things up and he could relax about her.

Elaine breezed out of the office and went to the fridge.

"There's still some salad in the covered bowl in there," Jan offered from the table.

"Thanks." Elaine prepared a plate for herself and brought the jar of Jan's homemade buttermilk dressing with her to sit across from Jan. "This day is flying by," she commented as creamy dressing oozed on to the pile of greens, chicken, sunflower seeds, and dried fruit.

"Yes, it is. Brian says they'll be coming by for the parade after we close. I told him they could join us on the porch. And I may let Amy and Tara know too. I'm not sure they've heard about the change in plans since yesterday."

"It is too bad that Bob isn't here, Jan."

Jan stopped pressing the buttons on her phone screen. Elaine wore such a look of sympathy that Jan nearly coughed.

"You're as bad as Brian," she said. "It's like you two have been talking."

Elaine's mouth dropped open a smidgen. She looked down at her salad and kept eating.

"I'm *fine*. Honestly. Bob and I FaceTimed again yesterday, and we're excited about all that's going on for both of us."

"I'm just looking out for you is all. Brian too."

"I know. Thank you. I love you for it. But I'm okay." Elaine looked like she wasn't sure whether to believe Jan, so Jan put her hand on her cousin's. "Really."

Elaine placed her other hand on Jan's. "Okay. I believe you." Then Jan placed her other hand on Elaine's and they playfully broke their hands away as if they were in a huddle.

CHAPTER TWENTY-SIX

"See, you just put your fingers in the Xs of the strings and pull them up and out, and then under and back up," Avery explained while Elaine placed her fingers.

Just as simple as that. "Like this?" Elaine asked, trying her best to follow the girl's direction despite feeling like she had six hands. It had been so long since she'd played Cat's Cradle, but waiting on the porch for the parade to begin had seemed like a perfect time to Avery, who'd asked for and received some yarn from Jan's knitting basket.

"Yep. See the new crisscross it made? And now you've got the string, and it's my turn."

The chairs on the porch were filled with Brian and Paula and their girls, Van and Amy and their boys, and Jan, Rose, Brent, Emma, Nathan, and herself. Amazingly, they still had leftover cookies from last night, and Avery and Kelly had made chocolate-covered pretzels to share as well.

Since Forrest High was actually in Penzance, the parade had already done a route through that town right after school. But because so many students lived in Lancaster, everyone traveled the few miles to do it again there. It was unusual, but it was tradition, one that was convenient for the Tea for Two owners and their guests.

Elaine checked for Nathan's assessment of her Cat's Cradle skills and was rewarded with a nod.

"Impressive, right? I'm a quick study," she kidded.

"There it is, everyone," Jan called out. She was pointing down Main Street, where a fire truck was poised to start the processional. Its siren blared, and from somewhere behind it the sounds of the Forrest High marching band started up with the peppy notes of the school song.

The kids squealed, and Avery abandoned the string game to lean over the railing.

"Can we watch near the street, Mom?" Kelly asked Paula. "I want to catch some candy!"

That request set off a chorus of "Please, can we?" from the other four kids until Van led them down the porch stairs, followed by Rose and Brent.

Elaine saw Paula nudge Brian and urge her husband to help watch the kids near the road.

Instead of moving that way, however, Brian shook his head and gestured silently behind him toward Jan. Elaine couldn't see if Jan was noticing this exchange between her son and daughter-in-law, but Elaine thought Brian could be more subtle about the care they'd agreed to show Jan, considering Jan's touchiness about the subject lately. He obviously didn't want to leave his mother without him on the porch.

Paula gave him a look that was just shy of annoyance, but it did communicate that she thought Brian was overdoing it.

"Nathan," Elaine interjected, "why don't you and I watch from the street with them?"

"I'll join you." Jan shot out of her chair. "Brian and Paula, why don't you have a date watching it together up here? We'll keep an eye on the girls for you." She headed down the stairs before anyone could respond.

Elaine wasn't sure what just happened, but she and Nathan followed Jan down the stairs.

The fire truck was passing Sylvia's Closet and was nearly in front of the tearoom when the candy started flying through the air from volunteer firefighters perched on the truck. Elaine waved to Tag King, Rachel Leon, Russell Edmonds, and Marcella, who'd been allowed a special seat on the truck next to her dad. The young girl threw a handful of candy toward Max and Riley, who scrambled as far as Van's and Amy's arms would let them to collect the goodies from the road.

Along the roadside, other people had set up chairs, and soon the men in their group dug out lawn chairs from the garage and set them up to make their new viewing area more comfortable.

The marching band came next, led by a baton twirler dressed more warmly than she would have been for a summer parade. They all looked resplendent in their pristine gold-and-black uniforms and plumed hats, bearing shiny instruments of every variety that thundered with each musical beat through the town.

Next came the floats. Students from many clubs and sports were decked out in Pirates gear to walk beside and ride on the creative conveyances.

"They protected their work well," Jan yelled over the noise. "The floats look wonderful."

The floats trundled by, from freshmen through senior, and Nathan pointed out to Elaine that the floats' themes told a four-part story of a winning football game. Each one had a scoreboard on it, with the seniors' scoreboard showing a winning score of 34-18.

"How creative is that?" Elaine was impressed. "That's positive thinking for you."

When the senior float passed by, she looked for some of the students she'd met that week. Trace and Derek both had places on the float. Dori was walking alongside it. Dori waved to someone on the other side of the street that Elaine couldn't see. When the float moved on, Keri and Chris Cosgrove were watching the parade, standing where Dori had waved. Neither one was part of the parade because both went to Claremore, but obviously their ties to Forrest High were strong. They seemed to be getting along well, joking and looking like old friends. And, she noted with some wonder, both of them were wearing black and gold, not the maroon and gray of their own school.

And halfway down the block, Elaine spotted Bridget Donahue sitting in a lawn chair near Annie Richardson. Only Bridget wasn't talking with Annie. Instead her focus seemed zeroed in on Keri and Chris.

CHAPTER TWENTY-SEVEN

It took Jan a second to recognize who stood in the doorway, only because she wasn't used to seeing the girl in her own kitchen. The grandkids and Emma had gone up to the tower room to play after the parade, and the adults were gathered around deciding what to order for takeout from the Pine Tree Grill.

"How are you, Dori?" she asked over the noise while she wiped her hands on the towel over her shoulder and gestured for Dori Richardson to have a seat. Brian got up from the table and offered his chair.

Dori smiled politely. She was still dressed in the Pirates jersey, black leggings, and sneakers she'd worn during the parade, and her ponytail swung as she sat down. "I don't mean to bother you, but I forgot to ask you and Mrs. Cook something last night."

"Oh?"

"Thank you for hosting the party, by the way. It was a lot better than wasting the night moping because of the rain." She set her keys and cell phone on the table.

Jan brushed it off. "We were happy to do it. It looks like today will be much better."

"It looks pretty perfect," Dori said. "Hopefully the field will have had enough time to dry, but if not, it'll be better than not playing at all. At least the wind died down."

Elaine sat down with them. "You said you had a question for us?"

"Um, yes. Actually, it's from several of us girls. And it's late notice, so I'm sorry. But you see, we had planned to decorate the senior players' rooms before the game yesterday afternoon. We got all the decorations together last weekend and painted posters for each of them, with streamers and other stuff. We were planning to split up and put up the decorations during the guys' final practice yesterday, right after school but before the parade." She stopped for a breath. "But the rain messed us up, and we haven't had time to get into their rooms today, not with their parents' permission and all, and with some of them home since it's Saturday."

"It's too bad all your work was for nothing," Jan said. "I assume you have a Plan B, and that's what you wanted to talk to us about?"

"Well, we'd still like to surprise them because they've worked so hard, you know? And we've still got the posters, which we can have some guys put in the locker room so they'll see them. But we'd also like to give them some special desserts."

She started shaking her head as if she feared what she was asking would be a nuisance. "If it's any trouble, please just say no. But we thought you two would be the best chance of getting something creative on short notice. We'll totally help."

"I love the idea." Jan wanted to make this work. They'd taken a break from making the desserts for the dance to watch the parade and game, so the kitchen was orderly and ready for this new project. She looked around at the other adults.

Nathan pushed himself away from the island. "How about if the rest of us scatter and eat at the Grill instead of bringing it here? That would give you space to work your magic, Jan."

The others were already moving on his suggestion, but Elaine said she'd stay behind to help.

Jan wouldn't hear of it. "You go enjoy dinner, Elaine. I'm happy to stay behind. I can snack on fridge food while we work."

"The other girls would like to help too," Dori added. "We just didn't want to bombard you with all of us at first. I told them I'd text when I knew your answer."

Jan was already standing up and reaching for her apron on the pantry hook. "The more the merrier. I've got some ideas, and if they get here quick we'll have an hour to work some miracles."

Dori's smile was huge as she said a heartfelt thanks and thumbed a text on her way to the front door to wait for her friends.

"Mom, we can stay if you…"

Jan's upheld hand stopped Brian. "Thank you, dear, but that sounds like too many cooks in the kitchen. This is my space now, so skedaddle, all of you." She playfully waved toward the back door. After collecting their kids from upstairs, the four couples, including Elaine and Nathan and Rose and Brent, headed out the back door.

Jan felt a little guilty when she heard Avery complain to her mother that she wanted to help Grandma. She couldn't resist including her oldest granddaughter, who loved the tearoom. And it would mean a lot to Avery to be included with the high school girls, so Jan pushed open the door and called to her. "Come here, sweetheart. You would be a big help."

Paula's face was full of gratitude as her daughter's eyes lit up and she bounded back up the stairs into the kitchen. Jan waved one more time and blew a kiss to the rest of them. "We'll see you soon!" Then she got Avery's striped apron, and together they started pulling out cake pans and ingredients.

Within a few minutes Jan was joined in the kitchen by Dori and two other girls also still dressed from the parade. Dori introduced them as Megan, a fair-skinned blonde who also worked in the training room with her, and Skye, a Pirates cheerleader with glistening black hair in a short pixie cut. Brian needn't have worried. Jan wasn't alone in the least.

When Jan was stationing each girl around the kitchen and doling out tasks, a fourth girl trailed in, out of breath but full of energy. Jan was surprised to recognize Keri. Keri was still in black and gold, and her red hair and freckles looked even more vibrant with the cold-air flush still on her cheeks.

"How can I help?" she asked cheerily.

CHAPTER TWENTY-EIGHT

Jan was pleased at the girls' quickness in the kitchen and delighted that they thoughtfully included Avery, and not as a little sister but as a peer they wanted to get to know better.

While they measured and mixed, Dori asked Avery if she had fun at the corn maze, since it had been at Dori's farm. Skye wanted to know what activities she was involved in, and when Avery told her she loved to cook, Skye told her it was a good thing Avery had stayed because it would take all of them to get this surprise done for the football players.

Megan had taken cello lessons for three years, so Avery connected with her about that. They were impressed to hear that she'd made first cello in orchestra last year. "Good for you for picking that instrument," Megan told her. "There aren't many of us."

And when Keri heard that Avery took gymnastics at the Boys and Girls Club, she insisted on seeing Avery's back handspring. Avery promised she'd do one for her outside if there was time after they were done. Jan might have been suspicious of Keri, but the way Keri was acting with Avery was undeniably sweet.

Flour dusted every inch of the kitchen island, and smudges of chocolate batter hung from the stand mixer and were smeared across the counters. However she'd describe it, Jan was having a lot of fun with all of them, listening to their hearts and adding her input from time to time. Sometimes the spontaneous, unexpected moments ended up being the sweetest.

"Okay, girls, you're doing a great job with that batter. Just fill the sheet cake pan over there with it and put it in the top oven, and then you can start mixing up the second batch. I'm going to pull frosting ingredients together, and I'll show you how we can cut out football shapes to decorate. If we can finish it all, each senior should end up with several mini football cakes."

As they worked, pouring batter into pans and whipping up butter and powdered sugar, Jan spoke over the buzz of the appliances. "So girls, Dori told me you all have been working on the surprise since last weekend?"

Four heads bobbed up and down, and Jan heard a couple of yeps.

"And none of the boys suspect anything?"

"Not that we know of," Skye answered.

"I'm sure they'll love it." Jan looked at their clothes and winked at Keri. "But one of you is not like the others," she said mischievously.

"One of these things just doesn't belong," Keri sang the next line of the old familiar *Sesame Street* song, tipping her head coyly. "Nope, I'm a traitor right now. I admit, these colors make me look confused." She checked her watch. "And I've got to go soon so I have time to get home and change into my cheer uniform."

Right then, Jan put two and two together. "You must be the one who planned to decorate Trace's room."

They all nodded at their friend.

"Yes. They were nice enough to include me, even though I'm not an official Pirate. I was happy to defect temporarily for this," she joked. "But I do need to show up to cheer for my own school."

They all laughed.

Jan wondered how Keri had gotten Bridget's permission to decorate Trace's room, but with that thought another piece fell into place. Elaine had filled Jan in on what she'd overheard from the group of girls. This may have been what they were talking about when they asked what Bridget would say when she found out. Perhaps Keri didn't ask Bridget if she could decorate Trace's room before last night, and then didn't need to ask because the rain postponed the game and changed their decorating plans. If that was true, she must really not have wanted to broach the question to Bridget.

Then Jan thought of something else. "By any chance were you all making the posters and getting the decorations together last Sunday afternoon?"

They looked as though they thought the question was odd, but Keri, Skye, and Megan all answered yes.

Dori reminded Jan that she was on the trail ride. "Skye and Keri were supposedly at a cheer clinic that day, and since I'm not a cheerleader I couldn't use that excuse, so I just went on the trail ride and caught up with them later. But it worked out okay because after the trail ride, Skye's cousin came with me to help finish up the posters with the others."

Skye explained that her cousin, aunt, and uncle were in from out of town and had gone on the trail ride too.

"I met them!" Jan exulted. "So you're the cheerleading niece they came to watch." She remembered the quiet couple with the daughter about Avery's age.

"Norah, my cousin, loves horses and couldn't pass up a chance to ride."

One way or another, Jan was going to talk with that family.

But Keri was saying more. "Trace wanted me to go horseback riding with you all, but that was the best day for us to do the posters, so I had to make up the excuse. I'll have to come clean about it after the game." She snuck a taste of cake batter. "I think he'll forgive me."

So Keri was not the prankster after all. She was with the other girls on Sunday, and if she hadn't been, certainly one of them would have spoken up.

When the cakes had cooled enough to cut into football shapes, Jan popped them into the refrigerator on plates to help them cool completely. Once the treats had her okay, she and all five girls settled at the table and island with spreading spatulas and bowls of brown and white frosting. In no time, dozens of adorable chocolate-cake footballs were ready to go. As Jan grabbed some takeout boxes from the tearoom supply and helped pack up the goodies, she drew near to Skye and asked for her aunt's phone number. "There's something I'd like to follow up on with all the riders from that day. Do you think she'd mind a call from me?"

"Oh no, Aunt Joanne is supersweet." It didn't take long for Skye to send her aunt's contact information in a text to Jan.

After the older girls coaxed Avery into demonstrating her back handspring and then cheering her on while she performed it successfully on the front lawn, the teens gathered the cakes and headed out.

Jan draped her arm around Avery's shoulders and they waved good-bye as the older girls jogged down the steps, trailing a chorus of thank-yous behind them.

Jan turned to Avery. "Did you have any fun at all?"

Avery put her arms around Jan's waist and squeezed tightly. "I want to do that again when I'm in high school."

Seeing how grown-up Avery was becoming, Jan knew that day would come all too soon.

CHAPTER TWENTY-NINE

I'm not sure I can be much help, Mrs. Blake," Joanne Quinn said over the phone. "Of course I'll be happy to talk with you though. We're leaving for supper with my niece and her family soon, but I have a few minutes."

Jan had taken a chance and called Skye's aunt before the game, hoping her own family would linger long enough at the Grill so she could ask Joanne a few questions.

"Thanks so much, and I won't keep you. I understand wanting as much time with your relatives as you can get when you live far away. And please call me Jan."

"Okay, Jan, what are you still trying to figure out about the accident? I felt so bad for Mrs. Donahue. Do you know how she's doing?"

Jan assured Joanne that Bridget was recovering well and would be at the game tonight to help cheer on the team. "I was riding behind most of the rest of you, so I didn't even see it happen. I heard that Leopold got fidgety and then bucked, causing Bridget to fall. But no one seems to have seen anything that might have caused him to do that." Jan told her about hearing laughter from the woods and asked if Joanne or her husband or daughter had also heard that.

"Just a minute, Jan."

In the background, muffled sounds like voices talking carried to her, then Joanne's clear voice again.

"None of us noticed anything at the time. Or maybe I should say none of us paid attention to it at the time. But we were talking about it a couple of days later, and my husband said he was wondering if he'd seen a flash of something in the woods."

"Really? Anything more specific?"

"He thinks it was a flash of black, but Leopold was so big and black that Sam's first impression was that the horse's wild movements were a blur. You know how the eyes can trick us sometimes."

"Maybe. Could you ask Sam if it might have been someone wearing black who could have been in the woods?"

"*Ooh*, that's a little creepy." Joanne's voice had dropped.

"I'm thinking a prankster, not someone with criminal intentions. Nothing scary."

"That's better, I suppose."

Jan heard more muffled voices before Joanne came back with Sam's response. "He says it might have been a person. Although he still doesn't trust what he might or might not have seen."

"And you and your daughter haven't remembered anything more? Maybe one of the other riders raising an arm?"

For a third time Jan waited while Joanne consulted with her family.

"No, none of us saw that. As far as we recall, everyone had their hands on the reins like we were supposed to."

Glad she'd made the call, Jan thanked Joanne for her time and complimented her niece's kitchen skills and pleasant nature.

She decided to make one more call and punched in Kit Edmonds's number. When she had Kit on the line, she asked if she, Marcella, or Russell might have noticed a flash of black in the woods. She explained that her reason for the question was because of another rider's observation.

Once again, Jan waited while voices talked in the background. It took a couple of minutes for Kit to come back on the line.

"Sorry for the wait, Jan. Marcella wanted to talk through it, wondering who was in the woods."

"I'm sorry. I didn't mean to upset her. Do you think talking about it is helping her?"

"I think we're getting there. She'll be okay. But back to your question. None of us saw anything in the woods. Just a big black flurry of horse and rider, and then Bridget's fall."

"Okay, I expected as much..."

"Just a sec, Jan." Then another minute of muffled voices before Kit returned. "Marcella just told me she saw Leopold look toward the woods before he 'jumped up,' as she calls it."

Could that be something? "He looked into the woods? At the ground or higher up, like at the leaves?"

Kit relayed the question, and Jan heard Marcella's girlish chirp: "He looked at the ground first, Mom, and then he started moving his feet funny. And then he looked right into the trees. And that's when he jumped up and the lady fell."

"Did you forget that when Mrs. Blake came over?"

"No."

"Marcella, is there a reason you didn't tell her all that when she was here?"

"She didn't ask me where the horse was looking. She only asked me about the arm motions."

Jan laughed outright. Of course Marcella was entirely right. Jan hadn't asked that, hadn't even thought to ask it. It wasn't rocket science: if you wanted answers, you had to ask the right questions. *Silly Mrs. Blake.* Her thoughts finished with a child-like *Duh* to herself.

But she felt she'd just made huge progress thanks to the keen eyes of a child who'd clearly seen two different things the horse had done. Leopold had looked down and gotten fid-gety—from the snake. Then he looked higher, right into the trees, and bucked—from a flash of black and someone giving him a hand signal to do so? Jan was nearly convinced that's how it happened.

"Oh, Kit, please tell Marcella that she is a trouper, and I'm so glad she's so observant."

Kit said she was glad to help and that she'd pass along Jan's compliment to her daughter.

Jan wasn't sure she'd ever had more fun investigating than she'd had recently talking through clues with this girl.

It was just a little fact, but one they'd needed proof about, and one that could mean a lot: Leopold had looked into the woods, not just on the ground, and had seen something—or someone.

CHAPTER THIRTY

Even before her group made it through the ticket line at the entrance, Elaine could see that Forrest High's stadium had taken on a life of its own. Beneath the lights, bleachers rose on both sides of the field and were overflowing with fans. The Pirates' band filled the grassy middle and were entertaining the spectators with a rollicking song, while the cheerleaders and dance troupe performed a pregame routine. Behind the bleachers on the home-team side, windows opened out of the fieldhouse wall, where people were lined up for hot dogs, popcorn, cocoa, candy, and other concessions.

Bundled in warm outerwear and with arms loaded with blankets to keep the cold at bay, Elaine and her friends and family sidled past others trying to find empty seats. From up ahead, Nathan turned back to point out a section and then led the way up to it.

When at last she was seated between Nathan and Jan, Elaine took a deep breath and exhaled loudly. "Phew! I didn't get my walk in this morning," she joked. "I'm out of breath climbing these risers."

"I'm using the excuse that it's the cold." Jan wrinkled her nose in jest. "Chills the lungs, you know."

Elaine liked that rationalization. Much better than feeling like she was out of shape, which she was not, she assured herself. She looked down their row and the one behind them, where Jan's kids and their families were settling in. Jack Weston had found Tara near the entrance and was sitting with her. Jan couldn't help notice that they were sitting so close their arms touched. And Rose, Brent, and Emma had met Rose's dad and were seated nearby.

The marching band moved off to the sideline, and from a microphone in the announcer's box above them, a rumbly voice called out, "Ladies and gentlemen, fans and alumni, please give your attention to the north end of the field, and let's give a big welcome to the Claremore Raiders!"

From the opposite side, cheers went up for the maroon-and-gray team who ran out single file on to the field and then veered over to their coaches on the sideline, where Elaine knew Keri was one of the cheerleaders waving pom-poms and jumping up to welcome them. A smatter of sportsmanlike applause drifted through the home bleachers.

And then one of the band's drummers started a staccato beat that built in volume, and the home fans rose a little higher on their seats, collectively knowing what was coming next.

"And now!" the announcer thundered dramatically, as fans lower in the stands began to stomp their feet on the bleachers in rhythm with the drum. "Please give it up for this year's Penzance Pirates varsity football team!"

Cheers exploded all around as a wave of people stood up to clap and the announcer called out each player's name and year, and then his number and position. Trace Donahue, number thirty-two, and Derek Jameson, forty-four, earned some of the loudest applause and bleacher stomps. Elaine looked over and saw Jan cover her ears with mittened hands, looking like she was having fun nonetheless.

When all the players had been introduced, the national anthem had been sung, and both teams' starters had taken their positions on the field, Elaine listened for the referee's whistle and watched the starting kickoff soar through the air. The teams merged toward each other, and the game had begun.

Only four minutes into play and with the Pirates in possession of the ball at their own forty yard line, Trace faked a handoff to a running back, then a second later threw a surprise pass to Derek, who caught it handily and took off down the field toward the end zone. Elaine stood on tiptoe to watch him soar past a Raiders defender at the fifty yard line. He kept going and blasted between two more Raiders at the forty, then with some fancy footwork he wove around another one as three fellow Pirates roared up to block for him.

The crowd was full of excitement. No longer covering her ears, Jan was jumping up and down, waving her arms and shouting for Derek to *go, go, go.* He reached the fifteen yard line before being forced out of bounds for a first down.

Elaine leaned over and spoke right into Jan's ear. "That ought to make him stand out!"

"Derek is *really* fast on his feet," Jan said loudly back.

"Freaky fast," Nathan added, grinning.

From below them in the stands, Bridget's voice could be heard hollering for the team she clearly loved and worked so hard to support. Elaine and Jan looked at each other and smiled. "You've got to appreciate her," Elaine declared, and Jan gave a big nod.

The Raiders didn't give up any more yards for the next three plays, but then as tensions were high so close to the end zone on fourth down, Derek got open again for a pass and rammed his way through a gaggle of Raiders for the first touchdown of the night. The blast of an air horn cut through the cacophony in the home seats while the cheerleaders did back handsprings down the sideline and the band broke into the school's fight song.

The Pirates missed the two-point conversion, so the Raiders took the ball with a 6–0 score. The rest of the first quarter was filled with a lot of back-and-forth possessions, a couple of frustrating errors, timeouts for coaches to huddle with their players on the field, and not many first downs as the two teams proved they were well matched both offensively and defensively. Chris led with precision as the Raiders starting QB, and Trace matched him on the Pirates team.

The second quarter didn't go as well for the Penzance-Lancaster boys as the team faltered, allowing an interception and two painful Raiders touchdowns, plus both extra points.

With twenty seconds left in the quarter and the Pirates trailing by eight, Nathan groaned in frustration and offered to go get snacks before the concession lines got long at halftime. From down the row, a number of requests for popcorn, hot dogs, and cocoa trickled back to Elaine. Wanting to stretch her legs, she said she'd go with him and followed him down the stairs.

Elaine knew they'd fight crowds, but it was even worse than she thought. Apparently a lot of other people had the same idea to try to reach the concession stand before halftime began. It seemed to take forever to inch their way down to the ground from the stands. The teams had already exited the field and entered the big doors of the fieldhouse locker rooms. Then Nathan and Elaine ran into a number of neighbors and friends as they walked toward the concession area, where more spectators were in line deciding what they wanted and waiting for the ones ahead to finish up. Nathan led them to what looked like the shortest of the three lines, but neither had seen the large family ahead of them in that line, with several children tucked out of sight among the taller adults.

By the time the parents filtered their kids' requests from all the chatter, then altered their order after their little ones changed their minds, then managed to pay while keeping their crew in tow, the doors of the fieldhouse opened, signaling to Elaine that halftime was ending soon.

Finally it was Elaine and Nathan's turn. They ordered and paid quickly, and with arms full, they met the stream of Forrest High players jogging back to start the third quarter. The team looked official in their Pirates uniforms, if somewhat smudged with dirt and grass stains from the playing field.

Elaine recognized a few faces and called out "Good luck!" to Trace and Derek as they passed right by her. Both looked, startled, in her direction but smiled and waved when they recognized her. Their black jerseys gave them an intimidating presence, she thought. And then she noticed something unusual about Derek's jersey right before he passed by her.

As she followed Nathan up the bleachers, she considered what she she'd just seen. She'd been close enough to see that Derek's jersey was torn, which probably wasn't an unusual thing for a football player. But it was a small tear, and not just a straight rip of the fabric. A piece of his jersey front was missing right above the first four in his number forty-four. It stuck out to her because of the gray pads showing through the hole. But it also stuck out to her because the hole was about the same size and shape as the piece of fabric she'd found on the branch near Old Man Warner's grave.

If she was correct, and it came from Derek's jersey, when was he by the grave? Had he been there with friends, as teens sometimes did for fun? She hoped that was the reason, but she wasn't sure.

An uneasy feeling nagged her, and she didn't want to make the connection that was playing at her thoughts. Was it possible that Derek was near the grave not so much to see the grave, but to watch the trail ride come through there? How could he have gotten there from the stables, and what could it mean?

CHAPTER THIRTY-ONE

Halftime had consisted of an intricate band formation that made a big "P" on the field, followed by the cheerleaders, who ended their performance in a tall pyramid. Jan recognized Skye at the top, who got down from her perch by doing a flip through the air and landing in the arms of two of her squad mates. Jan and Avery looked at each other and gave four thumbs up. And Jan saw Dori and Megan jog out to the team's benches to fetch some things they must have needed for players back in the training room.

Jan was happy to stay put and watch the performance. She could even stretch a few muscles when the grandkids went off to the restrooms with their parents. She scooted down the bleacher bench to give Tara a hug and visit with her and Jack.

Tara's nose was red from cold, but when Jan pointed it out, she just laughed and touched Jan's nose. "You're one to talk, Mom. Yours is nearly the color of the apples on the trees at Orchard Hill."

Jan reached over and tapped Tara's big hoop earrings that had unique red stones wired into them. "New creations?"

Tara's fingers met hers. "Do you like them?"

"Very lovely. I hear your stuff sold like hotcakes this week."

"Yes," her daughter answered indulgently. "So fun. Make sure you get your order in soon for Christmas. I'm booking up fast."

Jack was watching the exchange when another man who looked to be in his upper twenties appeared on his other side and got his attention. When Jack recognized who it was, he clapped him on the back. "Hey, man! It's been a while. How've you been?"

Tara gave Jan a shrug to mean she didn't know who he was. They didn't have to wait long to find out. Jack was still shaking the man's hand when he turned to include Tara and Jan in the conversation. "This guy's little brother is playing well tonight. Ladies, meet Colby Jameson."

"You must be Derek's brother," Jan said. Of course he was; he looked just like Derek, only with a few more years of weathering to his features.

"Yes, ma'am."

How sweet; he even called her *ma'am* just like Derek had when she first met him. "It's a pleasure to meet you, Colby. I've really been impressed with your brother tonight. He can outrun all of them out there."

Colby's pride in his sibling was unmistakable, even if the score wasn't in their favor at the moment. "He'll come out blazing in the second half, I'm sure. He wants to win this one so badly."

"Colby and I worked together years ago," Jack explained, "back when he was fresh out of college and I was a newbie starting up the fish and game office here. But we haven't seen each other since he moved away."

As halftime had wrapped up and the teams were reentering the field, Jan saw her kids with their children clamber up the bleachers.

"It was nice meeting you, Colby. Let's hope our team makes a comeback." Jan had squeezed Tara's hand and moved back down the row as Nathan and Elaine returned with buckets of popcorn and foil-wrapped hot dogs, napkins, and condiment packets. Somehow they were balancing two Styrofoam cups of cocoa on top of it all. Jan helped unload them and pass the food down. She ended up with a popcorn, which she shared with Paula, who'd switched seats and was now sitting on her left.

Jan was so busy talking with Paula and trying to pay attention to the game, that it was nearly the end of an uneventful third quarter before Jan noticed that Elaine seemed quieter than usual. After Elaine told her she'd explain later, Jan kept talking with Paula.

She learned that Paula had finished painting the bathroom that morning and loved how it turned out. Jan didn't know what to think when Paula joked that once she finally got Brian to help move the toilet and remove the mirror so she could paint behind them, she was able to finish the project quickly.

"Paula," Jan said directly, "I want you two to drop off the girls next weekend and get away together. Just the two of you."

Paula adjusted her knit hat and started to reply, but Jan held firm. "No arguments. I'll get the girls to whatever activities they have. It'll be fun for me, and I want to do it."

"My, Jan, that's wonderful of you. I don't even know where we'd go."

"You talk with Brian and let me know, okay?"

Satisfied that she could do this much to help this precious couple, Jan popped a couple of pieces of popcorn into her mouth and appreciated the warm, buttery comfort food.

The fourth quarter started like the first, with a bang, courtesy of another pairing of Trace's and Derek's skills. Trace narrowly missed being sacked and just in time flipped the ball to Derek, who seemed to run on air all the way for their second touchdown. Coach Delaney obviously was going full out for every point, because they ran a two-point conversion play that succeeded in tying the score 14–14.

With four minutes left on the clock and the homecoming game hanging in the balance, the Raiders were able to score again. Fortunately, they weren't able to add any extra points, and the score remained 20–14.

"These four minutes are going to be the shortest ever," Nathan quipped. "And the longest. I'm getting too old for this."

"No, you're not," Elaine said, leaning into him, and for a moment Jan wished Bob was there with her. But she turned back to the game.

The Pirates had to get another touchdown, and if they didn't want to risk overtime, they also had to either kick an extra point or run it in for two—and succeed. She clasped her hands to her mouth and blew her nerves into her mittens.

The teams faced each other again, the players crouched in position as they waited for the snap. Trace's "Down, set" rang all the way up the stands, then a pause as everyone leaned in … and then "Hike!" The field burst into motion and the clap of pads against pads echoed throughout the stadium.

Jan couldn't see the ball or tell what was happening—it all looked like a blur. But then her breath caught when an enormous Raider plowed into Trace and knocked him back and to the ground.

CHAPTER THIRTY-TWO

Gasps went up, and Jan heard a cry that sounded eerily like Bridget's from nearly a week ago. She scanned the crowd in the direction of the cry and saw that it actually was Bridget, moving awkwardly on crutches off the bleachers toward the field, aided closely by a man Jan thought might be Trace's dad.

All the players took a knee while coaches and trainers congregated around Trace's prone form. All the players except for one, number forty-four from the Pirates. Derek had yanked off his helmet and was running toward his friend.

Elaine didn't realize she and Jan had linked arms while they stared down at the field as time crawled. When the circle around Trace started inching backward and Trace's legs moved, a cheer went up from both sides.

Nearly across the grass on their way toward their son, Bridget and her husband stopped and hugged each other.

And Elaine noticed herself breathe again.

Next to her, Jan wiped at her eyes, apparently unbothered that popcorn was tumbling out of the container in her other hand. Who cared? Trace was starting to sit up now, albeit gingerly.

Applause broke out to honor the injured star. With Coach D holding one arm and Derek bracing the other, Trace got to his feet and limped to his parents.

Elaine's own eyes were moist by now seeing the concern and relief all around, across the sides. She figured no one must be surprised when Trace didn't return to the field, but she wasn't sure anyone was expecting what happened next.

When the teams re-formed for the Pirates' second down, instead of taking his usual position as receiver, Derek was in as quarterback.

Jan's mouth was an O, and Elaine felt her own jaw drop.

Jan nudged her and pointed to a man next to Jack a few seats down. "That's Derek's brother."

Elaine lifted her chin to acknowledge she'd seen him, then sent up a silent plea that the next three minutes would shine favor over Derek and the rest of the team.

The Pirates seemed shaken. They got pushed back five yards on the second down, followed by a penalty that cost them more yards. Coach D called a timeout and met with his players, which seemed to help because on the next play Derek made a solid handoff to a running back, who recovered the distance they'd given up plus ran for twenty more yards.

That new first down brought a momentary respite, but the pressure was on more than ever. Derek seemed to be settling back into his old position. He led well to another first down, but when the clock stopped it showed only twenty-two seconds remaining, and they still had a ways to go. It was now or never for a big break.

The Pirates cheerleaders sounded hoarse leading the crowd to keep up the strong support. Bridget and Trace's dad had returned to their seats on the first row, and Trace was sitting with a team logo blanket over his shoulders on a bench next to the water jug.

Elaine watched as Derek looked over to him, and Trace held his arm out, waist level and palm up, then raised it quickly to make a fist in the air.

A broad grin flashed over Derek's face, and he responded by holding his right fist up in the air. Then he pivoted to join his teammates in their offensive lineup.

Jan grabbed Elaine's arm and shook it. "That's the signal!"

"What...?"

"Leopold's signal! Did you see it?" And then Jan raised her arm and made a high fist.

Elaine didn't have time to answer because Derek bellowed, "Hike!" and the teams exploded yet one more time in a flurry to track where the ball was.

She looked for a handoff but didn't see one. No ball flying through the air either. But then she caught sight of Derek with his arm cradled around the football, cruising away from the mass of bodies and blazing toward the Pirates' end zone with four Raiders on his trail.

Seventeen seconds.

Thirty yards to go, and it wasn't a straight shot.

He wove around someone gunning toward him from the side.

Eleven seconds.

Another Raider dove for his feet, but Derek hurdled over him, then spun around one more opponent.

The crowd's noise was deafening.

He crossed the twenty yard line. All Elaine could think was he was *so* fast.

Six seconds.

With two seconds on the clock, Derek Jameson shoved away another defender and made a headlong dive across the line, holding on to the ball. The air horn blew. The touchdown was good. Derek had tied the game.

Elaine's throat hurt from yelling. When the kick cleared the posts two minutes later for the win, she wasn't sure if anyone's feet were still firmly on the ground. She felt like she was floating, carried by the exuberance of it all.

Jan stopped clapping long enough to point to the center of the field, where Derek was being carried by his team and dozens of fans who'd rushed out to congratulate the hero of the night.

CHAPTER THIRTY-THREE

I don't know about you, but I'm exhausted," Jan croaked.

"You're as hoarse as the cheerleaders," Elaine teased.

"I think I'm worse, actually. They're used to it."

After the game ended and the stands cleared of fans, Jan, Tara, Elaine, and Nathan had hung back with Jack and Colby when they saw the players come out of the fieldhouse locker room. Despite the hours of baking for the homecoming dance she still had to do that night, Jan decided another few minutes wouldn't make much difference. She'd like to congratulate Derek and Trace. She felt a connection with the team now, thanks to the past week and last night's party in particular.

Dressed in street clothes and carrying sports duffels, Trace and Derek were outside the fieldhouse doors being smothered in support from their parents and friends, who parted when Coach Delaney came out of the fieldhouse along with two men Jan hadn't seen before. Both were dressed in college logo coats. The three men approached Trace and Derek and began talking with them and their parents.

Beside Tara, Jack nudged Colby, who nodded.

Colby's reaction had Jan's attention now. His eyes looked moist, and he seemed moved at his brother's good turn of events.

Together they all watched Derek's and Trace's futures play out in front of them.

"I'm so happy for them," Elaine commented.

"They both earned it," Nathan added. "They played a terrific game."

With a swipe over his eyes, Colby strode up to his brother and parents, introduced himself to the two men, and offered his hand to shake. They talked, and after the men walked away, Colby gripped Derek in a bear hug and lifted him off his feet, sending a loud *whoop* into the air.

When he let go, Derek stumbled, laughing. It was the happiest and most lighthearted Jan had seen him look since she'd met him. She and the others couldn't resist moving closer to offer well wishes to the future college football hopefuls.

After more jesting, ruffling of hair, and some happy tears, the Donahues and Derek's parents left, and Jack clapped Derek on the back as he'd done earlier to Colby. "Derek, I've known your brother since he was a little older than you are now. He was a lot of help to me when I was starting up the fish and game office here. Now, a few years later, he's got his own booming vet practice. It's been good to see him again tonight, so thanks for such a great game to watch."

Derek stopped laughing and looked at his brother. Jan couldn't miss the subtle change in his demeanor. He shifted his weight and the bulky duffle and started jiggling his keys.

"In fact, Colby, we could've used your help this week," Jack added. "Jan here had a run-in with a Pueblan milk snake a few days ago. Colby used to be my reptile guy, always bringing in specimens he'd find in the woods."

Derek glanced away toward a group of girls, where Trace was waiting for him now too. "Um, good to meet you, Jack, but..."

But Jack didn't seem to hear. "It was the craziest thing. I brought the snake back to the office after Jan found it on the trail where Bridget Donahue broke her leg. I put out ads to try and find its owner, even offered a reward. But a couple of days later it disappeared right out of my building."

Colby listened, frowning.

"I haven't had any luck figuring out what happened."

Maybe it was the cold that made Derek's face look pale and Colby stiffen slightly and glance at his brother. Derek cleared his throat and mumbled an excuse about needing to get going, then hurried to catch up to Trace and the girls.

Jan was sure something other than the cold had caused Derek's abrupt freeze. And her stomach felt like lead from the certainty that her instincts would prove right.

"I HATE THAT I think Derek had something to do with it," Jan moaned to Elaine at home. "I know we haven't talked with him yet, but he obviously panicked when Jack talked about the snake."

With Rose's help, not to mention a constant flow of caffeinated tea and Elaine's company to keep them going, she'd finished making the last of the pecan tarts and cheesecake squares by two o'clock in the morning.

Five hundred desserts would stay chilled in containers on the screened porch, tucked safely away from Earl Gray's reach. The cat had come in while they were putting the containers out there, which was a good thing since all three women were sure they were too bleary-eyed to have thought about cordoning off an area had they not seen him appear during his nightly prowl.

All in all, the after-hours project had gone well and had even been fun, especially when Elaine put a Christmas music CD into the player in the office and streams of Nat King Cole floated into the kitchen.

"As much as I love Christmas music, I'm not sure I'm ready to think about all that just yet," Jan had said with a tired laugh as she used a flat spatula to move tarts from the baking sheet to a cooling rack.

Now, with Rose sent home and the cousins finally changed into flannel pajamas and fuzzy socks, they sank onto the sitting room sofa to decompress for a few minutes before bed. What a night it had been, with more highs and lows than most days held. They caught up on what they'd each noticed at the football game, details that had taken a back burner during the baking extravaganza.

"I don't like suspecting Derek either," Elaine answered her cousin.

"And if he did have something to do with it, something tells me he hates it too."

Elaine agreed with Jan's wisdom and assessment of Derek's likely involvement in the snake's disappearance. "But we still don't know why he would have done it. What would his motivation possibly be for pulling a stunt like the accident? I can't get my mind around the thought of him trying to injure Bridget."

"No, I can't either. And I don't think that was his true intention. And we don't know the extent of his involvement. He could have been working with someone else. After all, as far as we know, he was back at the stables when Bridget fell."

They reviewed the expanding ways he seemed linked to Bridget's accident. The scrap of black jersey fabric lay between them on the sofa. Elaine had explained the whole scene to Jan when she saw the torn hole in Derek's black game jersey.

"That's why you seemed quiet when you came back up from getting the food," Jan said. "I wondered if you were miffed from having to schlep all that greasy food up to us."

Elaine brushed off Jan's ribbing. "No, I just didn't want things to point to him. Especially when he was playing the game of his life. He looked horrified when Jack talked about the snake and in the same breath mentioned Colby's interest in reptiles."

"But we still don't know who the snake belongs to or where it is now. Or why exactly Derek looked so...caught," Jan reminded her. "I don't think Jack had a clue how his words were affecting both Jameson brothers."

"Me neither," Elaine said, grinning despite the seriousness of it all. "Did you notice Colby look at Derek? Why would a Pueblan milk snake trigger anything with him?"

"I don't know. And another thing we don't know is if the snake and the hand signal are even related. Derek could have been responsible for leaving the snake on the trail but not the hand signal."

Elaine shook her head. "But that would mean two different people were playing two pranks at the same time and the same place. That's pretty unlikely."

"Unless they worked it out together."

"True."

Jan sat up straighter, and her fingers came out like she was ready to count. "Okay, one: we don't know if it was Derek in the woods at the time of the accident. But two: when Jack brought up the snake, we both saw that Derek got very uneasy, even looked guilty, like he was about to get caught for something."

"Three," Elaine broke in: "if we're right and he put the snake on the trail, did he also hide there to make the hand signal?" She dropped the counting. "If Derek is guilty, why on earth would he come to us for help, asking us to solve the mystery?"

"My question exactly. Also, was Derek the one who took the snake back from Jack's office? Maybe he looked nervous tonight because he was covering for someone else who was in on it."

"It's possible," Elaine said.

Jan didn't say anything more right away, and then Elaine saw another thought dawn on her. "What is it?"

"Who knows, maybe Derek's own suggestion that Trace was the real target was correct. The school newspaper story didn't go into why the football position changes were made, but maybe Derek wasn't okay being switched from the quarterback position. Like Lucy seemed jealous of Bridget for all the advantages she seems to have, Derek might feel similar things about his good friend Trace. And then to lose that position to him might have been harder than we've stopped to consider. He did say that Trace doesn't need a scholarship to go to college, but Derek does. Maybe he figured his best chances were as the quarterback, the position he knew best and was used to playing."

Elaine listened quietly as she absorbed Jan's logic, which made a lot of sense. Maybe there was more to Derek's feelings about football and his friendship with Trace than he let on. "But still, playing a trick like that on his friend, who really did need to be in top shape for the game. That part doesn't make sense."

Jan seemed to think about that.

Elaine kept going. "He was the only player who ran to Trace when Trace did get hurt. Derek wasn't faking that concern, regardless of any tension they may have had over Trace's selection as quarterback."

Jan fiddled with some fringe on a pillow. The conversation lulled while each was lost in thought.

Jan finally broke the silence. "Well, I think we need to talk with Derek."

Elaine sighed. "I agree. And the sooner the better." Elaine yawned and reached over to give her cousin a quick hug. "I hope you had fun tonight, Jan. Hope it wasn't awkward with the rest of us couples, and without Bob..."

"I had a blast," Jan said.

She hoped so. "Love you, Jan," Elaine answered and left it at that.

CHAPTER THIRTY-FOUR

On their way out to Jan's Camry after church the next morning, they decided to celebrate the end of a successful Fall Fest by treating themselves to lunch at the Grill. The energy of a town celebration was always fun, but Jan was happy to pause after the crowds were gone and enjoy a visit with Mel and Bianca Stadler, the cowboy boot–wearing siblings who ran the restaurant. Bianca's bracelets jingled on her wrist as she took the water pitcher from the server and came over to fill their glasses herself. Sturdily built and always with her makeup perfect and her hair large, Bianca filled the room with brightness. She and Mel made the restaurant what it was just by being themselves.

"Pretty quiet in here, isn't it? The first few days after the tourists leave are always a shock to my system," she joked, snapping her gum. "Did you ladies have a good festival?"

"We did," Elaine answered for them. "I don't know if it's something about fall or what, but this time of year brings out the shoppers in droves."

Bianca waved a hand at Elaine, sending her bracelets jingling again. "I know what you mean. I think Christmas coming is part of it too. Makes everyone feel good to get a head start. Me? I spent most of my time here, but that's why I have this place, so I can socialize all day every day."

Looking over the menu, they decided they deserved to indulge a little after their hard work all week. "We don't give in often, right?" Elaine quipped.

"I'm sure I heard somewhere that calories don't count on Sundays following festival week," Jan added deadpan, drawing a sly look from her cousin, who didn't argue. They both ordered comfort food, regardless of what it might do to their waistlines.

After burgers, fries, and salads, they went home to relax in front of a romantic comedy. Jan changed into lounging pants and a soft zipper jacket and joined Elaine on the sitting room sofa.

While Elaine was choosing a movie for them to watch, Jan made a quick call to let Bridget know the desserts for the dance were ready for pickup and delivery to the commons area at Forrest High, where the homecoming dance would be held. Bridget would send a couple of Booster Club members by within the hour.

Jan agreed to Elaine's movie pick, not really caring much what they watched, happy to be in their snug home. They paused it when two cars drove up to take the food to the school and then went back to the movie when the crew was gone. Although the story was interesting and she liked the characters, before long, Jan noticed Elaine looking sleepy. She realized her end of the sofa seemed to be enveloping her as well and let her eyelids close.

She awoke with a crick in her neck from her cramped sleeping position, unsure how long she'd been out. Careful not to disturb Elaine curled up at the sofa's other end, Jan caught the final scene, in which the main character, the former owner of a small family-owned bookstore, gave in and kissed her true love, the owner of mega-bookstore, who also happened to be her former rival.

She'd seen the movie before and liked it, but the nap had been refreshing. Jan turned off the television as the credits began to roll and left Elaine to sleep on while she went downstairs to the kitchen.

After some rest she was ready to get a jump start on the week. A check of the refrigerator ingredients revealed enough to make a pork tenderloin and Asian cole slaw for supper. She mixed together an easy marinade for the pork and set it back in the refrigerator so the flavors could meld. Next, she whisked soy sauce with lemon juice, brown sugar, and a few other seasonings, then pushed chunks of red cabbage and carrots through her food processor and tossed the colorful mound of cabbage in a large bowl with her sauce. That bowl went into the fridge too, and she started cleanup.

With their supper prepped, Jan went to get the dust cloth and crept through each room, enjoying watching the shine return to each piece of furniture. She finished the downstairs rooms and went upstairs. In her room, she cleared off some paperwork from her bedside table, culling through a few pieces of mail she'd dropped there last week and tossing the junk mail into the trash bin. She stopped when she came to the school newspaper and took another look at the front page. She'd meant to read the entire thing and still wanted to. She dropped it on her bed on her way out the door to dust the rest of the upstairs.

She finished up in Elaine's room and the sewing room. Elaine still slept when she peeked into the sitting room, so she decided the dust bunnies would survive another day in there. Thinking she'd work on a crossword puzzle, Jan went back to her room and saw the newspaper still on her bed.

She chose that instead and curled up on her quilt to read the latest from Forrest High. She remembered Lucy working on this very publication as part of the journalism club in their day.

The pictures showed the changing times and styles, but the stories warmed her heart and made the passing of time seem so fast. There were updates on other sports teams, a reminder about auditions for the winter play, a meet-the-teacher article, a report from the student body president, and other smaller features.

When she reached the back page, Jan was surprised to see a feature article about Derek. It appeared to be a story for a regular feature highlighting a noteworthy student, and Jan was pleased for Derek that he had been chosen for that week's story.

She remembered seeing Lucy doing interviews in the school cafeteria or library, or even sometimes jogging to catch up with someone in the hallway for a quote to add to the current story she was writing for the paper. Jan could imagine a fellow student doing the same recently to get the scoop on what Derek Jameson was involved in at Forrest High.

The article detailed his leadership on the football team and his plans for after graduation. It also gave a few fun facts about how he'd become interested in football when he was in elementary school playing catch with his older brother.

It was all heartwarming and positive, until the writer switched focus and the tone changed slightly. Jan sat up straight on her bed and reread the paragraph to be sure she hadn't confused the writer's words. And then she frowned.

This could explain everything.

CHAPTER THIRTY-FIVE

It made sense to Jan now. Here was a clue they'd been missing about the motivation behind the accident. There were still answers to be sought, but she felt they were very close to knowing how and why Bridget's accident had happened.

The writer apparently had asked Derek how he was enjoying the wide receiver position, to which he answered that he was having fun. And yes, it had been a learning curve and an adjustment to his expectations to play first-string quarterback his senior year. Yes, he and Trace had worked through it and still made a powerful team on the field and were great friends and cocaptains of the varsity team.

But the next part was what made Jan take notice. The interviewer had probed further into the way the transition had occurred. She reread Derek's response.

"Well, the coaches make those decisions, not anyone else," Jameson commented. *"But yes, I understand why Mrs. Donahue suggested they should pick Trace as quarterback. She's right: he's a great athlete, and we're all family on and off the field.*

The nature of competition includes accepting and making the most of changes, and seeing them as opportunities for growth. Which is exactly what we've all done."

Derek sounded remarkably upbeat and unfazed in his response, not to mention confident and articulate. The smoothness of his answers to a somewhat confrontational line of reporting impressed Jan, but she wondered what Derek, and Trace as well, thought about this story, because she figured they had to have seen it. And Bridget, had she heard about it? The story drew attention to a difficult situation that the boys had had to work through, and Jan felt uneasy for them, even though they seemed fine about it. But had that always been the case? How fine had Derek felt when he'd first heard he was getting ousted from his favorite position? And how fine had he felt knowing the woman he'd thought of as "family" had been behind it all? Jan groaned and shook her head.

The recent clues that seemed to point toward Derek having a hand in the accident a week ago meant Jan was viewing the circumstances through a new set of facts. And now to learn that Bridget had been the one behind Derek losing his quarterback position to her son, his best friend...

"What's putting the frown on your face?"

Jan looked up to see Elaine leaning against her bedroom door frame, running her fingers through her hair to smooth it after sleeping on it. Jan had been so caught up in her thoughts that she hadn't heard her cousin stirring down the hall.

She thought about calling Bridget to get her take on what had happened and if she'd felt any negativity from Derek after the position changes were made. But she didn't want to impli-cate Derek to Bridget without talking with him first. She had another idea. "You should read this article," she told Elaine. "And then I'd like to swing by the homecoming dance after supper to pick up our food containers."

AFTER SHE READ the article, Elaine had been up for Jan's suggestion. They ate supper and then got into Elaine's car to make the short drive to Forrest High to pick up their food containers themselves. It would save the Booster Club members some cleanup and a trip back to the tea-room, and it provided the perfect reason for the cousins to show up at the homecoming dance. They wouldn't push for answers on the night of the dance, but if Derek was there and an opportunity presented itself, they might find a way to ask him about the article in the school newspaper and see how he responded to a casual comment that they hadn't known Bridget had influence on the decisions of the coaching staff.

Driving down Main Street on the dark autumn eve-ning, Elaine pointed out several cars parked by the shore of Chickadee Lake, and several groups of couples in suits, dresses, and heels over by the lake. "Look, some of the high schoolers are taking homecoming pictures. What a perfect place for it by the water." There wasn't much of a breeze that day. The shore area was lit by car headlights, but the lake behind the kids disappeared in blackness.

Jan leaned over to see out the window. "Oh, stop a minute, will you? That's Trace and Keri…and Chris with Megan. She helped with the football cakes. And there's Dori. It looks like she's going to the dance with Derek."

Sure enough, six of the teens were ones they had gotten to know somewhat. They all looked wonderful. The three girls looked like they'd had their hair professionally styled, and they wore dresses cut just above their knees. Keri's was kelly green with a flowy skirt and long-sleeved bodice with cutouts on the shoulders. Megan had chosen a peach dress with full-length sleeves and a V-cut back, and Dori wore a wine-colored strapless with a matching bolero jacket. Their dates looked suave in the latest cut of suit.

"They must have left the dance to take pictures. Now isn't a good time to chat with Derek," Jan decided out loud.

"No, I agree. Let's just wave and go get our containers."

They parked near the public swimming area and didn't even get out, but rolled down their windows when Dori pointed to the Malibu. Bridget and Annie were both there taking pictures and gesturing placements to the teens, but the mothers paused to wave at the smiles from Jan and Elaine.

Derek waved along with his friends, and then Elaine pulled back out on to the street and headed east.

"We'll have to figure out another time to talk with him," Jan said. "It was a long shot tonight anyway."

"It's been a while since our days of school dances, and we're definitely underdressed, but I can't resist," Elaine told Jan as she kept going toward the high school.

The expansive commons area had been transformed. As a sea of beautifully dressed teens socialized and danced beneath dimmed mood lighting, Elaine stood inside the door and took it all in. Lengths of shimmery black and gold gossamer were draped everywhere, giving the institutional room a classy ambience. A decked-out archway marked the throne area for the homecoming court, and without much trouble she picked out the king and queen in their crown and tiara. She didn't recognize them, but Jan started pointing out students she did know. She recognized the song playing and was tempted to join them out on the dance floor.

"Looks like our treats are going fast," Jan said, going over to the line of tables covered in crisp linen tablecloths. Elaine followed for a closer look at the spread.

Punch, water, and soda cans filled one table. The next one held a gigantic fruit and vegetable canape work of art. Farther down there were trays of crackers, sausage slices, and cheeses. And finally, the desserts. Along with their pecan tarts and cheesecake squares, the caterer had prepared slices of baklava, crème brûlée cups, petits fours, and tiramisu. There was even a coffee bar near a group of round, cloth-covered tables with tea lights. Half those tables were filled with partygoers sipping espressos, mochas, and tea in the romantic half-light.

The cousins recognized a couple of women they'd served at the tearoom who were manning the food tables and stayed to chat with them while several songs played and students mingled and laughed all around them.

"Next year you ought to be in charge of the food, Mrs. Blake and Mrs. Cook," a voice said behind them.

Dori Richardson stood there. Elaine had been about to suggest to Jan that it was time to go, but she changed her mind when she saw the rest of Dori's friends, including Derek, talking near the coffee bar. Elaine commented on what a beautiful color of burgundy Dori's dress was.

"And those crystals on the bodice, just gorgeous," Jan added.

Bubbly Dori briefly looked shy but thanked her.

"You're here with Derek?" Elaine asked.

She nodded. "He went to get us coffee." Over at the coffee bar Derek was reaching for two cups the barista was holding out for him.

"How's he feeling with that incredible game behind him?" Elaine wanted to know.

"He's been kind of quiet about it, but he said he's really excited!"

"We saw that his coach introduced a couple of scouts to him and Trace," Jan went on.

"Yeah, that made his year, I think. I expected him to be talking about it more, but he is kind of a quieter guy." Dori toyed with the charm on her gold necklace.

"Well, maybe he's feeling overwhelmed by it." Elaine could see that being the case. It had been an emotional few days. "He might need a little time to process it."

"Probably," Dori answered, looking over at Derek again.

He was still over by the coffee bar, looking around. Dori waved to get his attention, and he started toward her but faltered a step when he saw Elaine and Jan. Instead of continuing, he raised a cup to say hello to them and motioned Dori to an empty table.

"By the way," Jan began, "I've been meaning to return your school newspaper that I picked up after it fell out of your bag the other day. It was enlightening to read through it."

Dori didn't seem to know what Jan was talking about.

"Did you get the zipper fixed on your school bag?" Elaine asked, hoping to refresh the girl's memory.

"Oh, that." Dori rolled her eyes. "Ugh, what a pain. Yes, my dad got it unstuck for me." She addressed Jan. "You can keep that paper. Or toss it. I don't need it back, but thank you!" She smiled from one cousin to the next, then excused herself to rejoin her date, who had chosen not to come say hello to the women.

"Two guesses why he didn't want to talk to us."

Elaine frowned. "I don't think I'll need the second one. My guess is he knows we saw how much he didn't want to talk about the snake last night and doesn't want us to ask him why. After this, I'm not sure he'd talk with us if we called him. I think it may take another trip to Forrest High after school tomorrow."

Ready for the refreshment of sleep, Jan and Elaine got help locating their containers and left the dance.

CHAPTER THIRTY-SIX

Jan slept in until seven o'clock Monday morning. After show-ering and dressing, she read her Bible for a while curled up on top of the quilt on her bed. It was eight o'clock by the time she made it downstairs. She would have to bake quickly to make up for the lost early-morning hours, but a good night of sleep felt totally worth it.

Right now Elaine was sweeping the front porch and ready-ing the tearoom for the day, and Jan was standing in the office studying the photo print of the painting. She needed to get to the day's baking, but she had seen the print on Elaine's desk when she'd gone in there to write a note about a flour order she needed Elaine to place.

If only she could stare long enough at the artist's mark, maybe somehow it would give her a sense of where he'd been when he created the art, what type of man he'd been, the hus-band and father whose history still held unknowns to Archie.

All that was absurd, she knew. Staring at the layered ini-tials, HAB for Harley Archibald Benningham or Henry Arthur

Bentham—so English—would no more help her know what he was like than if she'd sat at his graveside talking to thin air.

She struggled to pull herself away from the mesmerizing scene. She ran her fingers over the glossy photo paper, remembering the feel of the dried layers of paint, the varying thicknesses made by the brushstrokes on the original. The artist had skillfully created the contours of the tiny leaves on the park trees and outlined the brick on the fireplace in the foreground, where Benningham's mark was, and on the buildings in the background. And she traced the line of the steeple behind them.

She looked more closely at the park scene, noticing for the first time details the artist had painstakingly included. The small figures of people he had added to the outdoor part of the painting could have been real people in his life. She imagined what it would be like to sit on that bench in the courtyard, how the view might have been different from eye level instead of from far off and above, where the woman in the apartment was sitting.

Elaine came up next to her while she was looking at the people on the sidewalk around the courtyard. "Any revelations yet?"

Jan sighed. "None. But I am enjoying touring it in my imagination." She touched the black baby buggy pushed by the young mother. "Who do you think the little person was in that stroller when Archie's father painted this scene? Do you think those were real people he saw, or did he just imagine them into the picture?"

Elaine looked over Jan's shoulder at the picture. "I haven't looked at it that way. I bet they were real. I wonder if he knew any of them. It's possible, since they shared a courtyard."

Jan was looking at the tiny characterization of a man and a little girl walking on the path. Archie's father had painted them from the front, as if they were approaching the apartment building. Only a very close-up look revealed the intricacies.

"Look how detailed he was to show them looking at each other," she pointed out, "the father looking down and the girl looking up, as if they weren't flat people just planted there, but were really enjoying the time they had together. I love it."

"In the meantime, you can share this much with Archie. Who knows, maybe some of these people his father depicted in the park were special to him, real glimpses into his life."

"*Ooh*," Jan's eyes went big behind her glasses, "that would be so meaningful. I'll mention that to him."

As they moved into the kitchen, Archie appeared, looking for a clean tablecloth to replace one he noticed had been stained. Elaine soon returned with another one for him. He remained while Jan told him of their latest thoughts about the painting. She was pleased to see how affected the stoic Englishman appeared to be over the idea that his father might have depicted real people from that era of his life.

"There's so much thought that went into this scene that it wouldn't surprise me if we continued to discover more of who he was just by studying what he chose to reveal here," she said. Throughout time, many artists shared hidden parts of their hearts through their work—sculptors, writers, musicians, and painters too.

A peaceful look came over him. "I have always been proud of my father, long before I knew of his success as an artist. He was a wonderful father, and I still miss him. Thank you both for your interest in my family history and for helping me unearth clues to who he was. There's so much more to learn, but already you've been an immense support."

Elaine squeezed his arm. "We're happy to do it, Archie. We appreciate you, I hope you know."

Jan nodded.

"And I you." He returned the kindness. "I know we've already talked about this, but I continue to believe firmly that God orchestrated your finding the painting, and I hope to one day know the path it took getting from my father's home all the way across the ocean to Maine, and here with you. All the while knowing I would run across it."

Jan was every bit as awestruck by the hand of God on the whole process. It had been a miracle, and she sensed there were more miracles to come as God led them along the next steps in learning the painting's history, and Archie's as a result.

"There's nothing coincidental about any of it," Elaine confirmed. "Which makes me all the more happy to have you on board here, Archie. It wasn't chance that prompted you to submit an application to work here."

His head shake was one of agreement, as if he was feeling as Jan was, still gripped by how much God had worked behind the scenes of all their daily lives. It was a sense of awe that wasn't soon to fade. "I am so grateful you found the painting, Elaine. But it also leads me to wonder who owned it prior to you. Did it pass hands many times?"

Jan agreed those were important questions. "Archie, let's keep praying that God will show us the answers."

Her faith felt a welcome boost, and she assured herself that God was also at work in the lives of Derek and Trace and everyone they'd talked with this past week since the accident. God would continue to help them figure it out.

For now, they all had a tearoom to run, so Elaine and Archie moved off to their various tasks.

Jan took one more look at the picture, lingering on the tiny father and child figures in the park, before setting it back on Elaine's desk. She could almost hear their precious conversation about boats and life lessons and great big love that would carry any child successfully through life.

She thanked God for her life on Chickadee Lake, and all the joy He'd given her. And she thanked Him most for his fatherly love for her and everyone she had come to care about.

CHAPTER THIRTY-SEVEN

After enlisting Archie and Rose to close up the tearoom for the day, Elaine and Jan drove out to the high school and arrived as the last classes were letting out. "Maybe we can meet up with Derek before football practice," she told Jan and suggested Jan park near the fieldhouse.

"I feel a little uneasy about this," Jan admitted after they got out of the car.

Elaine wasn't sure how this was going to go either. "I hope he is honest with us right off the bat. We may not know yet what he really intended to happen on that trail ride, but we do know he was involved."

"There he is," Jan said under her breath.

Derek was walking out of the school building, heading to the fieldhouse. Dori was with him. Both had their school bags over their shoulders.

"I imagined us talking with him alone," Elaine said. She didn't relish asking him tough questions when a girl he might really like was standing next to him. But she didn't have time to figure out a smooth way to ask him for a minute or two alone, so she decided to keep it simple and be frank. "Derek!" she called.

He and Dori looked over in surprise, but he followed Dori over to them.

"Hi, Mrs. Blake, Mrs. Cook." Dori showed her usual cheerfulness, but Derek merely gave the cousins a thin smile.

"We're wondering if we could talk with you, Derek." Jan kept her tone light and unassuming.

Derek looked back at the fieldhouse. "I've got practice now," he hedged.

"We won't keep you long," Elaine assured him.

Derek still didn't look willing but told Dori he'd catch up with her later. With unspoken questions on her face, she said she'd better get to the training room. After she was out of earshot, Elaine caught Jan's nod to go ahead. She told him first how happy they were for his game on Saturday and congratulated him on garnering the notice of at least two colleges.

He nodded and scuffed his shoe against the pavement. Elaine couldn't help thinking that he wasn't helping his own cause by looking as guilty as possible.

"We wanted to follow up with you about your request that we find out more about the accident last week."

At that he looked up. "I asked if you would look into the Raiders' involvement."

Elaine nodded. "Yes, but we didn't find anything there."

"Well, the game's over and Trace is fine, so I was worried for nothing."

Elaine wasn't going to let it drop that easily. "That must have been a great relief. I saw you run over to see if he was okay."

"Of course I did. He's a great friend."

"And his mother?"

Derek's brow furrowed. "What about her?"

"Are you concerned that she's in any danger?"

"Oh no. I'm sure whatever happened was all a fluke."

"Derek, does your brother own a snake?" Jan asked. "I'm curious whether you mentioned our missing snake to him. What with his interest in them, according to Jack."

He drew back, then awkwardly tried to recover. "Um, Colby? I don't know...well, maybe. He likes snakes, I know that. He had some a while ago, but I don't know if he has one now."

The cousins waited. Elaine had a hunch Derek was caving under a healthy conscience beleaguered by secrets he hated owning. She tried a different tack. Reaching into her coat pocket, she took out the scrap of black jersey fabric.

He stared at it in her open palm.

"This is one of the clues we uncovered near the accident site," she explained.

She could see it dawn on him as he rubbed the back of his neck. *"Hmm."*

"I was exploring the woods near Old Man Warner's grave and ran into the branch that was sticking out. It looks to me like it came from a jersey. Maybe a Pirates jersey."

"Which points to someone from Forrest High," Jan added gently but plainly. "A football player."

Elaine hoped their efforts to draw him out would work quickly. She wanted him to admit it so they wouldn't have to point the finger at him. She thought he had enough character to be honest, but she knew he was in a tough spot.

Finally he shoved the strap of his duffle higher on his shoulder. "Forget it, I can't do this anymore." As if a weight instantly fell off of him, his head lifted and he looked directly at Jan and then Elaine. "That's from my jersey. And Colby does have a snake. I took it from his house when he was out of town, and I planned to return it that same day. He lives in a small town outside Bangor. I wanted to leave it on the trail just as a joke. You know, to kind of surprise Mrs. Donahue. But that's all it was. At least at first."

"Because you were still upset at her for taking the quarterback position away from you?" Jan's eyes held understanding and truth at the same time.

She could see that he wondered how she knew that, but he just nodded. "I was going to return the snake to Colby's place that day, before he got back from his trip. He'd never know. It wasn't like I gave it a lot of planning. When Trace and I worked things out, I mostly let it go—the disappointment, you know. Losing the QB position made me sure I was done as far as football, because I needed every chance to get a scholarship. I was so mad at Mrs. Donahue for a long time. But it wasn't worth losing Trace's friendship. So I guess in a subconscious way—I don't know, maybe I was still a little angry too—I wanted to play a prank on her on the trail. Sort of make a point with some humor, but maybe hoping she'd see how much what she did affected me."

His face filled with emotion, and Elaine figured it was likely a combination of feeling betrayed by Bridget and feeling bad that he had hurt her too. Elaine completely understood why he'd battled so many feelings about it, and she told him so. "Did you use the circus signal on Leopold?"

"I promise you, I never wanted her to get hurt. Not even when I was hiding in the woods to see what would happen. But something came over me when I saw Leopold's uneasiness when he spotted the snake. Trace and I have used those signals so many times on Leo; it felt like my arm made the signal on its own." He was shaking his head and brushed a tear from his cheek. "At first it was kind of funny, but when I saw her fall, I felt sick to my stomach."

"I thought I heard someone laugh in the woods," Jan said, almost feeling relief that she hadn't imagined it.

"That was me, I'm sorry to say. But I wasn't laughing when I saw she was really hurt. I didn't know what to do. With all those people around and the doctor coming to help her, I panicked and got out of there. And I feel terrible about that too."

He explained that he had chosen that spot on the trail because he'd visited the gravesite with friends a few days earlier and had thought about Old Man Warner's story, how the man had lost his land. "I guess I was feeling sorry for myself and could relate to him because I thought I'd lost my future too."

Even that made sense to Elaine. "Did you leave a pile of pinecones on the grave too?"

He looked like he felt silly about that but admitted he had left the "memorial."

Jan touched his arm. "Derek, I can't tell you how relieved I am to hear that there wasn't some malicious motive behind what you did."

"No, definitely not. But it's been eating me up that I did what I did. I shouldn't have been there at all."

That reminded Elaine. "Speaking of that, how exactly did you make it to the gravesite all the way from the stables? Jan said you stayed back there when the riders left."

He looked embarrassed and proud and humble all at once as he scuffed the ground again and jammed his hands in his jeans pockets. "I'm a pretty fast runner."

They laughed then, and even Derek wasn't hiding a smirk very well.

"And during the game, when Trace made the hand signal to you and you returned it," Jan probed, "what was that about?"

"That was his idea, actually. A while back when we were learning our new positions and working through our feelings about that, we were talking one day about strategies on the field and leading the team. Well, he said that should be our sign for running the ball instead of passing it. We hadn't used it before, but by gesturing with the signal to me when I got put in as quarterback, he was telling me to go for it—don't pass it, run it. It meant a lot to me to know he was behind me for the win."

"I love that," Jan said. "That's a much better reason for the signal than what it looked like to me. To be honest, it helped me connect you to the accident since we've been wondering who might have signaled to Leopold on the trail."

Elaine felt lighter than she had since after the game when she and Jan had become nearly certain that Derek had had a part in causing Bridget's broken leg.

"Where is the snake now?" Jan asked him, always thinking of the details.

"Back at my brother's. I figured it wasn't breaking and entering because Jack's office wasn't locked and I was only returning the snake to my brother. I went over there after school to see how I might get it back, and I lucked out when Jack left. I snuck in real quick, got the snake, and left before he came back. I hadn't counted on you calling Jack to come get the snake in the woods, Mrs. Blake. I'd planned to take it back right after the prank. But when Jack took it, I got scared because I couldn't remember if I'd ever told anyone about my brother's snake."

"And so you made up the story about the Raiders not wanting Trace to play in the game to make them look guilty."

He admitted to that too. "I wanted to throw off any possible connection to me in case I had told someone about Colby's Pueblan snake and they put two and two together. And when the flyers and ads came out, I really got scared."

Elaine understood. "Colby looked at you like he suspected something after hearing the story from Jack."

"Yeah, I've got some explaining to do to him too. And to Jack. What do you think he'll do?"

Elaine didn't know for sure, but Jan said she thought Jack would be very smart about how he handled things when Derek told him the truth.

"And," Jan added, "I think when Bridget hears your story, she may see how hurt you were to lose the quarterback position."

He looked a little relieved but said nothing more about that. Instead, he held out his hands. "I asked for your help before, and if you wouldn't mind, I'd love some advice on how to make this right."

Elaine thought for a moment, then she smiled. "I've got an idea...How would you like to play another prank?"

The appalled bewilderment on their faces was so rewarding that she wished she could go back and ask the question again.

CHAPTER THIRTY-EIGHT

The sun was slipping below the horizon the next evening when Derek showed up at the tearoom after football practice. Not long after that, the front doorbell rang again, and Jack Weston entered the house and followed Jan to the smaller west parlor where Elaine and Derek were sitting. The women invited their guests to have some hot cider and pumpkin bars from the plate on the table.

Jan knew Jack was smart enough to realize this had something to do with the snake. She wasn't in the habit of inviting Jack to the tearoom, and the snake was the key reason she and Jack had talked in recent days. Now for Jack to show up and see Derek there as well after he'd left the conversation so abruptly when Jack brought up the subject of the snake after the game ...Jan could see Jack's wheels turning.

Fortunately, Derek seemed more confident now than when he'd admitted to the cousins his part in the accident. He didn't wait for Jan or Elaine to begin but looked Jack in the eye and explained why he owed him an apology. He began with the reasons for wanting to play the prank on Bridget and then admitted the whole path of his actions that had gotten him to this point.

"My brother didn't know I took his snake, so he was surprised at the game when you talked about the one in the woods. He knows all about the hard time I had accepting what Mrs. Donahue did getting me replaced, and it didn't take much to figure out that I had something to do with the snake and her accident. There aren't many people who have Pueblan milk snakes, but he's one of them."

Jack had listened that whole time without speaking. Jan was glad he kept his professionalism and didn't scoff or act critical. Derek knew what he'd done wrong, and now he was stepping up and doing what was needed to make amends. That seemed to count for something to Jack. It did to Jan, and Elaine too, she knew.

"Have you talked with the Donahues yet?" was Jack's first question.

"Just Trace. But Mrs. Blake and Mrs. Cook are helping me with a plan to do that soon."

Jan couldn't completely hide her amusement. She was looking forward to that part of Derek's apologies because she felt in her heart that it would go over well and even begin to repair some of the damage done by both sides, Derek's as well as Bridget's.

"I understand that what I did was trespassing." Derek swallowed before continuing. "And I'm prepared for whatever punishment I earned. I hope you know that I didn't mess with any of your things. I didn't touch anything except the tank. I only went in your office to get my brother's snake back and get out."

Jack rested his elbows on the table and steepled his fingers. "How did you know I would leave for lunch when I did? Most people eat much earlier than that."

Derek's shoulders rose and lowered. "I didn't. I drove to your office after school that day, debating whether I'd end up having to come clean to you to get the snake back. I was dreading that, so it seemed like a lucky break to see you drive away as I was turning on to your street. I grabbed the snake and ran. But when I managed to get away with it without anyone finding out—it ate me up. I felt worse and worse until finally Mrs. Blake and Mrs. Cook sort of cornered me. Sounds weird, but it felt like permission to finally do the right thing."

Jan considered that a life lesson. She was sure Derek was the type to learn from his mistakes and not repeat them.

Jack must have been thinking similar thoughts because he said some of those very things to Derek.

With the strong hand of his brother's old friend and boss on his shoulder, Derek wiped a few tears and listened with Jan and Elaine as Jack told him no harm had been done and that he even admired Derek's character in correcting his wrong.

Jan felt like throwing another Fall Fest just to celebrate the good that had come out of the first one, as crazy as it had been at times.

At the door, Jack reached for Derek's hand to shake. "You finish this season like you've been playing lately, and you'll have no trouble making it in a college program. And if you keep showing the integrity I've seen in you tonight, you're going to be a winner in life. Got that?"

Derek wore a smile bigger than Jan had ever seen on his face. "Yes, sir. Thank you, sir."

"I see no reason to bring the subject of the snake up again. And drop by anytime to say hello. Door's open." Jack gave a quick nod to Derek, then tipped an imaginary hat to Jan and Elaine and grinned. "Thanks for the snacks." Then he left.

NOT LONG AFTER that, the Malibu followed Derek's truck up the Donahues' driveway, mostly swallowed in darkness except for the swath of a flashlight's beam up by the barn.

Both vehicles turned their headlights off to maintain the surprise. When they parked, Trace walked up to Elaine's car, holding the flashlight while he opened her door. Derek came over to open Jan's. He held a vase of yellow roses. Trace nodded when he saw them and gripped Derek's shoulder supportively.

Derek had told them he'd already come clean to Trace. After Trace had listened to the truth, he'd taken a deep breath and said he forgave Derek and told him he believed his friend hadn't really meant harm to his mother.

Now Derek nervously cleared his throat and followed Trace toward the large, overhead barn door. It was closed, but a long sliver of light showed where the bottom of the door met the concrete pad. Bridget was inside.

Derek stood a few feet from the door and placed the vase on the ground. Then he returned to the others standing in the shadows off the side, but close to the barn door, where they could see—but wouldn't be seen—when the door opened.

Trace handed a remote opener to Derek. "It's all yours, man."

Derek took another deep breath, held out the clicker, and pressed the button. With a rumble the door began to rise. When it was a foot off the ground, he clicked the remote button again. The door stopped rising and stayed there. The guys chuckled quietly, and Jan and Elaine smiled at each other.

Looking more at ease now, Derek pressed the button again. Again it rose, and this time he let it go a couple of feet higher before stopping it. Inside the barn, Jan could see the lowest horizontal boards of the nearest stalls.

"What in the world...?" echoed from within.

Trace and Derek were laughing harder now, and their efforts to keep quiet wouldn't last much longer, Jan figured.

When the door was lifting higher for the third time, they could see Bridget up to her shoulders, wearing her barn coat and supported by her crutches. Her casted leg hung slightly bent. "Who's there? Is this some kind of a joke?"

The vase of flowers sat waiting for her outside the barn, and Bridget bent forward when she saw them. "What are those? Who left flowers outside my barn? Clive, is that you?"

Jan couldn't decide if it was concern or humor she heard in Bridget's tone.

Derek pressed the clicker a final time and let the door finish rising all the way. Bridget straightened with her hands on her hips. She smiled, sort of, and pointed at the flowers, then squinted into the darkness outside the halo of light cast by the light in the barn. "They're beautiful, but I'd love to know who's so generous to bring them for me." She laughed then.

"She's trying to figure out how to react," Elaine confirmed at Jan's side.

Derek headed for the roses, bent to pick up the vase, and approached Bridget. Trace followed his friend, which struck Jan as thoughtful. She and Elaine stayed back in the shadows and let the rest play out.

It didn't take long for Bridget's disoriented expression to melt into a broad smile when she saw the boys, and she looked shocked when Derek held out the vase to her.

"I feel like we're snooping, but I can't not watch this," Jan whispered.

"Me too. But Derek asked us along for moral support, so I think we're okay."

Still, Jan and Elaine decided to let the three have their private moment. They could catch up with Bridget later, so they stayed quiet and out of sight while Derek, Trace, and Bridget spoke. The cousins tiptoed back to the car to watch, determined not to disturb the trio as they worked things out.

Derek was talking, shuffling his feet now and then as Bridget listened straight-faced for several minutes. At one point her eyebrows shot upward and her jaw dropped. She looked sternly at Derek and started to say something, only for Trace to hold out his hand to quiet her. Trace talked next, looking like a peacemaker, and Bridget's expression softened. She looked at Derek, who was swiping his palm over his face, and her face melted as she reached out to pull him into a hug, no matter the vase, which was still in the crook of his arm.

Their conversation continued for several more minutes, with Bridget doing most of the talking and gesturing with her hands like she was trying to explain something.

After a while, the three traded more hugs before leaving the barn and walking toward the house, Bridget working her crutches between the two teens. Derek clicked the button one more time, and the door lowered.

As the light from inside the barn faded and Jan and Elaine were left beneath the moonlight, Jan knew some things between Bridget and Derek had been illuminated.

Bridget hadn't known Jan and Elaine were in on it, but she had been all smiles after talking with the boys.

She heard Bridget offer a supper invitation to Derek for the next evening. "And Trace," Bridget said, "why don't you see if Keri would like to join us?"

Elaine looked just as relieved as Jan felt as they got in the car to go home.

CHAPTER THIRTY-NINE

G randma, you're not s'posed to eat that yet!" Max held a small fist to his hip and was wagging a finger at her.

Jolted into submission, Jan stopped midbite. The chocolate chip cookie teased her from inches away.

"You haven't eaten your supper!" Riley hollered next to his brother.

Duly reprimanded, she apologized for her faux pas and put the cookie back on the napkin on the counter. "Can't get away with anything when you two are around, can I?" She reached to tickle them, but they wiggled out of the way and bolted giggling from the kitchen.

"Nice try, Mom," Van teased. He was stirring a big pot of taco soup on the stove.

"Obviously they've heard the 'no treats right before supper' rule," she answered wryly.

"We're training them well," Amy added from across the island.

Jan went to get a bag of tortilla chips from the pantry. Two days had passed since Derek had come clean to Bridget.

It had been good to resettle into her normal routine, and Jan looked forward to sharing a big family supper. Paula had texted her to say they were running late but would be there soon, and Jan thought she heard Tara's car pull up outside when she returned to the refrigerator to pull out sour cream. Then with a few pulses of the food processor, she had a bowl overflowing with shredded cheese. Amy balanced those items with a dish of chopped avocado and took them all to the dining room table.

Elaine was still upstairs trying to find the neighborhood shown in Archie's father's painting. They had worked on it last night but hadn't found the pot of gold, as they were calling it now. The exact neighborhood eluded them, but they continued to remind each other that it was only a matter of elimination before they were sure to land on the place represented in the painting.

The porch door swung open and clapped shut, and Brian and Paula's family followed Tara into the kitchen. Avery and Kelly hugged Jan, and Avery asked where Elaine was. The two had developed a close relationship over the months.

"She's upstairs working on a special project. Why don't you run up and tell her we're ready to eat?"

Avery bounded off, still holding on to a couple more girlhood years as young womanhood kept sneaking closer.

Everyone moved into the dining room and swapped places a few times before they were all settled and Brian prayed. After thanking the Lord for the food and their time together, he said a special thanks for her. It was all she could do not to squirm on her chair when he asked that God would help her not to be lonesome and to enjoy having all of them around a lot.

"Ame—"

"Let's eat!" She exhaled the short sentence.

The conversation moved on, and supper was festive. Jan was even relieved to see Brian and Paula showing each other affection. He held her chair for her when everyone was first sitting down, and they were smiling and Brian even winked at his wife over something private she said to him.

Subtly observing them, Jan had never been happier to realize she'd been wrong. The couple seemed close and in love as ever.

What she'd thought was friction between her son and his wife must have been because of his concern for her. Content, Jan turned her attention to the other end of the table. "So Nathan is working late tonight, Elaine?"

Elaine nodded, chewing, then swallowed. "He's getting some final things straightened out for an auction tomorrow. He asked me to say hello to all of you."

After supper, Jan was at the sink washing a few nondishwasher things while the others hung around and helped with cleanup. She overheard Paula tell the girls to get their coats because they had school the next day, when Brian picked up a hand towel and began to wipe the clean, wet soup pot.

"Mom, do you need anything this week? I can stop by to check the pipes before winter hits, or I..."

She couldn't help herself. Without thinking about what she was doing, she flipped the sopping dishcloth in her hand right at his chest. It struck with a wet *fllpp* and fell to the floor, leaving a dark spot on his sweater.

Everyone in the kitchen stopped.

Jan's hands flew to her mouth. The next instant, she broke into giggles as Brian and the others stared at her.

They all must think she'd lost it.

Feeling a little embarrassed, she apologized to Brian, took the dry towel from him, and dabbed at his sweater. Her eyes darted over the room, and Van's smirk almost started her laughing again.

Clearing her throat and setting her shoulders, she regarded her son. "Brian, I love you dearly. You are so thoughtful to care so much and look out for your 'old' mom. But son, *I am fine.* I'm happy even."

"But Elaine and I…" His sentence dropped off when Jan turned to Elaine.

"You've been talking?" She wagged a finger between them. She wanted to laugh again but would let them sweat it a little.

Elaine's fingers were covering her own lips, but she dropped them to mouth an "I'm sorry." She shrugged sheepishly.

"I'm fine, both of you. Bob's in Baltimore. I miss him, yes. But I'm here. I'm good. And thanks for caring so much about me."

Elaine seemed relieved that Jan wasn't upset or angry. She sighed. "That's all it is. I just want you to be happy."

"I *am* happy. Very happy. I've got you here. I've got my kids and grandkids close by. And I've got a home and business that I'm having so much fun with."

She inhaled dramatically for effect and nodded animatedly, obviously overdoing her arguments. "Who could ask for more?"

Elaine seemed satisfied. "Okay then. I believe you."

Jan was glad to hear it, but she couldn't let Brian keep feeling confused or bad either. He had such a good heart. She placed a hand on his arm. "I just need you to believe that too and let me move on. And," she looked at Paula, "I meant it when I offered to take the girls for a weekend. Every couple needs time away together."

Brian followed her gaze to his family, who looked as though they might either burst into giggles or crawl away mortified. They opted for giggles, and soon everyone was laughing at what Jan had done.

His surprised look switched to disbelief. "Have you been thinking Paula and I are having troubles?"

She held out her hands. "Well, you've been hanging around here so much, and she had a hard time getting your help with the girls' homework that one night, and she had to wait to get your help with the bathroom…I didn't know what to think. But tonight made me realize that you two are fine."

At that, Brian leaned back and howled with laughter. With broken sentences, he pointed between them. "You were thinking…and I was thinking…and we're both okay." He calmed down and wiped a laughing tear from his eye. Waving Paula over, he told her quietly what Jan's concerns had been, and she smiled and assured Jan that she and Brian were good as gold.

"I kept telling Bri that he was hovering around you too much, but I guess we can't fault the guy for being a mama's boy, can we?"

"We'll definitely take you up on the offer to kidsit though," he said.

"Can't wait," Paula agreed.

Jan pulled both of them into a hug, feeling happy and content. It was good to see her son drop his seriousness, even momentarily. They settled on the next weekend, and Jan was already looking forward to precious time with her granddaughters.

JAN'S FAMILY HAD gone home, and the cousins had changed into pajamas and made tea to take upstairs. On a side table, two napkins still held crumbs from the chocolate chip cookies they'd finally gotten to eat.

The sitting room glowed with light. Jan covered a yawn and massaged her sore neck muscles. "We did it," she said with a satisfied smile.

"Yes, we did. We solved another one," Elaine agreed. "I never doubted we would."

The events of the recent days had certainly made for full hearts, Jan thought. She was sure Derek and Trace's friendship would grow even stronger from having to work through a tough situation. And Bridget seemed to have had her eyes opened to how her influence could be detrimental if she wasn't careful. And maybe she'd come to really like Keri once she got to know her. That would be helpful to both Trace and Keri. Derek had survived and grown from having to deal honestly with some bad decisions he'd made. Jack had told Derek he didn't see a need to bring up the snake again. And Derek's college hopes were brighter than ever.

"What a week of mystery," Jan told her.

"Thankfully, it all ended well for everyone. Even Old Man Warner got some respect, thanks to Derek."

Although she'd never met him, Jan was pleased for the old guy. She was having trouble thinking of him as an old curmudgeon anymore. Derek had made that good contribution to his memory. Jan exhaled, long and contented. Life was good.

She looked at her cousin and friend. "Every time we've helped someone figure out a mystery, I have peace that we didn't just stumble on this house, just as we were saying to Archie that it wasn't coincidence that his father's painting crossed the ocean and ended up right here. God had a reason for putting us in this very place at this time in our lives."

Elaine squeezed her hand. "I've been so sure you must be heartbroken since Bob left that I've even bugged you at times, I think. But you really are doing okay, aren't you?"

Jan nodded peacefully. Tenderness about Bob's absence was in her heart, sure. But she felt the glow of peace more strongly. "This week is a big part of why I'm feeling that way," she told Elaine. "Just look at how it happened. It wasn't a lifelong passion for horses that made me go on that trail ride. But from out of nowhere I felt the nudge to sign up for it, and I didn't really think about why, except that it sounded like something new, so why not give it a try? But I believe God wanted me to go because it opened doors to encourage other people and help them through some difficulties they were facing. The Donahues, Derek, little Marcella. Even all the extra baking with those girls and then even more for the dance. Being able to provide a place to help them make cakes so they could encourage their friends wasn't a chance thing. And to top it off, my granddaughter was another beneficiary of my being here to be a part of that. You would have loved to see the joy Avery had during that simple, unplanned hour." Jan paused in her revelations. "I don't feel like God is done with His purposes for me here yet."

Elaine reached over and gave Jan a hug. "Okay then. Let's pray and leave the authenticator's work—and the timing of it—to God and see what else He wants to show us so we can help Archie."

Just then, lightning flashed outside and the sitting room lamps flickered.

"Was it supposed to storm tonight?" Elaine looked toward the curtained window.

"Not when I last checked. That was this morning, but there was nothing in the forecast then."

"Spooky."

Jan caught Elaine's hint of mystery. Or maybe the hope of a new one to challenge them soon.

Outside, the wind picked up and thunder clapped. Inside the sitting room, the lights flickered again, as if somehow they could read Jan's thoughts.

And with smiles of anticipation to each other, the cousins said good night.

ABOUT THE AUTHOR

Tea and Touchdown is Erin Keeley Marshall's second published work of fiction with Guideposts, but she has also enjoyed contributing to the devotional book *Mornings with Jesus* since its beginning in 2012. She is the author of *Navigating Route 20-Something* and *The Daily God Book*, a collaborating writer for *365 Pocket Prayers for Mothers* and *Hope of Heaven: God's Eight Messages of Assurance to a Grieving Father*, and a contributing writer and editor for many other publications. Erin lives in Arkansas with her husband, Steve, and their kids, Paxton and Calianne. Visit her at erinkeeleymarshall.com and on Facebook and Twitter @EKMarshall.

MOM'S MOLASSES COOKIES

1 cup butter

1 cup sugar

1 teaspoon baking soda

1 cup molasses

1 cup sour milk (add 1 teaspoon
white vinegar per 1 cup milk
to make sour milk)

1 teaspoon salt

1 teaspoon ginger

1 teaspoon cinnamon

1 teaspoon baking powder

5 cups sifted flour

Cream butter and sugar. Add remaining ingredients and mix well. Drop onto greased cookie sheets (smaller cookies work better for this recipe). Bake at 350 degrees for ten to twelve minutes. Frost with confectioner's icing (powdered sugar, with a little warm water). Makes five dozen cookies.

READ ON FOR AN EXCITING SNEAK PEEK
INTO THE NEXT VOLUME OF TEAROOM MYSTERIES!

Steeped in Secrets
BY SUSAN PAGE DAVIS

Elaine Cook and her cousin, Jan Blake, put on their jackets and slipped out through the kitchen on to the back porch. The bright autumn leaves had fallen off the hardwood trees a month ago, but the lake was still beautiful, encircled by dark pines and spruces. Elaine loved all Lake Chickadee's seasons and moods, even in the cold months when the lake froze solid. Today the water looked gray, and a stiff wind raised frothy whitecaps on its surface.

She shivered and zipped up her fleece jacket. "Is it going to snow today?"

"I don't think so," Jan said. "I hope not."

They walked across the dead grass and between Tea for Two, the business they ran in their house, and Sylvia's Closet next door, around to the front door of the shop. Elaine loved shopping at the vintage store next to their tearoom. The unassuming house on the lakeshore was owned by Sylvia Flood, who lived in the rooms above her business, making her the cousins' closest neighbor. Her store held treasures from the past. Elaine couldn't visit too often, or she'd wind up with a closet full of vintage clothing.

Sylvia stood behind the counter, but she smiled when she saw them and came out to greet them. "Good morning. How may I help you?" She looked very smart in a pinstriped pants suit with a splash of color at her neck from a pink and turquoise scarf. She wore her long, dark hair in her usual style, a ponytail. Her oversized glasses with black frames made her eyes look huge.

"We've come to browse," Elaine said.

Jan nodded. "We're putting on a Victorian tea for an exclusive women's group named the Pegasus Club from Waterville, and we felt the urge to splurge."

"New outfits?" Sylvia asked.

"Yes, if we find the right thing," Elaine said. "We met with their social committee chairman yesterday, and I get the idea these women are upper crust—doctors, professors, wives of the same."

Sylvia smiled. "Got it."

"We have dresses we've used before," Jan said, "but we thought it might be time for something different."

Elaine nodded. "At least some costume jewelry and other accessories. Do you have anything that looks 1850ish?"

"Or even 1890ish," Jan added. "That's what's so great about Queen Victoria. She lived so many decades."

"True. She spanned a lot of fashions too. You don't want hoop skirts, do you?"

"I don't think we'd have room to serve in those in our dining room," Elaine said with only a small pang of regret. Crinolines were not her favorite fashion. "I think we'd better go with something more streamlined."

"Sure." Sylvia led them to a rack at the side of the room. "I keep the really old stuff over here. Of course, most of these gowns are reproductions, because you can't expect to go around in hundred-and-fifty-year-old fabric. Not for long anyway. Most fabrics that old are very fragile. Now, are you dressing for day or evening?"

"The event will be held at three in the afternoon," Elaine said.

"At your place?"

Elaine nodded. "In our dining room. We expect twelve guests."

"That's about the max for comfort in that room," Jan said. "And that's assuming they don't all show up in hoop skirts or bustles."

Sylvia smiled and pulled a gold satin gown from the rack. "This is one a woman had made for a costume ball. The quality of the fabric and workmanship is very good. It might fit you, Elaine."

Elaine studied the dress. "It's beautiful, Sylvia, but I think the neckline's a bit extreme for an afternoon tea."

Sylvia shrugged. "You could put a lace insert at the neck."

"That's a great idea, but I'm not sure it's your best color," Jan said.

"I'm afraid Jan's right." Elaine gave her cousin a quick smile. She didn't want to offend Sylvia, but the ball gown was far too formal and daring for her taste.

"Well, I do have a few crinoline dresses, but you said you'll be in close quarters." Sylvia pushed several hangers along the rack.

"Correct," Jan said.

"There's this." Sylvia pulled out a lavender gown with flounces at the waist and hem. "I think it was made for a Civil War reenactment."

"Oh, that's pretty." Elaine took the hanger and held the dress up in front of her. "Is it long enough?"

"It might fit Jan better," Sylvia acknowledged. Jan was a couple of inches shorter than Elaine.

"I like it." Jan turned the price tag over. "I'll try it on."

"Go ahead," Elaine said. "If it winds up too long for you, I'll try it."

Sylvia took it to the dressing room she had made in a converted closet, pushed back the curtain, and hung up the lavender gown for Jan. Jan entered and closed the curtain. The cousins had the shop to themselves at the moment. November was a slower month for Sylvia, as it was for the tearoom. By comparison, the summer months when tourists flooded the area and the fall foliage season kept them much busier.

Sylvia turned to Elaine. "I might not have anything for you. Most of what I have right now is twentieth century, I'm afraid. I sort of specialize in the 1920s to the '50s."

"It's all right," Elaine said. "We can wear our older dresses if we can't find something new. We just thought it was time to upgrade, and I like an excuse for a new outfit. Do you have any accessories from the Victorian period?"

"Sure." Sylvia slid the hangers on the rack back into place. "I have some very nice fans and gloves, and a darling chatelaine from the 1870s." She went behind the counter and a moment later set two trays of small items on top.

They discussed the items, and a few minutes later Jan stepped out of the fitting room wearing the lavender dress.

"That looks great on you," Elaine said immediately. The color set off Jan's blue eyes and her brown hair that showed only an occasional strand of gray.

"Really?" Jan walked over to the full-length mirror and turned this way and that.

"Yes, really," Elaine said.

"It almost touches the floor. It might even be long enough for you." Jan studied her reflection.

"Don't forget, you'll be wearing your boots with it, and they have a heel," Elaine said.

"Oh, right." Jan gave Sylvia a tentative smile.

"I can give you ten percent off," Sylvia said.

"You talked me into it. I'll take it." Jan smiled as she went back to the fitting room.

Elaine continued to look at the accessories. When Jan came out and handed Sylvia the dress to fold and ring up, she joined Elaine at the glass-fronted case where the display trays were sitting. Sylvia had unlocked the front so Elaine could examine the other merchandise more closely.

"What's this, smelling salts?" Jan picked up a small, bejeweled bottle.

"That's a scent bottle. Perfume," Sylvia said. "It's small enough to fit in a pocket or the tiniest evening bag."

"I like this one." Elaine leaned close over a blue-and-silver bottle with a metallic glaze.

"That's lusterware," Sylvia said. "It was made in what was Czechoslovakia. As usual, you have excellent taste."

Jan flipped the price tag over. "I'll say. You can sell your half of the business and buy it."

Elaine chuckled.

"That's actually not a bad price for it," Sylvia said. "But I guess you just want a few trinkets."

"It's beautiful," Elaine said quickly. "But you're right, we're looking for simple accessories we can wear while we're working."

Jan went to the checkout counter and paid for her purchase. Sylvia handed her the receipt.

"I doubt we'll be wearing gloves during the tea," Elaine said, "but you mentioned fans. That might be fun."

"No Victorian lady would attend an event without her gloves and fan." Sylvia replaced the trays and locked the case of perfume bottles and snuff boxes. She then took three very different fans from beneath the counter's glass top and laid them on the gleaming surface. "This fan isn't old, but it's pretty. It was made in Japan and would go nicely with a red or green dress. Or white or gray, for that matter. A bit of color." She pointed to the next one. "This one has a fixed handle. Again, it's not very old, but it's interesting. I love the bright turquoise and gold. This last one is actually made of fabric, not paper."

"Oh, I like that." Elaine examined all three fans and a couple more Sylvia brought out. She settled on one that folded into a plastic case that looked like ivory. "This will go with just about anything, and it has this loop so I can hang it on my sash."

"Nice choice." Sylvia laid it next to the cash register. "Are you sure you don't want to try on that gold satin gown?"

"Oh, no thanks," Elaine said. "What do you have in jewelry? I understand large earrings were popular during at least part of the period."

"Yes, they were," Sylvia said, unlocking a case beneath the glass top of another counter. "They got huge in the 1850s. This pair is a bit later, maybe from the 1870s. The black beads are jet. Or, if you want something more colorful, I have some garnet drops or maybe these gold filigree hoops."

They were still browsing the antique jewelry when the bell over the door jingled and two elderly women walked in.

"Hello, Mrs. Lovett," Elaine said with a smile. "And Mrs. Orwell, isn't it?"

"Yes," said Agnes Lovett, the younger of the two sisters. "You're the tearoom ladies."

"That's right," Elaine said. She had met the women once before, when their niece, Rue Maxwell, had brought them to Tea for Two as a treat. Rue was a regular customer and owned the Northwoods Bed-and-Breakfast with her husband, Ned. "I'm Elaine, and this is my cousin, Jan."

Sylvia came around the counter and approached them with a smile. "Welcome. How may I help you?"

"Well..." Agnes looked at her sister. Her white hair was curled in tight ringlets and her face was wrinkled, and she wore black half boots and rust-colored slacks, with a woolen car coat over them.

"We wondered if you buy jewelry," Beatrice said. Her hair didn't show any gray, and Elaine was sure it was dyed the chestnut it had probably been naturally many years ago, but it was well done, and certainly made her look more youthful. Rue had told Elaine that both the aunts were in their eighties. Beatrice's gray pleated skirt was less up-to-date. It looked as though it might have come from the wardrobe she wore forty years earlier.

Sylvia smiled warmly. "I certainly do, if it's vintage. Jewelry from the 1950s and earlier is very much in demand."

"Oh, ours is old," Agnes said.

"But not *too* old," Beatrice corrected her. "And nothing too valuable. Just costume jewelry."

"That's right." Agnes nodded vigorously, sending her tightly permed white curls bouncing. "We just thought we'd sell a few things to subsidize a little vacation."

"That sounds interesting," Sylvia said. "Where are you going?"

Agnes said in a conspiratorial near-whisper, "We're thinking a cruise."

"Someplace warm," Beatrice put in.

"Sounds marvelous. I usually take things on consignment, but I sometimes pay cash if the seller wants me to. I have to lower my price a little when I do that, in case it doesn't sell. Do you have the jewelry with you?" Sylvia asked.

"Oh no. We thought we'd inquire first." Agnes looked a little flustered. "We can bring it in later."

"Yes, after we decide which pieces we want to let go of," Beatrice said.

"You need to sell off those things you got from the office," Agnes said a bit archly.

"Office?" Sylvia asked.

"From when she worked at the statehouse," Agnes replied. "Bea has gifts she got fifty years or more ago, and she clings to them."

"I do not!" Her sister's brown eyes snapped with indignation.

"Well then, now's the time," Agnes retorted.

"You should talk," Beatrice said with mock injury. "You've got those Bakelite bracelets Rudy Hodges gave you. Mother always said that was a most improper gift—too personal. And yet you've kept them."

"Bakelite is very popular right now," Sylvia said quickly.

"And what about the mysterious lapis lazuli necklace?" Beatrice went on. "You've never said where that came from, but you had it before you married Jerry."

Agnes's face reddened, and she pulled in a sharp breath. "Well, I never."

Sylvia held up a hand and said graciously, "Bring in whatever you're ready to part with. I'm open until five today, and from nine to five tomorrow."

"We'll be back." Agnes turned on her heel. Beatrice followed her sister out the door.

"Well." Sylvia smiled at Elaine and Jan. "Always nice to have new customers and consigners."

"You could probably sell some of the things they're wearing now in here," Jan said wryly.

"Yes, I thought Agnes's car coat was quite retro-chic," Elaine agreed.

"And Beatrice's wool skirt," Jan said.

"I loved it," Elaine said. "Don't know as I'd wear it though."

Sylvia walked back behind the counter with the jewelry set out. "I hope she *will* bring me the Bakelite jewelry. It's made a comeback with collectors." She frowned slightly. "I've seen them before. They're related to the Maxwells, aren't they?"

"Rue's aunts," Jan said.

"Oh, right." Sylvia straightened a couple of items in the case of jewelry they'd been looking at.

Elaine picked up an enameled necklace. "This is lovely, Sylvia. It wouldn't go with the period costume I have, but I might find something else to wear it with."

She turned the tag, and Jan leaned in to look and raised her eyebrows at the price.

"That's a little more than I wanted to spend today," Elaine admitted.

"You could steal it while Sylvia's not looking," Jan deadpanned.

"Ha!" Sylvia smiled and shook her head. "I actually did have a shoplifter in here a few months ago. Maybe I should report you to the police." She winked.

"You know us," Jan joked. "Menaces to society."

It started with a chuckle until the laughter escalated—disproportionately so—and tears had started streaming down their cheeks. Finally, they calmed down, and Elaine laid down the necklace with a sigh. "I think I'll just take the fan today."

Sylvia was wiping tears. "Sounds good, if you're sure about that gold dress."

"I'm sure."

Sylvia rang up Elaine's small purchase. "There you go. I'll let you know if I get more Victorian-era things in. When's your special event?"

"The week before Thanksgiving." Elaine took her bag. "Thank you, Sylvia."

"I'm sure this dress will be perfect for me," Jan said. "Thank you."

They stepped outside and pulled their jackets closer against the wind.

"I'm glad you didn't get the gold dress," Jan said. "You need something brighter."

"I was thinking that enameled necklace might look good with my red blouse."

"Really? At ninety-five dollars?" Jan asked.

Elaine shrugged. "You're right. If I'm going to spend that much right now, it should be on a new costume that's right for the Victorian tea."

JAN LET EARL Grey, the cat who'd adopted them soon after they moved into the house, on to the back porch the next afternoon and poured cat food into his dish.

"Where have you been? I was looking for you this morning. It was cold out there."

Earl Grey cast her a look that reminded her of his independence, and Jan smiled. Although she and Elaine had taken in the stray cat when they moved into the house, he sometimes snubbed them.

"All right, have it your way, but your basket is here when you want it." She filled his water bowl and headed back into the kitchen. The tearoom would close soon, but she had scones baking and a triple batch of cookies for tomorrow's cookie of the day yet to go through the oven.

She had just closed the door when the phone rang.

"Hi. It's Sylvia. I got some new jewelry in today that I think you and Elaine might like. Some of it's from the 1940s, but I think a couple of the pieces are older."

"Sounds good," Jan said. "Elaine's in Waterville today though. Can we come tomorrow, after the rush?"

"Sure, anytime."

"Okay. We'll probably come after lunch tomorrow. Thanks, Sylvia." Jan hung up, glad that Sylvia didn't seem put out with her for her remarks the previous day. She would have to be careful tomorrow. Sylvia did not take teasing easily.

She looked up in surprise when a knock sounded on the back door. Jan walked over and opened it.

"I hope you don't mind me coming to the back," Rue Maxwell said. "The lake was so pretty today, I wanted to have a closer look, before it freezes up."

"That's fine," Jan said. "Come on in." Even though she was a bit windblown, Rue still managed to look put together, with a smart plaid jacket, turquoise gloves, and gray woolen pants. Jan glanced out at the water. The sun's last rays had turned the clouds orange and pink, and the colors were reflected in the lake's choppy surface as glints of color on the waves, with small whitecaps adding garnishes.

Rue glanced at the cat, who was eating as though he was half starved. "He's such a beautiful cat."

"Yes, he's fluffed out his winter coat." Jan looked fondly at the big gray cat, trying to see him through her visitor's eyes. Earl Grey appeared much larger in the cold months than when he had shed out in summer. "He has quite a personality too."

Rue stepped into the kitchen, and Jan shut the door firmly.

"Now, what can I get you?" Jan asked as she carefully washed her hands. "Muffins for tomorrow's breakfast, I'm guessing."

Rue chuckled. "I'm too predictable. Yes, and I wondered if I could get a couple dozen cookies as well. I'm packing a box lunch for some of our guests tomorrow. They're going over to Fort Knox and the bridge tower," she said, referring to Penobscot Narrows Bridge & Observatory.

"I hope it's warmer tomorrow than it has been the last couple of days." Jan pulled two white boxes from a cupboard and began to fold them into shape.

"The weatherman says warmer and less wind."

"Well, that's good. Now, any preference on cookies?" Jan rattled off the kinds they had on hand, and Rue chose two of her personal favorites.

"I've got blueberry muffins, raisin bran, and cranberry nut. Is that okay?"

"Sure," Rue said. "Four of each."

Jan lined the cookies up perfectly in the box and opened a container of muffins. "Oh, I saw your aunts yesterday."

"Were they in here?"

"No, over at Sylvia's Closet."

"That's nice," Rue said. "I'm glad they're still able to drive and get about on their own."

"Yes, they're very well preserved," Jan said with a smile. "They must have been beauties when they were young."

"Oh yes," Rue said. "And very modern for the times. Their father was a congressman, you know."

"Really? What was he to you?"

"My great-grandfather. Aunt Beatrice was a stenographer in the attorney general's office before she married."

"I didn't know that, but Agnes did mention something yesterday about her sister having worked at the statehouse." Jan lined up four blueberry muffins and reached for the container of bran ones.

"Yes, and she kept at it for quite some time," Rue said. "She only stopped working there when she had her first child, but she'd been in the office for more than ten years."

"Really? And they had the same attorney general that long?"

"No, she actually had three different bosses during her tenure, but she was so efficient each new one asked her to stay on."

"That speaks well of her."

"*Mmm.* She still likes to talk about it. She's always dropping names of famous people she met during that time. All the governors, of course, and other statesmen and celebrities. She met Mamie Eisenhower once, and Arthur Godfrey. I think he had a summer home in Maine."

"Wow." The timer bell rang, and Jan turned and took a tray of scones out of the oven. "When did Beatrice have that job?" she asked, sliding in two sheets of cookies.

"Oh, in the 1950s, I think. Maybe into the sixties."

"Does she miss it?"

"I'm sure. But she's a big wheel in the Augusta Historical Society now. Very involved, very dedicated." Rue shrugged. "Aunt Agnes is more of a homebody. She'd rather spend time with her children and grandchildren. They both have 'greats' now too."

"That's nice. I think once when you brought her in for tea, she said something to me about the Literacy Volunteers."

"Yes, that's Aunt Agnes's hobby now. She says she's taught twenty adults to read in the last twenty years. She's very proud of that."

"She should be." Jan closed the muffin box.

Their employee, Rose Young, came in from the tearoom with a tray. "One pot of chai tea, coming up. Oh, hi, Rue."

"I'll fix the tea if you can ring up Rue's purchases," Jan said.

"Sure. Come on out to the counter, Rue."

Jan took a kettle of hot water off the stove and took down a flowered china teapot. They kept a couple dozen mismatched teapots on the shelf for everyday use in the tearoom. Rue and Rose picked up Rue's boxed baked goods and went out into the entrance hall, where the checkout stood.

Jan made the tea and went back to her baking. After the tearoom closed for the evening, she hustled about, helping Rose and Archie Bentham, their other server, do the routine cleaning of the afternoon. Elaine wasn't back from her outing yet, so Rose cashed up the day's receipts and Jan put the money bag in the small safe in Elaine's office.

"I guess that's it," Archie said as he hung up his apron. Although he was past retirement age, Archie's polish and his British accent made him a favorite server with the customers. "It was a good day."

"Yes, it was," Jan said. She always counted it a good day when they stayed busy and the cookie of the day sold out.

"Good night, then." Archie headed out the front door toward his car.

"I'm off too," Rose said. "I've got class tonight."

Jan walked to the back porch with her. She was proud of Rose for pursuing a career and taking culinary courses.

"I'm glad you wore something warm," Jan commented, watching Rose tie the hood of her winter jacket in place and pull on gloves. "It's freezing out here."

Rose walked over and kissed her on the cheek. "Thanks, Jan. You make me feel like my mother's still watching out for me."

Jan gave her a little hug. "Good night. And say hi to Brent for me." She stood on the porch watching until Rose was in the boat and had shoved off from the dock and started the engine. Rose looked back and waved, then zoomed off down the lake. Jan sighed and turned away.

Movement caught her eye through the side window as she turned. She stepped closer and squinted toward Sylvia's building. A stranger was walking along the side.

FROM THE
GUIDEPOSTS ARCHIVE

This story, by Adam Hunter of New York, New York,
originally appeared in *Guideposts*.

I n high school I played varsity football. I wasn't a star, but
my senior year I was good enough to start at defensive and
offensive tackle. Four years of brutal preseason football camps,
sweaty shoulder pads and buckets of black eye paint all came
down to my last game. I urged my dad to bring our video camera. I wanted to capture the last plays of my football career
for posterity.

Dad got me to play football in the first place. I enjoyed
throwing the ball around with my friends, but I didn't think I
had what it took to play on a team. "I'm no football player," I
told my dad.

"You'll never know what you're capable of unless you give
it a try," he told me. So I did. I remember how proud he was
when I won the most-improved player award my sophomore
season, prouder than if I'd been the MVP, and the hug he gave

me after I received my varsity letter. There was rarely a game that Dad wasn't on the sidelines, cheering me on.

I waved at my parents before the opening kickoff, and put on my game face. Our opponents had the ball first. I crouched down and awaited the snap. My pads crunched as I made contact with the offensive tackle. I grabbed at the jersey of their running back bursting through the hole, and dragged him to the turf. A loud cheer erupted from the sidelines. *I sure hope Dad got that one on tape.* I straightened my helmet and looked over. There was Dad with the camera, cheering like crazy.

On the next defensive series, I did a spin move and burst through the line to sack their quarterback. Only the second sack in my whole high-school career. Another one for the highlight reel. A couple plays later, I made another stop of their running back. Great! My last game and I was turning my intensity up a notch. It seemed as if every time I came off the field, the coaches were congratulating me for another great play. By the end of the game, I had seven tackles and a sack—my best performance ever. A perfect end to my career. I ran into my dad's arms. I was sweaty and smelly, but he hugged me anyway.

I couldn't wait to watch the tape. Relive every moment. As soon as we got in the house, I took the cassette out of the camera and rewound it in the VCR. My dad, mom, sister and I sat down in the living room in front of the big screen TV and dimmed the lights. I pressed play.

The video started. The two teams, lined up before the snap, then the running back taking the handoff, running up to the line, me reaching out, and then... clouds. I could hear my dad, screaming, "Way to go, A!" as images of the sky shook up and down on screen.

"Where's Adam's tackle?" my sister said.

"Sorry," Dad replied, sheepishly.

I leaned forward to see the next big play…and the next and the next. Not one was on tape. Not even my sack! Every time, just as I was about to make a play, the camera would begin filming alternating bits of grass and parts of bleachers, the audio of my dad's loud cheering cutting in and out. "All right, Adam!" I could hear my dad yell. "That's my boy! That's my son!"

The tape ended and Dad was quiet. "I'm sorry, Adam," he said, finally. That's when it dawned on me. I didn't have any of my football glory caught on tape—I had something better. A perfect record of Dad's cheers, his excitement, his uncontainable joy in watching me play. His pride in me. They say you can't see love, but that day I knew I had. "I can't believe I didn't get anything on tape," Dad said.

I smiled. "Yes, you did," I said, and hugged him hard.

A NOTE FROM THE EDITORS

We hope you enjoyed Tearoom Mysteries, published by the Books and Inspirational Media Division of Guideposts, a nonprofit organization that touches millions of lives every day through products and services that inspire, encourage, help you grow in your faith, and celebrate God's love.

Thank you for making a difference with your purchase of this book, which helps fund our many outreach programs to military personnel, prisons, hospitals, nursing homes, and educational institutions.

We also create many useful and uplifting online resources. Visit Guideposts.org to read true stories of hope and inspiration, access OurPrayer network, sign up for free newsletters, download free e-books, join our Facebook community, and follow our stimulating blogs.

To learn about other Guideposts publications, including the best-selling devotional *Daily Guideposts*, go to Guideposts.org/Shop, call (800) 932-2145, or write to Guideposts, PO Box 5815, Harlan, Iowa 51593.

Sign up for the
Guideposts Fiction Newsletter
and stay up-to-date on the books you love!

You'll get sneak peeks of new releases, recommendations from other Guideposts readers, and special offers just for you . . . *and it's FREE!*

Just go to Guideposts.org/Newsletters today to sign up.

Guideposts®

Visit Guideposts.org/Shop
or call (800) 932-2145